He loved her.

She had come to mean more to him than he had ever thought possible. The chances of her loving him were slim. She had been pressured into marrying him, fought him at every turn and to think that she could love him now was insane.

The door to his room opened and he watched as Dee entered the room, closing the door behind her. She moved to the side of his bed and looked at him. She bit her lip nervously as she said, "I do not want to be alone anymore. Will you hold me?"

He could not trust himself to speak as he lifted the covers making room for her next to him. He drew her close to him as she rested her head on his shoulder. "Are you sure?" he whispered softly.

"Yes," came her whispered reply.

Dear Reader,

We, the editors of Tapestry Romances, are committed to bringing you two outstanding original romantic historical novels each and every month.

From Kentucky in the 1850s to the court of Louis XIII, from the deck of a pirate ship within sight of Gibraltar to a mining camp high in the Sierra Nevadas, our heroines experience life and love, romance and adventure.

Our aim is to give you the kind of historical romances that you want to read. We would enjoy hearing your thoughts about this book and all future Tapestry Romances. Please write to us at the address below.

The Editors
Tapestry Romances
POCKET BOOKS
1230 Avenue of the Americas
Box TAP
New York, N.Y. 10020

Montana Brides

DeAnn Patrick

A TAPESTRY BOOK
PUBLISHED BY POCKET BOOKS NEW YORK

Books by DeAnn Patrick

Kindred Spirits
Montana Brides

Published by TAPESTRY BOOKS

An *Original* publication of TAPESTRY BOOKS

A Tapestry Book published by
POCKET BOOKS, a division of Simon & Schuster, Inc.
1230 Avenue of the Americas, New York, N.Y. 10020

ISBN: 0-671-46685-2

First Tapestry Books printing June, 1983

10 9 8 7 6 5 4 3 2 1

POCKET and colophon are registered trademarks of Simon & Schuster, Inc.

TAPESTRY is a trademark of Simon & Schuster, Inc.

Printed in the U.S.A.

To Bunny, my mother hen

Chapter One

THIS WAS THE LAST SOCIAL ENGAGEMENT ON THE CALEN-
dar before the wedding and Katherine Gwyn was
relieved.

When she had accepted Paul Forbes's proposal of
marriage a year ago, Kat had not fully realized what a
strain the engagement was going to be. After a two-
year courtship and persistent pressure from Paul, Kat
had given in and agreed to marry him. But as the
engagement lengthened and outside pressures began to
crowd in on her, Kat began to feel reservations about
marrying Paul. It was only her love for her grandfather
and the help of her best friend, Dee Higgins, that
stopped Kat from throwing her hands up and calling
everything to a halt.

The strain of the past months had taken its toll. Her
delicate features were drawn and pale and her brown
eyes were dull with fatigue. Kat's nerves were on the
edge of collapse and she would find herself crying over
trivialities.

If it were not for Dee's lively sense of humor, Kat
knew she might not have been able to cope with the
many details involved in staging a society wedding in
New York.

Tonight was the culmination of a rash of parties held
in her and Paul's honor. It was one she would much
rather miss if she could and stay at home in the

1

comfortable upper Fifth Avenue townhouse where she and her multimillionaire grandfather, Patrick Gwyn, lived.

But being his only granddaughter had its responsibilities as well as its benefits. Kat had to maintain a position in a society that she did not really like or approve. She hated being on display as though she were a prime thoroughbred filly. It was increasingly difficult for her to be polite when asked rudely curious questions by prominent hostesses. As though their positions in society gave them the right to be nosy about her personal relationship with Paul, Kat thought heatedly.

As Dee had said earlier that day as they rushed between B. Altman, Siegel & Cooper's and Sterns Brothers attending to last-minute shopping before Saturday, "Kat, you mustn't let the old harridans upset you. They think their money gives them the right to question anyone about anything."

Kat recalled Dee's words as she slowly made her way through the receiving line with her hand on Paul's arm. Waiting to greet them was their hostess, Mrs. Astor, one of the nosiest of them all.

Dee must have been thinking the same thoughts, for she nudged Kat from behind and whispered in her ear, "Smile and let Paul do all the talking. She's a patsy for handsome young men."

Kat turned to look at Dee as she laughed softly. "I would not let our hostess hear you say that if I were you."

Dee gazed back, her green eyes wide with innocence. "Are you suggesting that she dislikes the truth?" Her lips curved into a gamin grin as she added, "But watch her, you will see I know what I am talking about."

"What are the two of you whispering?" Paul asked with a frown.

"They are plotting the overthrow of the government," Dee's escort, James Hyde, replied with a shrug.

Paul's eyebrows elevated and he turned questioning eyes on Kat as they moved through the receiving line. As eligible, handsome and successful as he was, Paul was not noted for a sense of humor. This was becoming a more irritating flaw the longer Kat knew him. But she dismissed it as a reaction to all the strain of the past few months. Patting his arm with her hand, Kat reassured him, "You know better than to listen to James. It was only girl talk, nothing more."

Paul looked back at the pair behind him and Dee tried to maintain a serious expression on her face as James feigned injured dignity. "Kat! How can you say such things about me?" he bluffed.

Smiling at him, Kat shook her head. "I am afraid that it is very easy, James. Your reputation precedes you."

As they neared the head of the line Kat wondered not for the first time how someone like Paul could have fallen in love with her. He was not like James or the many other young men who had tried to court her with one eye on her money and the other on furthering themselves by gaining a relationship with her grandfather.

Paul was a man of means in his own right as chief assistant to James, who was the head of Equitable Life Insurance Company. Paul was well educated and confident in his own ability to get ahead in the cutthroat world of business and finance.

Kat could hear Dee and James trying to muffle their laughter behind Paul's back and she motioned with her free hand for them to quiet down. They had accompanied her and Paul many times over the past months, and even though James was Paul's boss he was also his friend and loved to tease him whenever he had a chance. Kat had to laugh quietly to herself as she wondered if society was expecting an announcement of their engagement. She knew that it would never happen. James was far too interested in throwing lavish parties and showing off the wealth he had inherited from his father to consider settling down and marrying. It mattered little to him that Dee was the daughter of a Professor of Hellenic Studies at Columbia University and not the offspring of a rich family. James and marriage did not go together.

And Dee, for all her apparent joy in life, was not the scatterbrain that some labeled her. Her interests were in areas foreign to most young ladies. Dee preferred things she had come to know and love with her three brothers, such as hunting, fishing and working with animals. She had stated on more than one occasion that she had no intention of marrying.

Dee's soft voice broke into Kat's musings. "I see your grandfather."

Kat looked where Dee was directing and sighed to herself. Grandad would be with J. P. Morgan and Edward Harriman, two of his sometimes partners and most-times rivals in the world of finance, railroads and steel. They always managed to upset Grandad, and if she did not arrive in time to buffer things, he might cause a scene. Patrick's temper was widely known, and Kat could see by the way his eyebrows were twitching that he was on the edge of losing it at this very moment. Thank goodness they were at the head of the receiving line, Kat sighed inwardly.

"Katherine, my dear. And Paul. How nice you look tonight, dear." Mrs. Astor bussed each of them on the cheek.

Please don't make this take too long, Kat prayed, expecting to hear the sound of her grandfather's voice raised in anger.

"Tell me, Paul," Mrs. Astor crooned, "isn't our Katherine looking especially beautiful tonight? I bet you can hardly wait until Saturday, my boy."

Paul smiled diplomatically as he replied, "You are looking quite beautiful yourself, my dear lady. Lucky for you Mr. Astor saw you first or I might be tempted to throw caution to the wind and whisk you away from all this."

Their hostess giggled and blushed as she smiled approvingly at him. "Katherine, you should thank your lucky stars that you have been blessed with such a man. Why, I swear he could charm the birds out of the trees."

"So I have been told." Kat smiled, wishing she could join her grandfather and calm him down before he exploded.

Mrs. Astor had expended all the time she had allotted for them and now looked over Kat's shoulder toward Dee and James. Kat could feel Dee cringe as she and James were greeted. "And little Aphrodite! How are you, my dear?"

Kat could hear Mrs. Astor chide James on his ostentatious spending habits as she and Paul began to edge their way toward her grandfather.

Reaching Patrick's side, Kat was grateful that she had come at an apparent lull in the discussion and not in the middle of a heated debate. She kissed her grandfather and greeted his companions. "Mr. Morgan. Mr. Harriman. I trust you gentlemen are not ruining your digestion by discussing business or politics?"

From the guilty look in her grandfather's eye, Kat knew she had been close to the mark. Her experience over the years as her grandfather's hostess had shown her that whenever two or more of these gentlemen gathered, the talk inevitably revolved around mergers, acquisitions and government interference. Privately, Kat was of the opinion that more business dealings went on at social gatherings than in boardrooms.

Patrick laughed. "We were discussing this investigation that Teddy has instigated by the Justice people into our Northern Securities Company."

"I am sure that President Roosevelt must have his reasons for doing so." Kat eyed him warningly. She knew what a volatile subject this was where he was concerned. "Enough of such weighty matters, gentlemen. This is a party. Relax and enjoy yourselves." She tempered her order with a sweet smile at Mr. Morgan and Mr. Harriman, but Patrick knew she meant every word she said.

They had been caring for each other for the past eleven years and knew each other very well. Patrick was worried at the look of strain in Kat's eyes. Was he doing the right thing by her? Should he have pressed her into accepting Paul's proposal? Patrick frowned as he thought, Why, I have never heard her say she loves him. She has said she likes and respects Paul, but love?

Kat could tell by the expression on Patrick's face that he was worrying about her again. She had come to know that expression well over the years they had been together. Her parents had spent all this time pursuing the social scene on the Continent without the hindrance a daughter might cause. They had even wired their regrets that they would be unable to attend her wedding. But this did not upset Kat as much as some thought it should. She had the one family member she loved and she was content.

Dee and James joined them, having broken away from the fawning attentions of their hostess. Kat smiled at Dee, who rolled her eyes in explanation of the ordeal she had just undergone. Kat considered Dee to be the closest thing to a sister she would ever have. Dee's parents had encouraged their friendship over the years in the hope that Kat's influence would smooth what they called Dee's rough edges. But Dee was still Dee in spite of her parents' hopes, and Kat loved her the way she was and would not have her change for anything.

Dee gave Patrick a warning look of her own and he stirred uncomfortably. Trying to steer their attentions elsewhere, he said, "J. P., Edward. I am sure you know Dee Higgins and her escort, James Hyde."

"Yes, we both know Dee and James," J. P. stated. "How is Daniel, your father, these days, Dee?"

"He is happily pouring over his old books and scrolls, sir." Dee dimpled up at him.

"James, you must bring Dee and come sailing again with us." J. P. was very proud of his new yacht, the *Corsair III*, and loved to show it off by taking friends sailing whenever possible.

"We would enjoy that, J. P.," James answered him familiarly.

Paul broke into the conversation, saying, "If you gentlemen will excuse us. We really should be mingling, as the party is in our honor. We wouldn't want our hostess mad at us."

"Certainly, we'll excuse you," J. P. laughed.

"At one time or another we have all had our hostess mad at us and not enjoyed the experience," Patrick added good-naturedly.

Paul had not intended for his excuse to be taken in that way and was about to defend himself when Edward Harriman stopped him by saying, "I would like to speak with you about that matter we discussed the other day."

Paul hesitated an instant before replying, "I think I know what it is you are referring to, Edward." He gave Harriman a meaningful look before adding, "I think it would be more practical, though, if we meet tomorrow at my office where we can go over things at length. My bride-to-be might resent my discussing business at our engagement party."

The group laughed and the two couples made their way through the crush of people toward the younger set. As they moved away Kat could plainly hear J. P. exclaiming, "Damn it, Patrick. This Sherman Anti-Trust Act is a direct attack on the free enterprise system."

"So much for our warning," Dee whispered as she also heard the return to the inevitable topic. Dee would have been lost in the crowd if James had not kept a firm hand on her arm to guide her. She smiled her thanks, her green eyes glinting mischievously from her gamin face. "If I had to, I could always go through their legs."

"Katherine, speak to your friend," Paul ordered, appalled at what he had heard Dee say.

Dee wrinkled her nose at him as Kat tried to hide her own annoyance by saying, "Dee, not tonight, please?"

Dee straightened to her full height, which was closer to the floor than the ceiling, and teased, "Not tonight?"

James nudged Paul as he eyed Dee in mock horror. James was accustomed to the bantering that seemed to be a constant occurrence between Dee and Kat, and he wondered how they always managed to shock Paul as they did. "Dee," he warned her as he saw that Paul was not in the least amused.

Shrugging her shoulders and pushing through the crowd, she quipped, "I suppose it is more polite to arrive erect."

Joining their younger set they accepted the flurry of meaningless congratulations on the upcoming nuptials. The surrounding conversation quickly returned to the usual shallowness that Kat and Dee had come to hate. The chatter about the latest fashions, which resorts were the best vacation spots and the upcoming polo matches bored Kat and Dee to tears. After bearing it as long as they could they excused themselves, telling their escorts that they had to powder their noses.

Having broken away from the group they made their way to the ladies lounge, where they sat in two of the ornate chairs near the mirrored alcove. "Ohh, that feels better," Dee murmured as she kicked off her shoes and bent over to rub her sore feet. "I think we must have walked ten miles today shopping."

Kat relaxed, allowing herself to sink into her seat. "Closer to fifteen, I think."

"What's wrong with Paul tonight?" Dee asked as she massaged her aching feet. "He certainly is on edge."

Kat frowned. "I have no idea why he is acting like he is. But he is not happy with you for some reason."

Slipping her shoes back on, Dee grimaced. "I have noticed. You would think I had suggested skinny-dipping in the fountain or something."

"Please don't suggest anything remotely like that or I won't be responsible for what may happen to you," Kat warned her.

"Tell me to be quiet if you don't like what I am going to say, but really, Kat, Paul has no sense of humor at all! If I had known that when I introduced the two of you I might have had second thoughts."

"Paul has a sense of humor, Dee. It just is not as developed as yours," Kat told her as she rubbed her hand on the back of her neck.

"You would stick up for him," Dee accused as she rose from her seat and moved toward the mirrored alcove.

Dee's words brought back memories of the night three years ago when she and James had insisted that Kat accompany them to another of James's lavish parties. Always extravagant, he had outdone himself that night by having two floors of a restaurant done in a replica of the Palace at Versailles. It was literally breathtaking, as thousands of roses had been used in the decorations. Kat smiled as she recalled that Dee had been outraged that James could spend close to $30,000 on roses for a party. It was at that party that Dee had introduced her to Paul. They had spent most of the evening together wrapped in conversation. Kat had been astounded that their interests were so alike in music, literature and the theater. That night had been the beginning of a two-year courtship that had Paul asking her to marry him at least once a week.

Dee rejoined her and said, "I realize that you are taking Paul's side because you love him. But he is becoming a downright stuffed shirt."

"I am not sure I do love him, Dee," Kat said softly.

"What!" Dee exclaimed, almost jumping from her chair.

Kat raised troubled eyes to her friend. "I do not know how I feel anymore."

Dee moved to her side. "Did he say or do something to make you feel like this?"

"He has been terribly busy these past few weeks. He is so tied up with business. When I asked him about the sudden increase in his workload he became quite terse with me and said that he was only trying to clear his calendar so that we might have an uninterrupted honeymoon," Kat told her.

"Then you think he has been neglecting you?" Dee probed.

Kat shook her head. "No. Dee, I hardly even noticed that he was not around. In fact, I was almost relieved at not having to see him every day."

"Oh," Dee sighed softly.

"Dee, what am I going to do?" Kat asked her.

"You are suffering from an all-time classic case of prenuptial jitters," Dee informed her.

"I am?" Kat frowned.

"You are," Dee insisted. "And the best medicine for that is not to worry. We will rejoin the men and have a wonderful time. You will go home and get a good night's sleep and by tomorrow or the next day you will feel fine."

Kat rose from her seat with a sigh. "I hope you are right."

"Of course I am," Dee admonished as she steered Kat toward the door.

Kat paused at the doorway and glanced at her. "But what if you are wrong and I still feel this way?"

Dee took a deep breath. "We will cross that bridge if we come to it. Now put a smile on your face or the men will wonder what we have been up to."

They rejoined their escorts and Kat tried to forget her doubts and remember Dee's words of encouragement. Paul's asking her if she would care for something to drink brought her back to reality and Kat looked at him blankly for a moment as though she did not know who he was.

"Katherine?" he asked, frowning.

"Oh, forgive me. I was lost in thought," Kat apologized. "Something to drink would be nice. Thank you, Paul."

As he moved away to fulfill her request, Kat watched how his tall figure moved with assurance as he greeted friends and acquaintances with a seemingly relaxed air.

Dee leaned over and murmured quietly, "He can be charming when he wants to, can't he?"

Kat shushed her and watched as Elias Spencer, one of her grandfather's chief aides, stopped Paul and spoke to him. Paul glanced back at her as though checking to see if she was watching him before he answered Elias. He kept his remarks short, pausing to intercept one of the circulating waiters bearing a tray of drinks. Elias scowled as though he did not like what Paul was saying and this puzzled Kat.

She was even more puzzled as she viewed the looks exchanged between the two men as Paul excused himself and, carrying the drinks he had acquired, returned to her side.

"What did Elias want?" Kat asked curiously as Paul handed her a glass of champagne.

Paul sipped his drink before answering her. "Nothing important. Why do you ask?"

Kat could tell from the tone of his voice that he did not like her questioning him and wondered even more. "He looked angry as you left," she informed Paul.

Paul laughed shortly. "He wanted to discuss business and I told him to call me at the office."

"Oh," Kat said as though his explanation satisfied her. Maybe what Paul said was true, but Kat could not help thinking that Elias had looked too angry to have been told to call Paul at his office.

She secretly watched Elias through her lashes as she sipped at her champagne. He appeared to be upset by something as he moved across the room and joined her grandfather. Taking a peek at Paul, Kat saw that he was also watching Elias and there was a hard look on his face.

"Paul?" she ventured.

He tore his eyes from Spencer and gazed down at her. "What?" he almost snapped at her. Catching himself, he smiled suddenly and added, "I am sorry, Katherine. I guess I am tired tonight. You were saying?"

Kat felt an uneasiness that she could not explain and could not mention to Paul. "I think we should go over and thank our hostess for everything," she told him.

"Yes, I guess we should," Paul agreed as he took her arm and guided her in the direction of Mrs. Astor.

Later that night as she lay in her bed unable to sleep, Kat's mind was a jumble of thoughts. Why had Paul acted as he had? What possible reason could Elias Spencer have for being angry with him? And why did she feel so uneasy about everything? Nerves, she told herself. No, it was not only nerves. It was something else, but what she could not clearly see. Her final thoughts as she drifted into an exhausted slumber were uneasy ones.

Her uneasiness stayed with her in spite of Dee's encouraging words, through the next day and the rehearsal evening and dinner.

Saturday morning dawned bright and sunny but Kat's uneasiness had increased. She had come to a frightening decision in the lonely predawn hours. It was one she knew she had to make and she hoped and prayed that her reasons for making it were the right reasons.

With all the confusion of preparations Kat was unable to see her grandfather before it was time for her to dress and go to the church. She wished she could have spoken to him sooner but knew she would have to tell him there. She prayed that he and Paul would understand.

The strains of the Wedding March from Wagner's "Lohengrin" echoed through the air of the church, drifting into an expectant silence.

Kat wished with all her being that things did not have to be as they were, but she knew in her heart and soul that she could not go through with the marriage. She did not love Paul, and it would be tragically unfair to marry him. Why it had taken her so long to reach such a final decision Kat could not truly say. But she had admitted her decision to Patrick as they stood at the end of the long center aisle of the church.

Patrick was stunned at what Kat told him. He had sincerely thought Kat would be able to make a go of this marriage. But if she felt she could not go through with it, then he would support her in her decision. He loved her dearly and wanted only happiness for her.

Dee overheard Kat tell her grandfather of her decision and moved to her side as Patrick made the long walk up the aisle alone and spoke to Paul.

"It wasn't nerves after all. Oh, Kat." Dee's voice was filled with compassion as she tried to comfort her. Dee knew that Kat would not do something like this unless she truly felt it was the right thing for her to do. She knew what agony her friend must have put herself through before reaching this point, and she also knew the consequences and wanted to help Kat in anyway she could.

A growing rumble of comment filtered through the gathered congregation.

"Stood him up? At this late date!"

"I have always said it would never happen."

"The haughty Miss Gwyn thinks she is too good for him."

"Poor Paul! How could she do such a thing to him?"

These and many less complimentary outbursts began to override the air of shock among the gathered guests. Patrick's brow furrowed and his expression was not one of benevolent goodwill as he heard one of the female guests refer to Kat as a "spoiled bitch."

He rejoined Kat and Dee at the back of the church and they retired to the apse, away from public scrutiny and gloating eyes.

Kat stood, her breathing shallow and pained as she realized what an ugly chain of events she had unavoidably set in motion by standing Paul up at the altar. If only she had been able to reach him by phone before it had come to this. She had spent almost an hour trying to contact Paul and tell him of her feelings, but had not been able to reach him anywhere. Now it was a major scandal.

If only she had been more honest with herself and Paul from the very beginning. She had accepted Paul's proposal knowing that she did not love him as she would have wanted to love the man she married. But she had fooled herself into thinking that she expected too much and that maybe with time she could learn to love him as deeply as she should. She had been a fool and knew it. Now she had hurt Paul and her grandfather as well as herself. Why did she want so much more? She and Paul were as compatible as any of their married contemporaries. What was missing that she felt she must have? Could it be that she was looking for the impossible?

Patrick watched the play of emotions on Kat's face and his protective instincts were aroused. He knew that she would not do anything such as this lightly and he also knew what self-satisfied pleasure this incident would afford his enemies and rivals. As he watched the two girls he knew how vulnerable they both were. Dee would also be tarred with the same taint of scandal, innocent or not.

He had not attained his position of power and wealth without a clear knowledge of how New York's High Society could smile to your face while twisting a knife in your back.

Kat looked up at him with tears in her eyes. "I am sorry, Grandad. I never meant to hurt you or Paul like this."

He put his arm protectively around her shoulders and drew her stiff form into his embrace. "I would much rather that you not marry someone you do not love and end up divorcing him later than marry him because society expects you to do so. No, you did the right thing." He scowled at some of the departing guests who had started to move toward them. "We will weather this together."

"The three of us," Dee added as she placed her hand on Kat's shoulder.

Patrick knew this day would provide fuel for the malicious tongues and triumphant eyes of many. He hoped Kat and Dee would be strong enough to bear it all.

The next week was a living hell for both Kat and Dee. The headlines in most of the newspapers guaranteed that the world would know of this latest society scandal. The telephone rang constantly with calls from the curious and self-righteous. Dee insisted on being at Kat's side as she returned the many wedding gifts and refused the visits of the shamefully nosy.

At twenty-three, Kat was now considered by many a predestined spinster. The shock waves through society reinforced this prediction.

Many who had been unsettled by the intelligence held in Kat's dark brown eyes were thrilled to see her suffer. After all, they said to one another, women were not supposed to be so smart and outspoken. The playboys who had courted Kat's favor in the past and not seen past her beauty, only to have her quick wit and shrewd mind expose them for what they were, rejoiced at her downfall.

Patrick had been right in his assumption that Dee would also be tainted with scandal. As she was as resented as Kat by many she had outshone, her close association with Kat made her as guilty as though she herself had committed the same act. Even James no longer called. And his obvious absence had the gossip mill working at full speed.

Dee had done all she could to try and make things easier for Kat. She had even chased a reporter from the house when she discovered he had slipped in unnoticed through the servants' entrance.

The worst of it was over with the return of all the gifts and world news replacing them on the front page of the newspapers. But Dee still found that she was waiting for something else to happen.

Her wide green eyes were clouded as she watched Kat stare aimlessly out the large window overlooking Fifth Avenue. Kat had taken to doing this often since the terrible day at the church. Dee tried to smooth her curly blond hair into place as she shifted on the dark velvet divan, wrinkling her blue chiffon Panama skirt. Finally, she could stand it no more and said, "Kat, I am sorry."

Kat turned toward her with a rustle of silk petticoats beneath her beige cashmere tea gown. "Why should you be sorry? You have not done anything." Kat shook her head. "No, Dee. I have only myself to blame for the way things are. I allowed them to go too far."

"If I had listened to you when you tried to tell me how you were feeling instead of dismissing your doubts as nerves, things might have been different," Dee insisted stubbornly. "I should have paid more attention to reality and not what I hoped was reality."

Kat crossed her arms, hugging herself as she frowned at Dee. "That is utter nonsense and you know it. I was the one who was fooling herself into a false reality, not you. I thought I could learn to love." Her lips compressed into a thin line. "A mistake I will not make a second time." She shrugged, adding, "I sometimes wonder if I am capable of loving anyone but myself."

"Kat!" Dee exclaimed in shock.

"Katherine!" Patrick's voice boomed as he entered the room. "I will not have you speaking that way."

Kat jumped, startled at hearing his voice, "Grandad! What are you doing home so early in the day?" she asked in surprise.

Patrick moved to his favorite chair by the fireplace and sank into it as though the weight of the world were on his shoulders.

Kat ran to his side, filled with concern. "What is it? Are you ill?"

Dee hastily poured him a cup of coffee and placed it on the table by his chair. Patrick ignored the coffee as he gazed up at both girls. "I have received some dreadful news. I came straight home because I felt I should be the one to tell you."

"Tell us what?" Kat was mystified at what could possibly have upset him so much. She had never seen him this way before and it frightened her.

"Paul died this afternoon after falling from the seventh floor of the Blaine Building. They are saying it was suicide." Patrick's voice cracked with emotion.

"Oh, my God!" Dee gasped as she took Kat's cold hands in hers.

"I killed him," was all Kat said before she collapsed to the floor in a faint.

It was later the next afternoon before they once again met in the sitting room where Patrick had delivered his tragic news.

Kat was pale and still visibly shaken, and Dee watched her with concern as Patrick spoke. "I think it would be best if the two of you went away for awhile. The change of scene might do wonders for you. The way things are here, you are once again targets for the evil-minded to aim at." He raised his hand as Kat tried to speak. "Now, do not give me an answer right now. I want you to think it over tonight and discuss it between you. We can make any final decisions tomorrow."

"Leave town?" Dee speculated aloud.

"Run and hide is what he means," Kat murmured bitterly.

"Katherine! I said we would not discuss it now. I only ask that you think about it." He paused before adding, "I do have a few interests out West that you could inspect for me if you are willing to travel."

"I'm sorry, Grandad. I never intended for anything like this to happen," Kat answered him.

"Listen to me, Katherine. You had nothing to do with Paul's death," Patrick informed her sternly.

When this was greeted by a look of disbelief from his granddaughter he went on to explain further. "I have had some of my best men investigating things, and it appears that Paul may have been involved in some business dealings that ultimately resulted in his taking his own life."

"What business dealing could cause something like that?" Kat asked him, not willing to believe she was not the reason for Paul's death.

"I am not at liberty to go into any details. I should be receiving another report from my investigators within the next few days," Patrick informed her. "Hopefully the full story may be known at that time."

The telephone rang in the hallway, causing Dee to start at the unexpected sound. Kat looked toward the closed door and listened as the butler answered the call.

The door opened and the butler spoke. "A telephone call for you, sir. It is your office calling."

"Thank you, Haskins," Patrick said as he rose to take the call.

Their discussion about traveling was postponed as Patrick became heavily enmeshed in a crisis that had arisen at his office and neither girl saw him for the next few days, days that had Dee and Kat talking things over at great length.

Dee was doing her best to make Kat see the truth. She could not accept the fact that Kat insisted on blaming herself for Paul's death. Exasperated, Dee finally convinced Kat that they needed to get out of the house and away from the persistent telephone callers wanting to ask about things that were none of their business.

The two girls spent a day peacefully strolling through the Museum of Man, and the quietness of its setting helped to soothe their ragged nerves.

After stopping at a small, quiet cafe for afternoon tea and a snack, Kat admitted that the day had been what she needed. "Thank you, Dee."

"For what? What did I do?" Dee asked as she nibbled on the pastry she had ordered. "If you mean for today, then forget it. I have been craving one of these pastries for ages and used you as an excuse to have one." Dee pointed to the cream-filled crust that lay half-eaten in front of her.

Kat smiled. "You cannot fool me, Dee Higgins. I know the real reason you wanted us to do something besides sit at home. So do not try denying that you were worried about me."

Dee made a face at her, uncomfortable with Kat's gratitude. "What do you think about your Grandad's idea of traveling west?"

"I have not really given much thought to it at all. Why?" Kat replied.

Dee wiped her lips with her napkin and suggested, "If he wanted us to get away from the gossips, why couldn't we go to my parents' vacation place in the Adirondacks?"

Kat sipped her tea and replied, "You would have to ask him that question. I have no idea why we could not go there." She frowned. "Although I suspect that Grandad's reasons for sending us west are not purely unselfish. Something has been happening out there that caused the recent trouble at his office."

"What do you suppose it is?" Dee asked, placing some money with their bill on the tray by her cup.

Kat waited until the waiter had collected the tray and returned with Dee's change before answering. "I am not certain, but I have a feeling it has something to do with one of his railroads."

Dee counted her change and decided that it was an ample tip and left it on the tray as she rose from her chair. "When are we supposed to speak with Grandad again?"

Following Dee from the cafe, Kat replied, "I think he means to be home for dinner tonight. I suspect it will be sometime after we dine."

Kat was correct in her assumption and Dee was able to question Patrick after dinner that evening. "Why can we not go to my parents' vacation home?"

Patrick paused as he lighted his after-dinner cigar, then replied, "Dee, there have been reporters camped near there since last week. They expect you and Kat to show up at any time and are waiting to pounce when you do. No, you both will be better off if you travel west as I first suggested."

"Reporters?" Kat quizzed him. "Why would they be interested in either of us?"

"Because you are news, my dear," Patrick explained. "The series of events that began with your not marrying Paul and culminating in his suicide have editors frothing at the mouth. They all want their papers to be the first with an interview with either of you. Some of the newspapers will print what they want to even if they do have to make it up as they go along. They will do anything and everything they think necessary to sell newspapers."

"It sounds like it might be safer out West with the Indians and outlaws," Dee commented with a shake of her head.

"Aphrodite Higgins!" Kat scolded her with a smile. "This is 1903! There are not any wild savages or blood-thirsty outlaws left."

"What a pity," Dee grinned. "I was beginning to look forward to meeting them."

"I am told that Seattle is becoming quite civilized," added Patrick with a twinkle in his eye.

"Seattle!" Both girls looked at him in surprise.

"Yes, Seattle. A relaxing side trip to San Francisco might be arranged if you behave yourselves," he teased.

"When you say out west, you mean at the edge of the Pacific Ocean," Dee told him. "That is thousands of miles away. How do you suggest we travel such a distance? Obviously, we cannot go by wagon train, it would take too long."

"Wagon train?" Kat repeated. "Dee, you have been reading those Wild West books again! Haven't you!" Kat accused her.

Dee defended herself by saying, "What is wrong with that? I like to know what is going on in other parts of the world. Is that a crime?"

Patrick laughed. "Dee, you are as another grand-daughter to me, but would your father approve of your reading material?"

Dee tilted her chin defensively. "If he were not so lost in his own dusty books and scrolls, he might read mine. He also has an inquiring mind."

"Lucky for you he has not read your books or you

might have been named Pocahontas instead of Aphrodite," Kat quipped teasingly.

Dee knew that what Kat said was closer to the truth than Kat realized. Her father had wanted to name all his children after the Greek gods of mythology. Thankfully, her mother's common sense had prevailed. "Apollo Higgins, indeed!" had been her comment to his suggestion of a name for their firstborn son. As strong as Dee's mother was, she had prevailed through the births of Dee's two other brothers. But she lost the battle and the war at Dee's birth.

Dee had been the apple of her father's eye from the beginning and his wife was coaxed into agreeing to the name Aphrodite. So Kat had come closer to the truth than she would ever know and consequently Dee shot her a stubborn look and held her tongue.

"Enough you two," Patrick chuckled. "To answer Dee's question regarding transportation, I have made arrangements for you to travel in one of my private cars on the Great Northern."

"Why the Great Northern?" Kat asked him suspiciously. "I would think that the Union Pacific would be better."

Patrick eyed his granddaughter. "You know more than is proper for a young woman to know. The Great Northern will provide you with a safer and more relaxing journey." He stared at Kat, waiting for her to comment. When she started to answer, he cut her off by saying, "My reasons are not open to question."

Kat smiled slightly and tilted her head saying, "More infighting among your colleagues?"

Patrick cleared his throat and glared at her. "It has been decided you will travel on the Great Northern."

Dee enjoyed teasing Patrick as much as Kat did and asked, "When has it been decided that we are leaving?"

"Tuesday of next week, why?" Patrick asked her suspiciously.

"I thought since it all has been decided I should know when so I can be certain to be there," Dee said with a twinkle in her eyes.

Patrick threw his hands up in the air, exclaiming, "The two of you are the most frustrating pair a man could ever deal with."

Kat hugged him, saying, "And we both know you love us dearly. Why else do you think we tease you so much?"

Against his better judgment, Patrick asked, "Why?"

"We know we can get away with it," Dee told him with a laugh.

His lean face was thoughtful as he closed the door. Elias knew that he had been excluded from the reasons behind the decision that Katherine Gwyn and Aphrodite Higgins were suddenly traveling to Seattle. His mind worked trying to analyze each piece of this puzzle. Twice in the past few days Patrick had kept appointments that Elias had had no prior knowledge existed.

The drawer in Patrick's desk was now locked, when in the past it had always remained open. And what was in that sealed envelope that Katherine had carried as she left her grandfather's office?

Did the old man suspect something? Or was he being cautious for reasons of his own? Elias shook his head and sat down at his own desk. Taking a piece of paper from his pocket, he stared at it. Then, smiling to himself, he returned the paper to his pocket. He would wire ahead of the train carrying the young ladies and have them watched. That would cover any trickery on Gwyn's part.

It was close to two hours later when Elias closed and

relocked the drawer on Patrick Gwyn's massive oak desk. He heard the rumble of voices approaching the office door. Quickly looking around with a practiced eye, Elias made sure that he had left no trace of his leisurely perusal of the contents of Patrick's private papers.

Chapter Two

THE CLACKING RHYTHM OF THE TRAIN'S PASSAGE WAS THE only sound in the private railroad car. Patrick had spared no expense when he commissioned George Pullman to design and outfit his private car. All the rich upholstery on the numerous chairs and couches was of the plushest variety. The walls competed with one another, vying for attention with their rich hangings overlaying the hand-carved inlaid paneling. French bevel-plated mirrors were set at artistic locations to reflect the grandeur and richness of the car's many amenities.

All this splendor was lost on Dee as she chewed her lower lip pensively and tried to sit quietly so as not to disturb Kat as she reclined on the velvet couch across from her. Knowing that Kat was awake, Dee refrained from conversation for fear it might lead to further words about their journey. Dee did not want to mention any of her fears. She knew how Kat refused to take any of them seriously.

"Dee!" Kat's voice ordered from across the car. "Would you stop worrying about what might happen! Try and rest." Kat shifted to a more comfortable position as she added, "We should be stopping in an hour or so for water. Nothing is going to happen between now and then." She smiled, softening her words of rebuke.

"Where are we, anyway?" Dee asked as she noticed the rugged green countryside for the first time in hours.

Kat followed Dee's glance out the soot-blackened window. "We are still somewhere in the wilds of Montana."

Wilds is right, Dee thought uncomfortably to herself. Snuggling into a ball, she took Kat's advice and tried to rest. It was better than waiting for outlaws to rob the train, she told herself.

Kat smiled at Dee as she napped. She knew Dee's imagination had been working overtime since they left what Dee called the "Civilized World." For all Dee's extensive reading about the West, she was still apprehensive that something terrible might happen to them. The rest would do her good, Kat thought to herself, wishing the same were true for her. Her mind kept going over the events that had led up to the present. Her actions left her nothing to be very proud of, she decided.

The hypnotic cadence of the wheels on the tracks brought other, older memories to Kat's mind. Memories of when her grandfather had been proud of her and not anxious to send her away. She had been eleven and Dee was nine when Patrick and Dee's father had escorted them to the premier performance at Carnegie Hall. It had been the first grown-up occasion for either of them and they wore beautiful dresses and carried the flowers their escorts had given them. Kat remembered how Tchaikovsky had conducted that night and how ever since when she heard the same music it reminded her of that magical evening.

The sudden sound of metal screaming and shrieking shattered the slumbering silence. Kat cried out as she was tossed into the air like a rag doll, hitting the wall sharply before the upheaval of the car sent her crashing into the sideboard as it slithered into her path. Pain shot through her side and blackness descended as she hit the floor.

Dee woke to Kat's cry and to sudden terror. All the furnishings were careening around as though propelled by the invisible hands of an angry giant. The sound of glass splintering mixed with the tortured wails of over-stressed steel. Dee tried to curl even tighter into a ball in an effort to avoid the flying wreckage as she was tossed about. The bright flash of a large shard of glass from one of the mirrors caused her to instinctively raise her arms to protect her head and face. The world around her was coming to an end as it shuddered and heaved and wreckage rained.

Dust and soot clouded the air, making it hard to see and grating her throat with each breath. As quickly as it had started, the reign of terror subsided to be replaced by an even more frightening silence. The only sounds remaining were the settling of debris and the incongruent dripping of wine from the broken bottles of Patrick's private stock.

Dee slowly opened her eyes, straining to see in the murky light. "Kat! Kat! Are you all right?" she called frantically.

Silence was her only answer. Oh, God, please let her be all right, Dee prayed as she tried to wriggle out of her cramped position behind a mound of broken furniture. All her efforts were to no avail; she was trapped! Trying not to panic, Dee took several calming breaths that resulted in choking fits of coughing. When she could she called once more, "Kat! Can you hear me? Are you all right?"

A burning sensation in her wrist made Dee glance down. She had a long, wicked-looking gash that was oozing blood. Wrapping a piece of torn petticoat around it, she fought down her rising panic and called out, "Kat!"

A feeble moan sounded nearby. Then Kat's shaken voice answered her. "Dee? Where are you?"

Relief swept through Dee at hearing Kat's voice. "I am trapped over by where the window used to be. At least, I think it is where it used to be. Are you hurt?"

Kat turned to her right and faced the sound of Dee's voice. Shaking her head, she tried to clear it of the dizziness that was crowding in on her. Exerting great effort, Kat crawled toward the pile of once-beautiful furniture that now formed Dee's prison. "Dee? Can you hear me?" she called.

"I hear you. You sound awful," came Dee's reply. "You must be hurt. Can you tell how badly?"

Kat leaned against the upside-down sofa as she tried to remain conscious. "I must have hit my head and my left side hurts, but otherwise I'll live," Kat reported as she checked herself. "What about you? Are you hurt?"

"I cut my wrist and have a few bruises, but that's all," Dee answered her. "What do you think happened?"

"The train made an unscheduled stop." Kat tried to laugh but gasped at the lancing pain in her side.

"Very funny," Dee returned. "Have you any other bright ideas, such as what do we do now?"

Kat eyed the massive pieces blocking Dee's freedom. "There is too much for me to move alone. We will have to wait until help comes."

Dee viewed her prison and murmured, "If it comes." She realized something that Kat apparently did not. Their railroad car was the last on the train, with the mail car separating them from the main body of passenger cars. Would anyone think of looking for passengers in a rarely used private car, when they had their hands full with all the other passengers? Dee hoped that they would.

Kat's voice was strained and weak as she tried to reassure Dee that help was on the way.

It seemed as though hours passed before Dee heard thumping on the walls and voices calling, "Anyone in there?"

"Here! Yes! We're in here!" Dee yelled, her throat hoarse with grit. She hoped whoever it was hurried, she was very worried about Kat. She had not been able to raise any response from her for a long while.

Darkness was falling before Dee was startled by the nerve-shattering screech of their compartment door being wrenched open from the outside. Frantically, she called out, "My friend is hurt! Please help her!"

She heard a deep masculine voice issue orders for Kat to be carried out to a waiting wagon. Dee felt helpless trapped as she was and called out again, "Is Kat badly hurt?"

The sounds of someone moving closer through the tangled debris told her she was not alone. When the same deep voice she had heard before answered her, Dee was only partly relieved. "Your friend has an ugly bump on her head. The doctor will have to decide how serious it is. We will be taking her to him as soon as I find out where you are hiding." He sounded as though he were standing next to her.

"I am not hiding! I am trapped behind the sofa, desk and I don't know what else!" was Dee's indignant reply.

Her rescuer eyed the piled wreckage. "Is there room under all this?"

"I am under it and there is room for me!" Dee declared hotly, wishing that he would stop wasting time talking and get her out. She had to be with Kat.

"You must be mighty small," was the comment as the sound of moving wreckage filled the air.

Dee felt her cheeks redden in anger. "Please hurry, my friend needs me."

"We may be here for awhile. There is a mountain of furniture blocking you in there," said the deep-voiced stranger.

"A mountain?"

Hearing the strain in the girl's voice the big man said, "My name's Sven Thorsen. What's yours?"

"Dee Higgins," came the slow reply.

"Hang on, little one, I'll have you free in a moment," he reassured her.

Dee bristled at his calling her by that name, but the small glimmer of light that came into her prison as he lifted the weighty sofa made her hold her tongue. She caught a glimpse of a large muscular arm as the massive rolltop desk was heaved out of the way. He must be a giant, she thought to herself as she saw the ease with which he was working through the wreckage.

Sven was beginning to wonder if he had been hearing things. Surely no one could have been trapped in so tiny a space and survived. He moved a heavy pile of rags that were once elegant wall hangings and two wide eyes stared up at him, causing him to revise his opinion.

"Thank you! I was afraid I might be stuck in here forever," Dee greeted him from her cramped position.

Taken by surprise, Sven said the first thing that came to his mind. "You really are a little bit of a thing, aren't you?"

Dee craned her neck, trying to take in his massive physique in what little light there was to see by. "If you will forgive me for saying so, anything would look little next to you," she told him.

His booming laughter filled the demolished car and

Dee clapped her hands over her ears for protection. Her action brought her roughly bandaged wrist into view. Sven bent down and lifted her bodily from the rubble, saying, "Why didn't you say you were hurt? We will have the doctor take a look at that."

In her concern for Kat, Dee had completely forgotten about her own injury. Sven's reminder made her say, "Oh, you mean this." She held her arm up. "It is not anything serious, only a scratch."

Carrying Dee's small figure, Sven left the wrecked rail car and moved out into the evening air. Bearing her to the waiting wagon, he said, "We will let the doctor be the judge of how serious it is."

Dee's eyes widened at his words. How dare he say she did not have the sense to know if she were hurt seriously or not! Why, he is not only big, he is a bully!

Settling Dee next to Kat in the wagon, Sven checked on Kat's blanket-wrapped form before turning to the gathered workers and saying, "These are the only passengers in this car." He viewed the sweat-stained men and asked one of their leaders, "Have all the others been transported into town?"

"Hours ago, Mr. Thorsen," was the reply.

Sven looked down at the occupants of the wagon and said, "I will take these two to the lodge. It is too far and too late to take them into town."

"Whatever you say, Mr. Thorsen."

Gathering the reins, he started the team forward as he said, "I will check with you tomorrow, Ben. Tell all the men they did a good job."

Directing the wagon to the north, they left the mangled wreckage of the train behind them. "Where are you taking us?" Dee asked tentatively.

Sven caught the nervousness in her voice and knew that shock from the crash was starting to affect her. "To the lodge, where my brothers and I live," he explained.

Brothers! Dee thought fuzzily to herself before saying aloud, "You mean there are more like you?"

She could feel herself blushing in embarrassment as Sven's laughter filled the cold night air. She decided she had better keep her mouth shut if he found her so amusing.

The ride was a cold and frightening one. She knew she had never seen a night as dark as this one. She was accustomed to the streetlights and bustle of people in New York. But this Montana darkness was an eerie blackness with strange sounds coming from behind the dark shapes of unknown trees and bushes.

Dee heaved a quiet sigh of relief as they pulled onto a drive leading up to a building that she hoped was their destination. She could dimly make out the shape of the two-story structure, beyond the fact that it looked quite large from the outside. There was a covered porch with steps leading down to the front of the lodge, and light glowed from a window on the second story with another warm glow from a window on the main level.

She looked down at Kat lying unconscious by her side. I hope we can find help for you here, she thought to herself as Sven reined in the team and the wagon halted.

Climbing down from his seat, Sven bellowed, "Eric! Leif! Bert!"

The heavy front door opened and light spilled out across the porch, cutting the blackness. A tall figure came through the door and down the steps to the wagon.

Sven lifted Kat gently and started up the stairs through the open doorway.

"Wait for me," Dee called as she struggled to leave the wagon.

"Don't worry, Miss. She will be fine. Let's get you

inside," a friendly voice answered her as two arms lifted her from the wagon bed.

"I can walk, thank you," Dee insisted.

"So can I. What a coincidence," was the warm reply as the tall figure carried her up the steps.

As they entered the doorway Dee looked up into a pair of twinkling eyes and a smiling face. They moved into an entry area and Dee searched for Kat. She saw Sven disappearing up a staircase in front of her, bearing Kat in his arms.

There were sounds of activity coming from the passageway to the left of the stairs. The sounds confused Dee and she glanced around the entryway with frantic eyes. She saw a closed door to her right and a warm inviting glow from lamps in the room to her left, where she was being carried. She had only a few seconds to notice everything as they entered a comfortable parlor with three Morris chairs covered in leather and corduroy. There were parlor tables of oak with hand-carved claw feet conveniently placed near each chair.

She was taken to an overly large horsehair sofa covered with brightly woven blankets that was set in the center of the room to take advantage of heat from the natural stone fireplace.

Laying her down on the sofa, her bearer said, "I'm Leif. What is your name?"

"Dee," she answered as she had her first good look at this friendly-voiced companion.

He was tall with a slim, athletic build and curly red-gold hair. The same twinkling hazel eyes she had seen in the dim outside light beamed down at her as he accepted her appraisal. She felt an immediate liking for this young man and was not embarrassed to ask, "Where has my friend been taken?"

Looking through the doorway they had entered, Leif

replied, "Upstairs. There are bedrooms up there. I think she will be more comfortable until the doctor can look at her."

"Can he be trusted?" Dee asked, sorry she had asked as soon as she uttered the words.

Leif laughed. "Sven? I think so."

Heavy footsteps sounded on the stairs, which made Dee shiver as Leif's laughter brought Sven into the room asking, "What is so funny?"

"Our guest wanted to know if you could be trusted," Leif told him.

Dee gulped as she felt Sven's icy blue eyes bore into her as he stood towering by Leif.

"And what did you say, baby brother?" Sven asked suspiciously.

"Baby brother!" Dee gasped as she looked from one man to the other and saw the resemblance that was unmistakable.

Leif ignored her gasp and answered Sven with a grin, "I told her you had been fed and did not fancy tender young women, but preferred tough ole mountain cats for dinner."

Sven took a good-natured swing at Leif, which Leif easily dodged.

Sven was about to check Dee's bandaged wrist when a rough voice ordered, "Enough jawing, you two."

The figure of an older woman came bustling into the room carrying a pan of water and some lint bandages. Setting the pan on a nearby table, the newcomer smiled at Dee, saying, "Ignore those two lummoxes, dear. They would let a body bleed to death before they quit going on at each other."

"Bert!" came a chorus of protest from the maligned pair.

Bert looked them up and down and began issuing orders. "Don't stand there gawking. Go hurry your brother and have him look at that poor girl upstairs while I attend to this young lady."

Turning her back on them, she began unwrapping Dee's injured wrist.

"Another brother!" Dee mumbled in confusion as the men left the room.

Bert discarded Dee's makeshift bandage and competently began to wash out the ugly gash that was revealed. Dee winced as pain lanced up her arm and Bert took a firmer grip as she applied an antiseptic. "You said something about another brother. That would be Eric," Bert informed her.

Dee bit her lip and tears sprang to her eyes as the medicine flowed into her wound, burning it like fire. Gritting her teeth against the pain, she heard the older woman's voice through a haze.

"I should have known those two idiots would not have told you anything."

Dee tried to protest that she had not been there long enough for anyone to tell her anything but was cut off by Bert as she continued. "I am Bert. Those two that just left are my nephews, Sven and Leif Thorsen. I sent them after their brother Eric. He is a doctor."

Dee felt her mind whirl in a jumble of impressions. Everything was happening at once and she could not take it all in. The mention of the word doctor made her try to pull free and rise from the sofa, distress written on her face as she whispered, "Kat."

Bert's firm grip on her arm prevented Dee from rushing in search of Kat. "Hey, now!" Bert warned her. "You can go to your friend as soon as I am done here. Now sit still and let me finish."

Dee squirmed impatiently as Bert applied a bandage to her now throbbing wrist. Bert had sat back and was about to gather her supplies when Dee slid off the sofa and headed in the direction she had seen Sven carry Kat.

Bert shook her head at Dee's reckless haste and left the litter of her first aid to follow her.

Dee rushed up the long staircase and soon found herself on a landing with doors facing her no matter which way she turned.

"Where is she?" she called down to Bert.

"Most likely they put her in the corner room to your left," came Bert's response from the bottom of the staircase.

Moving to her left, Dee saw the door she wanted at the far end of the landing. Hurrying to the door, she opened it and entered a large, rustic room. Kat was lying motionless on an immense feather bed. Going to her side, Dee looked down at Kat's bruised form. There was a gash on her forehead with a large purple bruise spreading from the side of her temple into her hairline.

"I knew something was going to happen," Dee murmured, trying to hide the shock that Kat's appearance caused her. She looked back to the closed door, wishing the doctor would hurry. Oh, dear, she thought to herself, the doctor. Would he be qualified to treat Kat? Or was he a local horse doctor that treated people when the need arose? Looking back at Kat's unconscious form, Dee thought in dismay, I can't allow a horse doctor to treat her.

The sound of male voices on the staircase hardened Dee's resolve to take care of Kat. She patted Kat's listless hand and squared her shoulders, ready to face the men. She realized that she would have to be sure and express gratefulness for their care, but she would also have to explain carefully that she wanted only proper medical treatment for Kat. Listing in her mind what she was going to say, Dee felt she was ready, if only the room would stop spinning.

Entering the room, Eric found himself faced with a pint-sized roadblock when he tried to make his way toward the bed and his waiting patient. He stepped back in surprise as a small hand pushed firmly against his chest and a small female voice ordered him with a quaver, "That is far enough."

He looked down at his antagonist and frowned as he saw her dilated eyes and pale face. "I will see you after I have examined your friend," he told her. "Please wait outside."

Dee raised her eyebrows and stared at this third Thorsen brother. Were they all so bossy? she thought incongruously to herself. His golden hair, gray eyes and tall stature marked him a Thorsen, but was he a real doctor? "Are you a real doctor?" she asked him in a voice that she hoped was stern, but sounded more like a whisper.

Eric's head snapped back at her question. "What other type of doctor could I be?"

"A horse doctor," Dee informed him as he tried to pass her and she once again blocked his way.

"Horse doctor!" Eric jerked at this appellation. "Did you also hit your head?"

A sheen of nervous perspiration filmed her body as Dee said, "No, I did not hit my head. I cannot have anyone who is not qualified treating my friend."

Eric could not believe his ears or his eyes. This little bit of a girl was questioning his credentials and delaying his treatment of a patient. He picked Dee up by the shoulders and moved her out of his way, saying, "I suppose you wish to see my diploma?"

"That would prove that you are a doctor." Dee said, fighting the dizziness that came over her. "That is . . . if . . . you have a diploma to show me."

Eric could see that she was about to collapse at any moment and yelled, "Sven!"

Sven and Leif came at his yell. Hearing them enter the room, Eric said, "Tell this child that I am a qualified physician and one of you take hold of her before she collapses."

Sven shook his head at Eric's calling Dee a child. He knew from his own experience that she did not like that at all.

Leif put his arms around Dee's shaking shoulders and raised his eyes questioningly to Eric as she sagged against him for support, saying, "Leif?"

Eric shook his head warningly at Leif, telling him more about Dee's condition with that simple movement than with words.

Leif caught the silent message and said, "Eric's a doctor, Dee. I do not think that Harvard Medical School would appreciate one of its graduates being questioned as to his qualifications."

Dee looked up at Leif's blurred face and then over at Eric. "Harvard Medical School?"

Leif nodded his head as Eric bent to examine Kat.

Dee saw him and with a small sigh fainted into Leif's surprised arms.

Lifting her inert form, Leif looked at Eric for an explanation. Eric glanced over his shoulder at hearing Dee's sigh and said, "She is suffering from shock and possible loss of blood. I am not surprised that she fainted, only that it took her so long to do so."

Leif started to the door as Eric's voice stopped him. "Take her downstairs. If she does not come out of her faint soon, loosen her stays. Women usually insist on wearing them too tight to begin with."

Returning to the parlor, Leif laid Dee on the sofa and crouched next to her, cradling her hand in his. Bert moved over to them and seeing that she had fainted ordered, "Lift her up some, Leif. I have to undo her shirtwaist and loosen her bodice so she can breathe."

Leif pulled Dee's slight form upward until her head was resting against his shoulder. Bert quickly undid the numerous satin-covered buttons on the back of Dee's shirtwaist and, reaching under her corset cover of fine lawn, loosened the ties on Dee's corset.

Looking up at Leif, Bert saw something she thought she would never see: he was close to blushing with embarrassment. Taking pity on him, she said, "Sven. You come hold her up. Leif, go out into the kitchen and bring back a glass of cold water."

The brothers changed positions and Leif made haste to vacate the room. Bert and Sven exchanged amused glances and Sven cradled Dee against his chest as Bert continued to loosen the confining undergarments.

Slowly recovering from her faint, now that her restrictive underpinnings had been loosened, Dee felt mortified at her behavior. She wished that she could melt away and disappear and not have to face the owner of the broad chest she seemed to be resting upon. She knew from its muscular hardness that it must belong to Sven. Moving slightly, she stiffened as it became apparent to her that her clothing had been rearranged.

Sven knew by her tenseness in his arms that she was conscious. He could also feel her beginning to tremble uncontrollably as though chilled to the bone. "Bert, fetch one of the blankets here."

"I'll bring a heavy one," Bert said as she left to get a blanket from her large linen closet.

Dee tried not to scream for her to come back and not leave her alone with Sven. She tried to pull away from him, but he tightened his grasp, saying, "Be still now, little one. You have had enough shocks for one day."

What did he mean by that, Dee thought to herself.

Before she could renew her attempts to free herself Bert returned and tucked a fluffy wool blanket around her and Sven's arms as he held her.

"Leif must have gotten lost trying to find that glass of water," Bert said. "I'll go and make some coffee." She bustled from the room.

Dee wished she could stop shaking. No matter how hard she tried to control the tremors that shook her they continued. Why was Sven having this effect on her? She had been held in other men's arms and never started shaking.

Sven could feel the effort that Dee was trying to exert over herself and said softly, his voice rumbling in his chest, "Relax, no one is going to hurt you. It is a reaction from the wreck that is making you shake like a leaf. It will pass sooner if you don't fight it and relax."

It's not all from the wreck, she thought to herself. You are part of my trouble.

As her trembling eased Dee was ashamed to raise her eyes and look Sven in the face, partly because of her behavior upstairs and partly because she was afraid that he would be able to tell by looking at her that he had affected her as he had. Moistening her lips, she spoke softly, "You must forgive me. I do not know what came over me. I was only trying to do what I thought was best for my friend."

"Shh," Sven murmured, his breath stirring her blond hair.

Dee rested her head on the hard pillow of strength, too weak to fight any longer. Gradually she felt her body calm and a growing warmth from the blanket. She railed at herself for her weakness.

The sound of someone else entering the room made her bury her head and close her eyes. She could not bear having to face anyone just yet.

"Here's the water, Sven. The damn pump in the

kitchen was dry and I had to go out back to fetch the water," Leif said as he gazed down at the huddled Dee in his brother's arms before placing the glass on the nearby table. "Will she be all right?" he asked as he saw her pale face and closed eyes. "Surely she would have come out of a faint by now if nothing serious was wrong," Leif commented in a worried tone.

"Go fix up that other room, next to mine. We'll take her up there as soon as Eric has looked at her," Sven instructed.

Leif frowned slightly at Sven's tone. He was not a child to be brushed off so lightly. "I asked if she would be all right." He repeated his question in a harder tone of his own.

Sven looked up at him, startled at the sound of maturity. "I think so. But Eric will be able to tell us. Now go attend to the room; you know Bert can't manage the stairs because of her arthritis."

Leif departed and Dee sighed softly in relief. How she wished they had never left New York. At least everyone there knew how she was prone to put her foot in her mouth.

The sudden slow movement of Sven's hands on her back caused her to stiffen and try to push away from him. What was he doing!

"Easy, little one. I'm rebuttoning your shirt so you won't be embarrassed in front of the others," Sven explained easily.

Bert rejoined them carrying a tray laden with a coffee server and mugs. Setting it down on a table, she eyed Sven and the small bundle that rested against him. "Has Eric been down yet?" she asked.

"Not yet," Sven answered her.

"That poor girl must be hurt pretty badly, then," Bert observed aloud. "He's been up there a long time."

"Bert," Sven growled warningly as he looked down at Dee.

Bert followed his glance and saw Dee's wide green eyes looking back at her in anguish. "There now, dear. Pay no attention to the ramblings of an old woman. Your friend is probably fine. Eric is a good doctor and he can take good care of her. Now don't you worry."

Dee pushed herself away from Sven's unresisting hold and sat upright on the sofa as the blanket fell away from her shoulders.

Bert was quick to notice that the back of Dee's shirtwaist was buttoned and gave credit to her nephew's quick thinking in saving the child any embarrassment.

Dee accepted a steaming cup of coffee, even though she did not think she could drink it without spilling it all over her. There were occasional shivers that still rocked her. Watching Sven's hands as he accepted a cup of coffee, she wondered how such large hands had so easily managed the intricacies of the tiny buttons on her back. This thought caused another shiver to course through her.

Sven watched Dee as she shakily tried to sip her coffee and wear a facade of normalcy under abnormal conditions and wondered how such a small female could cause so much trouble in so little time.

Handing a cup of coffee to Leif, Bert took one for herself and sat down, saying, "Where are you from, Dee?"

Dee liked this rough-sounding woman. She had been more than kind in taking strangers into her home and caring for them. Dee smiled at her. "We are both from New York."

"New York?" Bert repeated as she looked over at Leif. "Leif might know your people. He is going to the university there."

"You are?" Dee said in surprise.

Leif shrugged. "I am finishing up my law degree." Turning to his aunt, he added, "But I doubt if I would know any of Dee's relations. There are many more people back there, Bert. Besides, most of them are too busy to know everyone else and they don't meddle in each other's affairs."

"Are you saying that I meddle?" Bert accused him.

Flashes of the scandal that had sent she and Kat on their journey west made Dee frown. "People in the East sometimes overly concern themselves with the affairs of others," she commented half to herself.

Leif threw a puzzled look at Sven and Bert but did not press Dee for a further explanation.

"Do either of you have any kinfolk that might be worrying about you?" Bert inquired. "We could contact them for you. What is your family name? And your friend's name, too, so's we can send word for you."

Dee had been so lost in their immediate problems she had forgotten that she would have to wire New York with the bad news. "I should contact our families as soon as possible. Kat's grandfather will be very worried." She spoke softly to herself before remembering that she had an audience. "Pardon me. I was thinking aloud. Something that Kat says I do too much." Dee tried to rearrange her position on the sofa and not spill her coffee.

Sven reached over and helped her, adjusting the blanket that partially covered her.

"Forgive me for being so slow-witted in answering your questions." Dee smiled self-consciously. "I am Aphrodite Higgins and my friend is Katherine Gwyn. We were on our way to Seattle when the train . . ."

Sven saw her features pale at the memory of the wreck and interrupted her, saying, "Is Kat any relation to Patrick Gwyn?"

"Why, yes!" Dee's shocked eyes looked at him. "How did you know that?"

"I didn't. But Patrick Gwyn is a partner with Jim Hill in the Great Northern Railroad. We do our shipping with his line," Sven answered her, noticing the increasing strain reflected in her eyes. He silently wished that Eric would hurry before she passed out again.

"Shipping?" Dee looked at Leif in confusion.

"Logs. We own and operate our own logging company," Leif explained.

Eric came into the room and went over to Dee. Lifting her wrist, he began to check her pulse rate. His arrival stilled the conversation.

Dee was torn between asking him about Kat and wishing he had not come into the room at all. In the glow of the parlor lamps he seemed to her to be a tall, avenging angel. Her questioning of his competence appalled her even more.

Seeing the bandage on her wrist, Eric turned to his aunt. "How deep was the wound?" He watched Dee closely as Bert answered him.

"It was deep enough. I do not think it needed any sewing. I cleaned it and dressed it," Bert said, explaining her ministrations.

Eric could see that Dee was still obviously shaken and he wondered about other injuries she might be concealing. Lifting her chin, he examined her eyes with clinical interest as he asked, "Do you hurt anywhere else? Is there any dizziness or nausea?"

"I did feel dizzy, but that is all. My wrist your aunt told you about," Dee whispered softly.

"Are you quite certain?" Eric probed. "If you would be more comfortable, we could retire to my office."

"No!" Dee exclaimed, "I am quite all right, believe me. There is no need for you to concern yourself about me."

Eric smiled, softening the hard planes of his strong face. "I thought we agreed earlier that it is my profession to be concerned."

"I would like to apologize for my behavior earlier, Doctor," Dee hastened to say.

Eric waved her silent as he poured himself a mug of coffee. "It was understandable under the circumstances. And my name is Eric." He sat in the remaining Morris chair and crossed his legs.

"Eric?" Dee had a hard time saying his name. "How is Kat?"

"She is very lucky. She could have been seriously hurt. As it is she has a concussion and some bruised ribs." He sipped at his mug before continuing. "I would like to keep an eye on her for a few days." Seeing the growing alarm on Dee's face he added, "But barring any unforeseen complications, a roaring headache and a tender side should be her only problems for awhile."

"Complications?" Dee seized on the word anxiously.

Leif reached over and took her hand, saying, "Doctor talk. They think it makes them sound important." He shot a warning glance at Eric.

Eric saw how Dee relaxed as Leif spoke to her and raised questioning eyes to Sven, who shrugged in response.

"Can I see her?" Dee asked.

"In the morning you may see her," Eric returned steadily. "I think you both need rest tonight."

Leif smiled at Dee and said, "I'll carry you up to your room, Dee."

"I think I told you once before that I can walk." She smiled back at him.

Leif looked at Eric for instructions and Eric said, "I think she knows what she is capable of doing, Leif."

He rose, allowing Dee to lean on him for support as

they made their way to the base of the staircase. Leif hoped she would not faint as they slowly ascended.

Reaching the top, Dee was more than grateful for Leif's strong arm. Her knees felt like rubber and her head was beginning to whirl with dizziness. She paused at the landing and asked, "Which room is mine?"

Leif grinned. "The door in front of us is my room. You know Kat's room. Nick's room is on the other side of hers." He directed her attention to the opposite corner room adjacent to his. "This will be your room. Sven is next to you with Eric next to him."

His obvious omission of a powder room made Dee uneasy. Looking about the landing she found that he had accounted for all the rooms but one and asked hopefully, "And the remaining room?"

"That is a mess right now," was his reply.

"What?" Dee did not understand what he meant.

"It was another spare bedroom until last week," he explained.

"What is it now?" Dee was almost afraid to ask.

Leif shrugged his shoulders and grinned even more. "Bert has a habit of ordering things from the Sears, Roebuck catalogue. Over the years, she has managed to send for almost everything and anything you could think of—"

"So?" Dee interrupted him.

"So, her latest order arrived last week and we haven't had time to finish installing it yet," Leif told her.

"Installing it?" Dee felt lost.

"Yes," Leif answered before plunging ahead with his explanation. "Bert ordered a complete indoor plumbing outfit with tub, lavatory and water closet."

"Oh," Dee murmured, surprised that they did not already have this normal convenience.

"Dee, this is not New York. Most of the people here have outside plumbing."

"Outside?" Dee gulped. She had read about facilities such as these but had figured they were in the same category as outlaws and savage Indians, a thing of the past. She never in her wildest dreams thought that one day she would be utilizing them herself.

Leif hoped he had not upset her too much. The young ladies he knew in New York would probably have fainted if they thought they would have to discuss such a delicate subject with him.

"Oh, well, as my father would say, 'When in Greece, do as the Grecians do.'" Dee stated gallantly.

"Isn't that Rome?" Leif said, surprised at her reaction.

Dee looked up at him and giggled. "You have not met my father."

It was not until she had persuaded Leif to take her down, after agreeing to let him carry her, and show her the primitive necessities and they had returned to her room that Dee thought to ask who Nick was. Leif had mentioned that one of the other bedrooms belonged to him. But who was he?

Probably another brother, she told herself as she slipped into the huge feather bed and drifted into an exhausted sleep.

Chapter Three

REJOINING HIS BROTHERS, LEIF WAS RELIEVED THAT HE had finally managed to settle Dee. She had been so insistent on seeing things for herself that he had begun to wonder if she would ever settle for the night. She certainly was not like any other New York girl he had ever met.

"What are you looking so pleased about? And what took you so long?" Eric asked him.

Leif related the trek to view the outside plumbing and Dee's attitude regarding its existence.

"You took her where?" Eric exploded.

"She was bound and determined to see it tonight, Eric. I figured if I did not take her, she might try to go on her own," Leif explained.

Eric was ready to lecture Leif when Sven cut him off, saying, "At least he managed to settle Dee. Which is more than you were capable of doing earlier, Eric. How did a feather of a female like that manage to get the best of you?"

Leif laughed. "I would not underestimate Dee, if I were you. She is quite a lady with a mind of her own."

"She is stubborn, all right," Sven returned.

Eric leaned back in his seat. "Quite a lady? What have we here? Love at first sight?"

Leif refilled his empty mug and took a seat on the vacant sofa before answering Eric's barb. "She stood up to you, didn't she?"

Eric glared at him coldly. "She took me unawares. Besides, she was suffering from shock and not accountable for what she said."

"You were the one who looked shocked when we came in to see what was happening." Leif grinned.

"Enough, baby brother." Sven stopped Leif from antagonizing Eric.

Leif quieted, content that he had managed to score a few points off the normally unruffled Eric. Dee must have unsettled him far more than I thought, Leif guessed to himself.

"Eric, is Kat seriously injured?" Sven asked now that Leif had let up.

"You heard what I told Dee," Eric answered slowly.

Sven grimaced. "Yes, I did. Now I want to hear what you did not tell her." Sven eyed Eric steadily. "I pulled her from the wreck, remember? I know there is more than you told Dee."

"I would like to know the full story myself," Leif interjected. "Now that Bert and Dee are settled for the night, you can tell us what Kat's condition truly is."

Eric reached into the box next to him on the table and withdrew a cheroot and lit it. Exhaling slowly, he mused aloud, "Lucky is what Kat is."

"Eric," Sven growled warningly.

"All right," Eric conceded. "Kat does have a concussion. I found no indication of a skull fracture. But from the depth of her unconsciousness and the length of time she has been out, I cannot be positive a hairline fracture does not exist." He crossed his fingers. "Other than that, I was being entirely truthful when I said that I would like to keep an eye on her for a few days. Her ribs and other injuries will heal with time and rest. It is her head injury that concerns me the most."

"Are you expecting complications, Eric?" Leif questioned thoughtfully.

"I am not expecting them, Leif. But their possibility always exists where head wounds are concerned," Eric replied.

"That decides it," Sven said with a hard look on his face.

"Decides what?" Eric asked with a wary voice.

"The ladies will stay here until they are recovered enough to continue their journey," Sven announced.

"What is it that you have not told us, Sven?" Eric asked flatly.

Sven frowned and answered grimly, "I do not think the wreck was an accident."

"What?" Leif exclaimed. "What makes you say something like that? Do you have any evidence to back up your feelings?"

"Only what my eyes and ears tell me," Sven answered. "When we reached that private car we discovered that the couplings had been tampered with, causing the car to derail."

Silence greeted this statement. Sven clenched a fist as he went on. "Those girls could easily have been killed. The cars in front of them jackknifed and could have crushed their car."

"Who would want to do something like that?" Leif asked as he rose and paced the room slowly.

"A few of the crew reported seeing riders hightailing it away from the train as we pulled up," Sven told him.

Leif ran his hand through his hair. "You think these riders the crew saw had something to do with the wreck?"

Sven answered his question with a hard stare.

"But why derail a private car?" Eric asked as he tapped ashes into an ashtray.

"Kat is Patrick Gwyn's granddaughter. Some people will stop at nothing when they are out to cause trouble," Sven pointed out.

"I don't like the way you are thinking," Leif said with a tight voice.

"Eric, do you remember that letter we received a few weeks back from New York?" Sven asked.

Eric thought for a few moments. "It was something about new shipping rates, wasn't it?" Eric tried to recall all the details.

"That's the one. It carried instructions for us not to sign any new contracts originating from New York unless they had Patrick Gwyn's personal signature on them."

"That's right. Now I remember. We thought it odd at the time, as we had signed a new contract only a month or so before the letter came," Leif interjected.

"This as beginning to sound like the start of a rail war," Eric observed. "Do you think that is what we have on our hands, Sven?"

"I can't say it is a full-scale rail war, but Gwyn and Hill are prime targets for trouble. They have always fought with the other rail owners over bringing help to the settlers out here. And they have done it in spite of the opposition," Sven explained.

"Over half the farmers out here owe something to Gwyn and Hill. Either a break on freight charges or new agricultural aid or prime stock has come from the Great Northern. And we all know that this has never sat right with the Northern Pacific or the Union Pacific," Eric added as he agreed with Sven that things did not look good.

The three brothers looked at each other in silent decision. "Kat and Dee stay here until we know exactly what is going on," Sven said for all of them.

"Of course they will stay here," Bert asserted from the parlor doorway as she entered the room, her dressing gown making a soft rustle on the highly polished floor.

"I thought you had retired for the night, Bert," Eric said easily. "You should know by now that eavesdroppers never hear anything good about themselves." He tried to lighten the tense air by teasing her.

"I came to take care of these dirty dishes," Bert explained as she grabbed Sven's mug and placed it on the tray, ignoring his startled protest that he was not finished. "All I did hear was more than enough to tell me that there is dirty dealings going on and somehow those two girls are caught in the middle."

Eric rose from his seat and taking the tray from her stiff fingers set it back on the table before clasping her to him in a warm embrace. "Now, don't you go getting all upset. We don't know they are in any danger."

She looked up at him and said, "You don't know that they're not, either. I haven't lived this long not to be able to smell trouble when it is coming my way. You know as well as I do that the railroads have been at each other's throats for years and violence is nothing new to them."

Releasing her from his arms, Eric handed her the tray, warning her, "Don't say anything to either of the girls. They have enough to cope with after what they have been through without worrying about more trouble."

Bert turned and started to leave the room, pausing at the door to say, "I may be old and slow. But I am not stupid."

Kat slowly fought through the layers of cotton that shrouded her mind, pressing her down. As each layer evaporated it was replaced by a growing awareness of pain. Fluttering her eyelids open, she closed them again against the glare that sounded alarm bells in her head. She wondered if her head would fall off, it hurt so badly. Remaining perfectly still, she took further inventory of her condition as innumerable aches and pains flashed through her, blending with the enormous throbbing in her head.

She tentatively moved her right hand and felt soft, fluffy material under her, not the hard, unyielding grittiness she remembered from the train.

Wincing, she forced herself to peek out at her surroundings. It was obvious she was in a bed, inside a room somewhere. But the question was, Where? The walls she could see were a soft white with a spartan cleanness that spoke of care. There was a small table with a bowl and pitcher for washing against the wall at the foot of her bed. Turning her head ever so slightly and seeing stars even with that small effort, Kat slowly focused on a plain three-drawer dresser of heavy wood and a large wardrobe that stood next to it.

Having surveyed as much as she could see, she tried to move for a better angle of view. The effort forced a low moan from her lips as her left side stabbed with pain.

A blurred figure moved into her line of sight. "Kat?" came Dee's anxious voice.

"Dee?" Kat's dry lips felt cracked as she tried to speak. Blinking, she tried to clear her vision.

"Yes, it's Dee," came the reply from the slowly focusing figure as Dee turned to someone standing next to her and said, "She's finally awake."

Kat moved her head on the pillow and soft hazel eyes, a smiling face and red-gold hair came into view.

Leif was relieved that Kat was regaining consciousness at last. He had spent most of the morning keeping an agitated Dee company. He had started to worry about Eric's "possible complications" himself. Looking down at Kat, his smile widened. "Welcome home. I am Leif and you are Kat. Now that the formal introductions are over, don't try to say anything. You still need lots of rest to get your strength back."

Kat tried to wet her lips with her tongue before whispering, "Where?"

Leif answered her soothingly as Dee appeared at his side. "I think I will let Dee tell you all that while I tell my brother that you have rejoined the living." He placed his hand on Dee's shoulder before moving out of Kat's line of vision.

Kat heard his footsteps recede and a door open and close. Dee took her hand in her own, saying, "I was so worried about you. But the doctor says that if you follow orders you are going to be fine."

When Kat tried to interrupt to ask, "What doctor?" Dee shushed her.

"You heard Leif. Rest and let me do the talking for both of us," Dee admonished her.

Dee's familiar chattering was something Kat thought she would never hear again. She smiled weakly as she listened to Dee explain in her own rambling fashion where they were and how they had come to be there, barely pausing for a breath as she spoke. At least I know Dee's all right, Kat thought to herself as Dee's words flowed over her.

"And Sven didn't believe that there was anyone trapped in that little space and I told him . . ." Dee explained.

Kat's eyelids were feeling heavy again and lethargy seemed to be creeping over her with every passing minute. She had to struggle to listen to Dee's tale of their rescue, only catching phrases and names as Dee rambled.

The door opened and closed and footsteps sounded in the room. Kat felt her wrist being lifted. Focusing her eyes, she saw a tall, blond man, who must be Eric from what Dee had told her, holding her wrist and monitoring her pulse rate.

Eric laid her wrist down on the quilted coverlet and bent to examine her head and eyes. She felt totally defenseless as a pair of penetrating gray eyes gazed steadily into hers. He had not said a word since entering the room, and Kat was beginning to wonder if he ever spoke.

As though reading her thoughts as he stared into her eyes, he spoke, and his voice was somehow exactly the way she thought it would be: warm and rich. "You have suffered a concussion and some bruised ribs. Plus, as I am sure you have noticed by now, many nicks and other bruises that may trouble you over the next few days."

He stood upright and Kat felt an odd sense of loss now that his eyes no longer gazed into hers. "You will have to take things very slowly," he continued. "I think that a few days of complete bed rest are in order before you should even think of rising." He paused. "After that, I might allow short periods of being up. But only if you promise not to try to do too much too soon."

Kat had begun to drift off into a twilight world where only Eric's voice existed as he was explaining her condition. Her eyes flew open painfully at hearing his laugh. "I wish more of my patients would follow orders as well as you seem to be doing."

Kat felt her cheeks redden. "I'm sorry," she whispered.

Eric smiled, the expression lighting his eyes. "You have nothing to be sorry for, Kat. It is your body telling you the same things I have been saying. Rest is what you need."

"The train?" Kat questioned, confused.

"Rest, I said, Miss Gwyn," Eric reminded her.

He had called her Kat before. Why the formality now? she wondered. "Kat," she said to him slowly.

"Kat it is." Eric understood her disorientation and wished she would sleep and give her system the chance to begin healing.

"Thank you, Doctor." she responded.

"Eric," he said, smiling.

"Eric." She barely whispered, liking the way his name sounded.

"You sleep now," Eric ordered. "Someone will be in later to check on you." He motioned for Dee and Leif to follow him from the room.

Dee patted Kat's hand and Leif smiled at her before they joined Eric at the door.

Returning to the dining room with its beautiful Colonial dining suite, Eric resumed his seat at the extension table of highly figured oak. He rested his hands on the molded edge and thought over his observations of Kat.

Leif seated Dee in one of the leather-upholstered box-frame chairs, ignoring her protests that she really was not very hungry.

Dee was anxious for Eric to say something about Kat. Eric noticed her concern and smiled at her, saying, "You had better have something to eat, Dee. Kat will be fine if we let her rest and watch her so that she does not try to overdo things."

Dee felt her worry ease and discovered to her surprise that she felt hungry. As Bert filled a plate for her, Dee marveled as she had at breakfast that in spite of the many difficulties of life here in the West, Bert had created a home of the finest appointments and comfort.

The table setting with its Haviland china of translucent white with very delicate pink, wild crabapple

blossoms and light green fern moss background could
have proudly graced any of the great homes Dee had
known in the East.

As Dee aided Bert in the kitchen after the meal,
Sven and Leif came in. Pulling on heavy work gloves
Sven grabbed some of the fruit that Bert had in a bowl
on the counter and, tossing a few apples to Leif, said,
"We are going to check on the cleanup at the wreck,
Bert. Sorry, I can't say how long it will take us."

Bert dried her hands on a dish towel, saying, "See if
you can salvage any of Dee's or Kat's things. They only
have the clothes on their backs, and heaven knows I am
not the same size they are."

Leif grinned. "Will do, Bert."

"Eric said he would be in his office if you needed
him. He has to complete some reports for the railroad's
insurance carriers," Sven told them as he and Leif
headed out the door.

When Bert told her that there was nothing further
she could help with, Dee went upstairs to check on Kat.

Kat was asleep and Dee sat by her side for a few
minutes, hoping that she might wake. I would like to
talk with you, Dee thought as she looked down at Kat.
There are so many things I am not sure of and I wish I
could tell you. You have always made molehills out of
my mountains. Dee's thoughts were admittedly selfish.
She desperately wanted to share her impressions of the
Thorsen brothers with Kat. She also wished Kat was
able to help her decide what they were supposed to do
next. Sighing, she whispered, "After all you are the
oldest. I haven't had to handle things without you for
years. Frankly, I don't think I like it very much."

Kat's eyelids fluttered as though she heard and
understood what Dee was saying. Dee felt a twinge of
guilt that she was unloading her problems on Kat. Kat
had enough problems of her own just trying to get well.

Straightening her shoulders, Dee scolded herself: I must learn to cope on my own. Kat can't always be there and it is unfair of me to expect her to be.

Having made this decision, Dee rose quietly from her chair by Kat's bedside and returned to her room. She tidied the room, making the bed and opening the window to freshen the air. She looked at the beautiful coverlet as she smoothed it over the feather mattress and wondered if Bert had made it or if some other Thorsen lady had spent the loving hours it took to create it. There was so much she would like to know about the Thorsens but knew it would be rude to ask.

Finishing the few things that needed doing in her room, Dee found that she was at loose ends and went back down to the kitchen.

Bert was busily working at the far counter, pausing only briefly to look up as Dee came in. "Why not go outside and get some fresh air, dear. There really isn't anything you can help me with right now," she ordered before Dee could say a word.

Having been banished from the kitchen, Dee decided that she might as well do as Bert suggested and went out onto the front porch.

She walked over to the railing that surrounded the covered porch and gazed out at the view. The area around the lodge was crowded with tall evergreen and ponderosa pine trees that Dee could not believe were real. Their scent was on the air as breezes stirred their boughs, and their size was something she had never seen. Under the trees were carpets of heather and field marigolds sprinkled like colorful gems amid the masses of fallen pine needles.

The numerous birds that soared through the trees called messages to one another or serenaded the day. Dee thought the scene of this musical rainbow was beautiful and, glancing over her shoulder at the front door, toyed with the idea of exploring farther on her own. But common sense prevailed as she told herself that she would probably become lost, everything being so new to her.

Descending the steps, she strolled to the side of the lodge and saw that there was a barn with a small corral next to it. She was very tempted to explore the barn but instead contented herself with walking around to the back of the lodge. She saw the water pump with its large handle and a way from that she recognized the tall outbuildings that Leif had shown her the night before. Around the corner the rear of the lodge was open to view. There was another porch off the back of the building with steps leading to ground level.

Seeing a large orderly patch of greenery, she went to investigate. She knew that it was a garden when she saw the neat rows with ditches on either side. But what the different types of plants were she had no idea. The sound of a door opening and closing made her turn around. Bert was coming toward her carrying a basket on her arm.

"I see you found my vegetable garden." Bert smiled as she set the basket down next to her feet.

"These are all vegetables!" Dee exclaimed in surprise. "But they are all so pretty." She stroked one of the leaves on a nearby plant.

"That is broccoli," Bert informed her with a grin. "I also have corn, squash, carrots, radishes, cabbage and beans," she pointed out with pride.

When Bert offered to teach her what was what and how to harvest the vegetables that were ready, Dee jumped at the chance.

The rest of the afternoon Dee and Bert worked together in the garden. That evening as she fed Kat some nourishing broth that Bert had prepared for her, Dee chattered like a magpie.

"You know all my gardening has only been with flowers," she reminded Kat as she launched into a colorful explanation of how she had landed on her seat in the dirt when she had tried to harvest a particularly stubborn carrot.

Kat laughed at Dee's description and was instantly sorry as her ribs protested. She put her hand to her side. "Maybe you had better not make me laugh, Dee."

"I will try not to, Kat. But you know how clumsy I can be sometimes—I outdid myself this afternoon," Dee told her.

Kat grinned up at her. "That must have been something. I have seen you do some beauties over the years."

Dee smiled back at her and made a face as she spooned some broth for Kat to sip. "Be careful what you say. I might make you feed yourself," Dee warned.

"I wanted to do that in the first place, but you wouldn't let me," Kat reminded her.

Dee paused with the spoon in midair. "Oh, that's right. Well, I guess that threat was empty."

Kat tried to move suddenly and yelped, "So's the spoon. You just tipped it all over me."

Replacing the spoon in the bowl, Dee hastily tried to wipe the broth from Kat's neck. "I am sorry, Kat," she apologized. "But you distracted me."

Taking the napkin from her, Kat cleaned herself up, saying, "It obviously doesn't take much to do that. Maybe I had better feed myself while you finish your tale of the garden."

"Spoilsport!" Dee accused.

Kat stared at her steadily, "Which is it to be, Dee? Either you feed me as you insisted upon doing or allow me to feed myself and be free to finish your story. You can't do both."

Handing Kat the bowl and spoon, Dee fluffed her

pillows so she could feed herself and sank back into her chair, saying, "You win, as usual."

Kat spooned some of the broth into her mouth and was thankful that it was still warm. With Dee's chattering and all it would have been cold before she had finished feeding her. "Go on with your tale. I'm listening," Kat told her.

That was all the encouragement Dee needed and she went on, "If Mother had seen me today, she would have died. You know she never did approve of my gardening. But it was wonderful!" Her arms spread wide to emphasize her feelings.

Kat could picture Dee's mother if she had seen her daughter grubbing in the dirt, as she described gardening. Poor Dee. She had a hard time fulfilling her mother's ideal of what a daughter should be.

"Did you know that broccoli was a flower?" Dee asked, not really expecting an answer. "I didn't know that," she admitted guilessly.

"How could you be expected to know it?" Kat inquired, as she enjoyed Dee's natural enthusiasm for things that were new to her.

"Well, I know now, so it is unimportant that I didn't know before," Dee explained to her. "Remember I said that I had outdone myself this afternoon? Well, Bert asked me to pick some cabbage and I must have spent nearly twenty minutes picking it."

"What is wrong with that?" Kat asked as she placed the empty bowl and spoon on the tray Dee had brought up with her.

Dee laughed. "Nothing at all, except you are forgetting that I had never seen a head of cabbage before today."

Kat started to laugh with her and stopped herself with her hand on her side. "What did you do? I can't wait to hear."

Dee smoothed the folds in her skirt, trying to draw her tale to a dramatic conclusion. Seeing that Kat was properly curious, she continued, "I unraveled a head leaf by leaf."

Kat could not stop herself from joining Dee in laughing when she heard what she had done. "Leaf by leaf?" Kat smiled.

"That's what Bert said," Dee informed her as they both laughed.

"I must agree with you, Dee. You really outdid yourself there."

When Eric entered the room sometime later, he found a yawning Dee seated next to Kat's bed. Looking at Kat, he saw that she was asleep. He caught another barely suppressed yawn from Dee, and helped her to her feet, saying, "Enough for today. You need your rest as well as Kat does. Now off to bed with you."

Dee shot him a stubborn look that was ruined as yet another yawn overcame her.

"You will find some of your things in your room. Sven brought back what he could from the train," Eric told her. "We had no way of knowing what belonged to whom, so we put everything in your room. You can sort through it in the morning."

"Thank you," Dee mumbled as she placed her hand over her mouth. "I am sorry. I don't know why I can't seem to stop yawning."

"It's the fresh air." Eric smiled down at her. "Besides, Bert told me of your helping her in the garden today. That will tire anyone out."

"Oh." Dee flushed and added, "Especially if that someone has no idea what they are doing."

"You'll learn." Eric grinned as he shook his head. "Leaf by leaf?"

Dee looked down at the floor. "Leaf by leaf," she admitted.

"You have more patience than I do," Eric said. "Now off to bed with you."

"Good night, Eric. Please say good night to the others for me. And thank Sven for bringing our things," Dee said as she moved to the door.

"I will. Good night, Dee."

It was a flabbergasted Leif who ran into Dee later that night. He had gone upstairs to his room and upon reaching the landing had been heading for his room when he heard a sound from Kat's room. Glancing in that direction, he was surprised to see Dee close Kat's door and start walking toward him. Her eyes were glazed and unseeing as she passed him. Reaching his door, she opened it and calmly walked inside.

He followed her, wondering what she thought she was doing. He watched as she snuggled peacefully in his bed. He did not know what he should do. "Dee?" He called her name but received no response.

He decided that he had better tell his brothers or they would never believe him later. Young ladies did not crawl into his bed every night.

Eric and Sven were having a final cup of coffee when Leif came into the parlor, saying, "You two had better come and see this. I think there may be something wrong with Dee."

"What?" Eric asked as he rose to follow Leif.

"She is in my bed," Leif explained as they started up the stairs.

"She is what?" Sven sputtered into his coffee. He followed, wanting to know how Dee had ended up in his baby brother's bed.

Reaching Leif's room, they saw what Leif had said was true. Dee was curled contentedly asleep in the middle of his bed. They both looked at Leif for an explanation. He raised his hands in self-defense. "Don't look at me like that. I didn't put her there."

"How did she get there, then?" Sven questioned with a raised brow.

Leif related what had happened and how it startled him as much as it did them. Looking at Eric, he said, "Why would she do something like this?"

"She was sleepwalking," Eric answered him.

"What?" Sven was not ready to believe Leif's story as easily as Eric apparently did.

Eric glanced over at Dee. "I will try to talk her back into her own room. It isn't wise to wake a sleepwalker. The shock might harm her."

"Wouldn't it be easier to pick her up and carry her back to her own bed?" Sven asked, unheard.

Leif and Eric were busy discussing how they would persuade Dee to move and not wake her. Tired of all the fuss, Sven scooped Dee into his arms like a toy doll and carried her past the startled faces of his brothers back to her room. Once there, he gently tucked her back into bed.

Having accomplished this, he returned to his now cold coffee in the parlor. His brothers followed him, Eric saying, "Sven, you could have awakened her doing that. You heard what I said about that being dangerous."

"The way you two college men were beating your gums, it would have been morning before you did anything," Sven told them. "This way Dee is right where she belongs, no worse for wear, and we can all get some sleep. So quit fussing at me."

Sven's practical method of doing things had always been at odds with his brothers' penchant for discussing all the reasons and possible results before acting. This time, Sven knew he, for one, was too tired to stand around all night while they made up their minds and took matters into his own hands.

Eric and Leif followed Sven to the sofa, trying to explain to him everything that could have gone wrong. He finished his coffee and stared up at them. "College men," he muttered, shaking his head.

They all looked at one another and began to laugh.

Chapter Four

DEE AWOKE THE NEXT MORNING FEELING REFRESHED AND eager to face the day. She could not remember when she had slept as well.

She found herself humming a carefree tune as she descended to breakfast. I guess country air agrees with me, she thought happily to herself.

The brothers heard her approach, and Eric motioned with his hand as he spoke. "Remember, not a word about last night. If she says anything about what happened, fine. If she doesn't, it will mean she has no recollection of it happening."

Dee joined them at the table. "Good morning, everyone. It looks as though it will be a beautiful day."

Leif grinned at her sunny disposition. "Morning, Dee."

Sven kept a wary eye on her as he asked, "How did you sleep last night, Dee?"

His brothers shot him looks of reproof that changed to smiles as Dee answered Sven, "Wonderfully well, thank you. And you?"

Sven directed his attention to his food as he grunted noncommittally, "Fine, I guess."

The meal passed swiftly. Dee offered to take Kat's food up to her after she'd helped clear the table. "After all, it is the least I can do," she said.

"Bert, I have to check on some of the train passengers that were taken to town yesterday. I won't be back until late," Eric said as he rose from his seat.

"If you can hold your horses for a few minutes I want to go with you," Bert told him. "I have some shopping I want to do and I would like to visit with Helga for awhile."

"Fine. I'll be in my office when you are ready," Eric replied.

"I think I will ride as far as the mill cutoff with you," Sven told them. "I want to speak to one of the foremen."

Dee looked around the table in surprise. Was she to be left on her own?

Leif saw her look and said, "I have some studying I need to catch up on. My vacation won't last forever."

Dee tried not to show her disappointment at being left on her own, but she was not very convincing. Leif chided her, "Hey, you won't be totally alone, Dee. I'll be in Eric's office if you need me for anything."

Dee would have liked to go into town with Bert and the others but found that she was too shy to ask. "I guess I had better take this up to Kat. She will think we have forgotten all about her," she said as she picked up the tray of food.

Carrying the tray into Kat's room, she called, "Wake up! Your food has arrived."

Kat slowly raised herself on her pillow, saying, "Do I feed myself?"

Dee quirked an eyebrow at her. "Do I look like your nursemaid? Certainly you shall feed yourself."

Placing the tray so Kat could reach everything, she stood by the side of the bed with her hands clasped behind her back and rocked on her heels. She watched as Kat nibbled on a piece of toast and said, "I guess we are on our own today."

"We are? Why is that?" Kat questioned as she sipped at her coffee.

"Everyone else has things to do and places to go," Dee told her wistfully.

Kat looked up at her and grinned. "Are you feeling left out?"

Dee looked sheepish as she answered, "A little. I haven't anything to do." She placed her hands on the back of the chair by Kat's bed and leaned on them. "How are you feeling today?"

"Better than yesterday or the day before," Kat told her. "I am still sore and I find myself tiring easily. Otherwise, I think I will survive."

Dee unconsciously fidgeted as she heard the others departing and the sound of Eric's office door closing. "Oh, well," she murmured to herself.

Kat heard her and said, "Do you want to talk for a while? I can't promise you I will be able to stay awake for a long time, but if you are willing to give it a try, so am I."

"I would like that. That is, if you promise to tell me when you are tired," Dee replied.

"I promise," Kat said, smiling.

Dee had so much she wanted to discuss with Kat that she did not know where to begin. She was afraid of wearing Kat out and prolonging her convalescence.

"I have an idea," Kat said. "Eric mentioned this morning, when he came in to check on me, that what is left of our things was taken to your room last night. Why not bring them in here and you can go through them while we talk?"

Dee welcomed the suggestion and went to bring everything that had been salvaged to Kat's room. Piling things on the foot of Kat's bed, she quipped, "If you are not careful I may bury you under everything."

"I will take that chance," Kat shot back at her as she finished her breakfast.

Shaking out a day dress that belonged to Kat, Dee removed a hanger from the wardrobe and hung the dress on it, saying, "How long do you think we will be here?"

"I don't know," Kat answered. "I asked Eric this morning and he said he would let me know when I was fit to travel. So your guess is as good as mine." She snuggled into her pillows. "Why? Don't you like it here?"

Dee paused in her folding of a chiffon petticoat. "Yes, I do like it here." She placed the petticoat in one of the dresser drawers. "I only hope we are not being a burden to anyone."

"Has anyone said anything that makes you feel we might be?" Kat asked her with a frown.

"Oh, no," Dee quickly responded. "It's only that I feel so useless most of the time. I am sure Bert would be better off not having to contend with my ineptitude in the kitchen."

"But you were never allowed near the kitchen back home. What do you expect?" Kat reminded her.

"Kat?" Dee hesitated, not sure how to say what she wanted to say. "What do you think of the Thorsens?"

"What do I think of them? You have seen more of them than I have. You tell me what your impressions of them are," Kat said.

Dee lifted a stack of underthings she had folded and carried them to the dresser as she formed her reply to Kat in her mind. "They seem nice enough. Leif is very friendly and helpful. Eric is a capable doctor, in spite of my unfounded and foolish misgivings when we first arrived. Bert is a dear for all her rough ways," she told her.

"And what about Sven?" Kat prompted.

"I am having a hard time deciding about him," Dee admitted as she folded a nightdress over her arm. "Every time I think I have him figured out, he does something I did not expect and confuses me."

"Confuses you?" Kat queried, intrigued. Dee was normally a fairly good judge of people and this knack had never failed her in the past.

Dee stopped midway in folding some hose and said, "I can't seem to think clearly when he's around. He unsettles me."

"I think I might know what you mean," Kat told her.

"You do?" Dee finished folding the hosiery.

Kat bit her lower lip as she went on. "Eric unsettles me."

"He does!" Dee exclaimed in surprise. "Have you any idea why?"

"No more than you do as to why Sven affects you that way," Kat admitted ruefully.

"Do Leif or Sven have the same effect?" Dee asked curiously.

"No," Kat replied. "What about you? Does Eric unsettle you?"

"No. Neither does Leif, for that matter. In fact, I feel the most comfortable around him," Dee explained.

"Does Sven know how you feel?"

"Does Eric know about you?"

They looked at each other and shook their heads. Dee finished sorting Kat's things and started on her own. Not wanting to dwell on the possible reasons for their odd reactions to the elder Thorsens, Dee changed the subject. "Kat, what do you think caused the train to derail like that?"

"I have deliberately tried not to think about the cause," Kat said, frowning.

Sitting on the foot of the bed, Dee asked, "Why? Do you think it might not have been an accident?"

"I am hoping that it was an accident," Kat told her. "I don't want to think it wasn't. Has anyone said anything to you about it?"

"No. No one has even mentioned the accident since we arrived," Dee informed her.

"Keep your ears open. Maybe someone will say something when they think you aren't listening."

"Do you think they are keeping secrets from us?" Dee asked.

"I don't know. But if they are, I would like to know why." Kat looked up at her.

Dee felt a chill run up her spine at Kat's words. "Please don't frighten me by talking like that, Kat. You know how I can be when I am frightened."

"Unpredictable?" Kat suggested with a small smile.

"I guess for lack of a better word that describes me." Dee smiled back at her.

"Seriously, Dee. I do not mean to frighten you. But we should face the possibility that everything is not as it appears. That way, maybe we will be in a better position to cope should things change suddenly."

Dee rose from the bed. "I know what you are saying." She lifted her folded clothes and said, "But that doesn't mean I have to like it."

Kat smiled at her as she stifled a sudden yawn. "I think I am getting tired. If you are finished with the clothes, you don't have to spend all your time with me. Why not go outside for awhile? I think I am going to try to take a nap."

"That's a good idea for both of us. You nap, and after I put these away"—she held up the clothes in her arms—"I will go outside and see if the fresh air will settle my edginess."

Dee left Kat to doze and carried her things to her room, where she deposited them where they belonged.

As she did so, she found her mind going over the things that she and Kat had said.

So Eric unsettled Kat, did he? Don't be so glad to hear that, she told herself. Sven still bothers you. Admit it, you had a hard time answering him this morning when you were at breakfast. So what if I did, she argued with herself. But she still recalled that she felt warm all over when he'd looked at her. Dee mentally shushed herself, saying aloud, "You need that fresh air Kat was talking about."

"I think I will ride into town with you," Sven told Eric and Bert as they neared the mill cutoff. "I can stop at the mill on our way back. I want to see for myself what Gwyn's reply will be to our wire." He kept his horse alongside the wagon as they passed the cutoff.

Nearing the outskirts of town, Bert broke the silence, saying, "You can leave me at Jensen's. I think I will visit Helga first."

Eric nodded. "I'll drop you off there and go to the telegraph office."

Stopping the wagon near Jensen's General Store, Eric helped Bert down from the wagon and watched as she entered the store. Sven tied his horse near the wagon and joined Eric as he watched their aunt disappear into the large building.

Together they strolled down the crowded street in the direction of the telegraph office. "Eric?" Sven said as they made their way through a group of farmers.

"Umm?" Eric replied.

"What do you think of our guests?" Sven asked him.

"I don't know. Why do you ask?" Eric said as he tipped his hat to some passing ladies out doing their morning shopping.

"Come on, Eric. You must have some opinion of them," Sven insisted.

Eric paused in his stride and eyed his brother. "You mean it, don't you? You really want to know what I think of Kat and Dee."

Sven straightened to his full height and challenged, "What is wrong with that?"

Eric continued walking as he answered, "Nothing, I guess."

"Well?" Sven pushed.

Eric glanced over at him, saying, "I think Dee is a possible problem child and Kat is a mystery."

"Problem child? Mystery? What do you mean by that?" Sven demanded as they neared the telegraph office.

Eric halted in his tracks and, placing his hands on his hips, said, "Don't think I haven't noticed the way you act around Dee. One minute you are a bear with a sore head and the next you are like a lamb. Has she gotten to you, big brother?"

"And what if she has?" Sven defended himself curtly.

Shaking his head, Eric chuckled. "If she has, you are not alone. I think Kat is beginning to get to me."

"You don't say!" Sven grinned broadly. "That makes fools out of both of us, then. We have only known them a few days and look at us, we're both mixed up as hell."

"That we are, brother, that we are." Eric laughed as he clapped Sven on the shoulder.

"Do you think they know how we feel?" Sven asked as they reached the door to the telegraph office.

"I don't know about Kat. She's a mystery to me, remember? But I think you have poor Dee going in circles. I have seen how she acts around you and it is not the way she acts around Leif or I," Eric answered him.

"You think so?" Sven said.

"I know so," Eric returned.

"Now for the big question. Are we going to do anything about it?" Sven asked with a serious look on his face.

"I don't know about you, but I am going to be very careful and see how things go. It may end up amounting to nothing as far as Kat and I are concerned," Eric told him.

"I don't know what I am going to do, either," Sven said. "Dee is probably too young for me, anyway. Besides, she's used to a different kind of life than I am."

They cut short their conversation as they entered the telegraph office. Nearing the counter, they saw that the clerk appeared unusually anxious to wait on them. Sven quirked an eyebrow at Eric, wondering what could have prompted this eagerness. Eric shrugged, took a piece of paper from the stack on the counter and wrote out his message.

As he wrote, the young clerk hovered nervously. Sven became increasingly suspicious as he viewed the clerk's edginess. "What's ailing you, Peters?" he asked.

The clerk's head snapped up àt hearing his name. "Nothing, Mr. Thorsen. But there has been a lot of excitement around town since the train wreck and I have been mighty busy sending wires all over the country." He glanced down at the message Eric was writing. "I suppose you are notifying the kin of those ladies you took out to the lodge?" he commented.

Sven glared at him stonily and the young clerk moved away from where Eric was writing. Leaning over Eric's shoulder, Sven whispered, "Better keep it simple. There's too many long noses around here."

Eric looked up from the completed message and handed it to Sven. Sven read, "P. Gwyn, Fifth Avenue, New York. K. and D. involved in train mishap. No serious injuries. Will wait for reply. Eric Thorsen."

Sven nodded as he handed the message to the eager clerk, who quickly perused it. An expression of disappointment crossed his face.

"Is there anything wrong, Peters?" Sven asked.

"No, sir," Peters was quick to reply.

"Then what are you waiting for?" Sven asked him in a hard voice. "Send it."

"Yes, sir!" Peters stuttered nervously as he turned to the telegraph key and began to tap out the message. Having completed the task, he rose from his chair, saying, "Will that be all?"

"We will wait for a reply," Eric informed him.

Peters shuffled his feet uncomfortably and cleared his throat before saying, "That could take a few hours, Mr. Thorsen. If you want, I could send someone to fetch you when the reply does come through."

The brothers exchanged looks and Eric nodded. "Fine, Peters. We should be nearby."

Peters tried to hide his sigh of relief but was not fast enough to fool Sven's keen eyes. Turning, Sven followed Eric outside. Reaching the wooden walkway, they paused and Eric said, "He was in an awful hurry to find out what we had to say."

Sven gazed around the street as he said, "Even more anxious to be rid of us once he knew."

Looking up the street to Jensen's, Eric saw his aunt out front with Helga. Seeing him, Bert waved for him to come. Eric stepped off the walkway into the street, saying to Sven, "Bert looks upset about something."

Sven looked at her and, seeing the distress in her face, said, "You go to her. I'll stay here and keep an eye on our Mr. Peters."

Eric zigzagged his way across the busy street to join Bert and Helga in front of the store. Bert took him by the arm and led him inside, where they had less of a chance of being overheard as she spoke. "Eric, Helga has been telling me that there is a lot of ugly talk around town about Kat and Dee."

Eric wondered why he was not surprised at hearing his aunt say this. "What kind of talk?" he asked the two women.

"It started with this," Helga said as she handed him a newspaper dated over a week old, with a New York banner across its top.

Bert pointed to an article on the front page and Eric read it in silence. Finishing, he looked at Bert and her friend. "Where did this come from?" he asked them.

"One of the passengers from the train had it with them," Bert told him. "Helga heard the talk and spoke with the man who had it. He offered to let her keep the paper. Then he went on to say that he suspected that the two young ladies who had been taken to the lodge were the same ones mentioned in the article."

"Where is this man now?" Eric asked Helga.

"I don't know. He has disappeared. I have asked around and no one else seems to know where he has gone," Helga told him.

"Odd," Eric murmured to himself.

"I can not believe what this paper says," Bert declared in a firm voice. "Kat and Dee are not like this at all."

"Unfortunately, Bert, this article has enough innuendo to convince anyone who does not know them as we do," Eric told her. "I think our missing gentleman deliberately left the newspaper where he thought it could do the most damage."

Sven watched from his vantage point as Eric went inside the store with Bert and Helga. Strolling over to one of the support posts for the covered walkway, he leaned against it. This gave him a view of both the telegraph office and the front of Jensen's Store.

He had been leaning there for a few minutes when he

saw Peters leave the telegraph office and scurry across the street, heading for the hotel. Sven knew that it was too soon for a reply from New York and wondered who Peters was in such a hurry to see. Maybe he was delivering a reply to one of the other wires he had said he had been sending since the accident, but Sven doubted it. Peters had a sneaky air about him that Sven did not trust.

Losing sight of Peters as he mingled with the crowd in front of the hotel, Sven turned his gaze back to the general store. Bert and Eric were coming out and heading in his direction. Eric was carrying what looked like a newspaper in his hand. Sven straightened from his casual stance and waited for them to join him.

Without saying a word, Eric handed Sven the newspaper and pointed to the article he had read earlier. Sven frowned as he read the words indicting Kat and Dee with slanderous subtlety as a possible murderess and a scarlet woman. He looked up at Eric, saying, "Where did you get this trash?"

Eric pointed to the paper. "Read on, there is more."

Sven finished the article, reading the barely concealed charges backed up only by gossip and sensationalism. He handed the paper to Eric. "I've no doubt that all our self-appointed guardians of morality are having a field day with this."

"There is ugly talk going around," Bert told him.

"But up to now it has only been hinted by mysteriously disappearing sources that the girls in the article might be Kat and Dee," Eric added.

"Mysteriously disappearing?" Sven asked.

"Some stranger from the train that has apparently vanished," Bert explained.

"Where did you hear all this?" Sven said in a cold voice.

"Helga spoke with the man herself. He is the one who left the paper with her," Bert told him.

"What I would like to know is how many other papers he left elsewhere?" Sven commented. "It would only take a few carefully placed words and one of these"—he shook his finger at the paper Eric held—"and the whole town will be up in arms."

Eric knew Sven was right and wished the reply from Gwyn would come so they could plan their next move. "What about our friend in the telegraph office?" Eric asked as he looked over at the building.

Sven related what he had observed and what he suspected, adding, "A long talk with New York may help us." He paused a moment. "A long, private talk."

The three retraced their steps to the telegraph office and went inside. The desk was unattended and they took seats in the chairs scattered around the room.

It was late afternoon before the Thorsens were able to leave the telegraph office and return to Jensen's General Store to talk.

It had required hours of painstaking communication on Eric's part and almost brute force on Sven's in detaining Peters as Eric tapped out his private messages to Patrick Gwyn.

Helga greeted them as they entered the store and escorted them to the back, where she and Karl, her husband, had their living quarters. She left them in complete privacy and returned to wait on customers, saying, "If you need anything, call one of us."

It was a solemn group seated around the bare wooden table; pieces of paper were piled in front of them containing their responses from Gwyn. Eric lifted the top sheet of paper and reread it. "He wants us to keep their true identities as much of a secret as possible. That is much easier said than done."

"Did he go into any detail regarding the blackmail threats he had received?" Sven asked as he read another sheet.

"He was deliberately vague on that. He said only that it involved some business dealing that he was opposed to and his granddaughter and Dee's safety had been threatened if he did not change his stand," Eric answered him.

"This is something that does not surprise me," Sven said as he held up the sheet he was reading. "This confirms that the train wreck was deliberate sabotage."

"Read it out loud, Sven," Bert instructed.

"I received word that the unscheduled break in Kat's and Dee's journey was a warning that my opponents mean business," Sven read.

Bert rested her head in her hands as she thought. The sounds of customers being greeted and waited upon in the front of the store drifted into the room. Lifting her head, she looked at her nephews and said, "How are we supposed to keep their real names a secret?"

"I have no idea," Eric replied.

"Gwyn certainly doesn't believe in doing things the easy way," Sven said. "We are instructed not to mention a word of the threats to either girl. Why?"

"He is afraid that if they knew, they might try to do something on their own and get hurt," Eric answered him.

"Would they be foolish enough to try something on their own?" Sven asked doubtfully.

"Gwyn seems to think so, or he would not have given us those instructions," Eric replied in a grave tone of voice.

"What happens when the girls come to town? People will certainly want to know who they are. You know how strangers attract attention," Bert said as she rose from her seat and began pacing.

"We will have to keep them from coming to town," Sven stated.

Bert paused in her pacing and looked at him as though he had lost his mind. "You know we can't do that forever. They will want to know why. What do we tell them then?"

Her question was met with silence. Bert stared at her nephews for a moment before saying, "We can't pretend they don't exist." She waved her hand toward the front of the store, adding, "There is speculation already as to why all the other passengers were brought to town and two young ladies were taken to the lodge."

Eric frowned at her. "Don't get so upset, Bert. Sit down and help us think this out."

Bert sat back down, saying, "Don't get upset! A few more days and folks will be dying of curiosity. Before we know it, they will be coming out to the lodge to see for themselves what is going on."

"She's right, Eric," Sven agreed.

Eric glared at him and continued to shift through the messages from Gwyn as though they might give him some clue as to what to do next.

Bert broke the prolonged silence, saying matter-of-factly, "You will have to marry them."

"What!" Sven exploded.

"That is ridiculous!" Eric argued.

"I haven't heard either of you coming up with any bright ideas," Bert told them. "Look at it this way. If you marry them, their real names will be Thorsen. We can say that they were your fiancées on their way here from back East. What would be more natural than that they should stay at the lodge?"

"Isn't that rather drastic?" Eric asked. "There has to be a simpler solution." He shook his head.

"If there is a simpler solution, I am waiting to hear it," Bert told him firmly.

"Even if Eric and I were to agree to your outrageous idea, I cannot see either Kat or Dee agreeing," Sven told her. "We can't even tell them why, thanks to Gwyn."

"How do you know they won't agree?" Bert insisted. "Don't think I haven't been noticing how Dee acts when she's around you. And Eric hasn't been himself since Kat arrived."

"Bert," Eric said warningly. "You are imagining things."

"Am I?" She stared back at him.

The brothers exchanged looks, remembering their earlier conversation. "What do you think?" Eric asked Sven.

"I think we are asking for trouble," Sven answered him.

Chapter Five

DEE WAS DELIGHTED THAT ERIC HAD SAID KAT COULD come downstairs for a short time, even though he had made them both promise they would not argue with him when he said it was time to go back to bed.

Kat smiled up at Eric as he stood by the side of her bed. "I promise!"

Dee rushed to get Kat's robe from the wardrobe, saying, "So do I!"

Kat knew she was pushing things when she asked, "Could I sit in the sun?"

Eric frowned at her. "I said you could get out of bed for awhile, not go touring the countryside." He wished she would not look at him like that; it made it hard for him to refuse her anything.

"All I want to do is sit on the front porch in the sunshine," Kat said, defending her request.

Dee looked at Eric with pleading on her face. She knew how closed in Kat had been feeling and how much she wanted a little bit of freedom.

Giving in to Kat's request, Eric said, "Only on the front porch and no farther. You are not to move from there, understand?"

Dee wasted no time in helping Kat don her robe. She stepped away from the bed as Kat started to get up. Her movements were slow and she tried to laugh them off by saying, "I think staying here so long has made me weaker than I thought."

Eric whisked the bedcovers away and, bending down, scooped her into his arms, saying, "You are weaker than you think you are. I'll carry you down."

Kat felt tingles run up and down her skin as she put her arms around Eric's neck and he started for the door. She could not understand why he was affecting her like this and it made her nervous. She tried to cover her nervousness by saying overbrightly, "Do you do this for all your patients, doctor?"

Eric's gray eyes stared into hers, sending shock waves to her very core. She shivered involuntarily as he said, "Only the special ones."

Eric narrowed his eyes as he felt the tremor flow through Kat's body. "Dee," he said. "Bring a blanket with you for Kat to put over her." He stood there with Kat in his arms as Dee gathered a blanket from the foot of the bed. "And Dee, ask Sven to move one of the parlor chairs out onto the front porch."

Dee opened the bedroom door and hurried down the stairs, calling, "Sven!"

She had reached the bend in the staircase and was turning to descend the next step when she collided with Sven as he was coming up. His hands went out to steady her and their grip on her arms made her even more breathless than the sudden encounter.

"Hey, there! Not so fast, little one. You could trip and hurt yourself." He smiled at her. "You wanted me for something?"

Dee had to think for a second before she remembered why she had been calling his name. "Oh," she said breathlessly. "Eric wants you to carry one of the parlor chairs out onto the front porch. He is bringing Kat down to sit in the sunshine."

"I will get right to it," he answered her as he released his hold on her and made his way back to the ground floor.

Dee clutched the blanket she was carrying against her middle trying to steady the fluttering she felt. Sven paused at the foot of the stairs as though he was waiting for her to join him. She took a deep breath and did, following him into the parlor, where he lifted one of the heavy Morris chairs as if it were kindling.

"Bring the footstool over in the corner," he instructed Dee as he headed for the door. "Kat will need something to rest her feet on."

Eric lowered Kat into the chair and, reaching over, took the blanket from Dee and tucked it over and around Kat's legs as he said, "No longer than an hour, understand?"

Kat nodded that she did and said, "Thank you, Eric."

"I will be in my office if you tire sooner. Dee can come and get me and I'll carry you back up," Eric told Kat as he moved away.

Sven had disappeared back inside after bringing out the chair and Dee knew she was not strong enough to cart another out for herself. Shrugging, she sat down at the top of the steps and wrapped her arms around her knees.

She and Kat had been sitting quietly as Kat enjoyed her first few minutes of freedom when the front door opened again and Sven appeared, bearing an old rocking chair Dee had seen in Bert's room. Bert was close on his heels carrying a large bowl filled with green beans.

Sven placed the rocking chair near Kat and smiled down at Dee, saying, "Would you like me to bring something for you?"

Dee answered him without thinking. "No, thank you. I am fine right here." The roughness of the edge of the step was pushing through the folds of her dress and the hardness of the wooden plank was not made for comfort, but Dee found she could not ask Sven to bring her a chair nor could she admit to him that she needed one.

Sven moved past her down the steps and turned toward the barn, leaving the girls and Bert to visit alone in the sunlight.

Balancing the bowl on her lap, Bert began to snap the stems of the green beans it held. She rocked gently to and fro as she worked, saying to Kat, "I thought I would keep you both company while I did some of my work. I hope you don't mind."

Kat was quick to reassure her. "No, I don't mind. I would enjoy having you with us. What is it exactly that you are doing?"

Bert grinned at her. "Nothing earthshaking." She lifted one of the beans and held it so that both the girls could see what she was doing. With a quick motion of her wrist the stem snapped cleanly away from the main body of the bean. Bert allowed the stem to fall back into the bowl as she set the bean to one side of the pile it held.

"That looks easy enough. May I try?" Dee asked.

Bert laughed. "I never intended for you to do my work for me, but I learned a long time ago never to say no when someone offers to help." She gathered a bunch of the unsnapped beans and handed them to Dee.

"May I try also?" Kat asked her.

"Only a few for you," Bert said. "I don't want Eric mad at me for tiring you out." She handed a small bunch of the beans to Kat.

Dee spread her skirt out on her lap and laid the beans on top. Taking one, she tried to imitate what she had seen Bert do. The bean bent in two and split in her hand. She looked up at Bert in dismay, saying, "But I did what I saw you do!"

Kat laughed at her. "Obviously, you did something differently."

Dee stuck her tongue out at her, saying, "I'd like to see you do it, Miss Know-it-all."

Kat took one of the beans from her lap and, watching once more as Bert expertly snapped another bean, tried to copy her motions. The stem on her bean snapped only partway off. When she tried to pull it the rest of the way she discovered that a long string of fiber came loose down the entire side of the bean. "Oh, dear," she said in dismay. "What are we doing wrong, Bert?" she asked as she saw Bert shake her head at her while Dee laughed.

"You both are trying to force it. You can't force it. You watch me again." She showed them how she did it and the stem broke away cleanly as before.

The girls kept trying and soon could manage to snap the stems away without crushing the beans, but they had to work at a much slower pace than Bert.

They were almost through with the large bowl Bert had brought out with her when Bert asked, "Do you girls know much about our way of life out here?"

Dee could not help but giggle. "I have read quite a bit about it. But none of my books ever explained how to snap beans!"

"You say you have read about it?" Bert asked carefully.

"Dee collects and reads what I think are called, by some, penny pulps," Kat explained with a grin.

Bert's eyes widened. "Penny pulps! Goodness, Dee, you must have a very distorted view of things."

Dee bristled, ready to defend herself, and Kat stopped her by saying, "She spent most of our journey out here waiting for outlaws or Indians to attack our train."

Bert laughed. "Were you disappointed when they didn't show up?"

Dee shook her head. "Not in the least. Kat is exaggerating when she says I was looking for outlaws or Indians to spring out at us at any minute. I know the chances of that were slight."

"We live a very quiet life-style these days," Bert told them. "But when I was your age things were different. Why, back then you never knew what might happen next. Maybe an Indian at your front door or outlaws shooting up the town. It was wild and woolly then."

"Do you miss it at all, Bert?" Kat asked as she saw the wistful expression on her face.

Bert sat back in her chair as she answered, "No. Not really. I was younger then, certainly, and did not have this confounded arthritis in my hip. But times are more settled now and peaceful." She laughed to herself. "Although I will admit that they can be too settled."

Dee frowned and asked, "Why do you say that?"

Bert waved her hand at her, saying, "Oh, nothing, girl. It's only people, that's all." She watched the two girls carefully from lowered eyes. She saw that she had intrigued them as she had meant to do and hurriedly followed up her advantage by saying, "Why, these days some folks think they know everything."

"How so?" Kat prompted her to go on.

Careful now, old woman, Bert thought to herself, you watch what you say. "Well, take, for instance, your being out here with us," Bert said slowly.

"What about our being here?" Dee asked her. "We aren't causing problems for you, are we?"

Bert deliberately hesitated before she answered Dee's question. "Nothing that won't fade with time, child."

"Bert," Kat insisted. "If we have caused trouble by

being here you must tell us. How else can we make things right?"

"Kat's right, Bert," Dee agreed. "You must tell us."

"I don't see how you can do anything about it," Bert started, "but if you insist on knowing I'll tell you. But you must not get the wrong idea about people out here. Not everyone is like some you might meet."

"Bert!" Kat urged her to go on.

"When I was in town yesterday, I heard some talk going around that made me mad, that's all," Bert told them.

"What kind of talk?" Dee asked.

"Some holier-than-thou types were saying that it was immoral for two young single ladies to be out here alone with three single men." Bert paused only briefly, not wanting to give either of them the chance to interrupt her before she had finished what she wanted to say. "They were making no bones about wondering out loud what kind of chaperone an arthritic old woman could possibly be."

"Bert! That's terrible!" Dee exclaimed. "How could anyone say such things!"

"Surely you told them how wrong they were," Kat said in a shocked voice.

Bert snapped the last few beans and nodded. "You are right, I did. But some people are worse than mules when they get a certain idea in their heads."

"Do Eric and Sven know what people have been saying?" Dee asked self-consciously.

Bert felt sorry for her but knew she had to continue now that she had started. "Yes, they both know. It did not set well with them, either. We have always been held in high regard by the townspeople . . ." Her voice trailed off.

"What is it, Bert?" Kat asked gently. "There is something you are not telling us, isn't there?"

Bert looked up at them and feigned an expression of guilt as she admitted, "I guess I lost my temper and said a few things I shouldn't have."

Kat and Dee looked at each other in alarm. What could Bert have said that had her so upset now?

"What did you say?" Dee tried to drag the full story from Bert.

"I am afraid that I said you were Sven's and Eric's fiancées come out from back East to get married." Bert played her part to the hilt.

"What!" the girls exclaimed in horror.

"Oh, Bert!" Dee said. "How could you say something like that? You know it isn't true."

"I know. I know," Bert agreed. "But something just came over me and before I knew it I had already said it," she explained. "And I am afraid I may have made things even worse."

"How?" Kat was almost afraid to ask she was so stunned by Bert's first revelation.

"Parson was standing right there when I said you had come out to be wed and he declared that the weddings should take place as soon as possible to avoid further scandal in the community." Bert released a heavy sigh as she waited for the reaction to this.

"And you were not going to tell us any of this!" Kat said.

"I figured it was my own fault and you should not be made to worry about it," Bert explained.

"How were you going to explain when we did not marry Eric and Sven?" Dee asked, appalled at what Bert had told them.

"It needn't concern you, girls," Bert told them. "In a few weeks you will both be on your way and wagging tongues can't hurt you."

"But they can you and Eric and Sven!" Dee exclaimed heatedly. "Why, all your reputations could be ruined!"

Bert smiled wanly. "I don't think it would go that far. Tarnished a bit, maybe, but not ruined."

"Bert! We can't possibly leave you to face this alone," Kat told her. "None of you asked to have us thrust upon you as we were. Why should all your reputations be smeared because of it?"

"But what could either of you do?" Bert asked, hoping she would hear the answer she wanted to hear.

Kat sat back in the Morris chair and thought to herself, And Grandad sent us west to get away from scandal. Sitting forward again she looked over at Dee and saw that Dee was as upset as she was. There was really no other way out to save the Thorsen good name than for Kat and Dee to go through with the marriages.

"We will have to marry them," Kat stated flatly as she looked at Dee.

Dee swallowed painfully as she replied, "I know."

Bert had all she could do to control her impulse to shout in triumph. Her maneuvering had worked. She knew that the only way she would ever get either of them to agree to the marriages was to make it appear that it was their idea. Now she had done it. A feeling of guilt swept over her as she thought, But did I do the right thing?

"Heavens!" Bert exclaimed. "I can't let you do a thing like that!"

"I don't see how you can stop us," Kat informed her. "Will you tell Eric and Sven or shall we?"

"Tell me what?" Eric asked as he came out onto the porch.

"Bert?" Kat questioned.

This part will be the hardest of all, Bert thought to herself. "I have some news for you, Eric," she said carefully.

"And what is that?" Eric asked curiously. He had come out to tell Kat that her time in the sun was over for the day and to carry her back upstairs. Instead, it appeared he had walked in on something. Judging from the paleness of Kat's cheeks and the agitated way Dee was twisting the hem of her skirt, it was something that had upset both of them.

"I know you will be mad when I tell you," Bert began.

"I will be mad when you tell me what?" Eric demanded.

Bert shifted in her rocking chair as she said, "I told the girls about the talk that was going around town."

"You what!" Eric thundered at her.

"Eric!" Kat interrupted. "Please don't be mad at Bert. It wasn't her fault. We forced her to tell us."

"You forced her to tell you?" He looked at Kat, perplexed, for he knew it was next to impossible to force Bert to do anything she did not want to do.

"That's right," Dee interjected. "And we can not stand idly by and allow you to risk your reputations on our account."

"What!" Eric exclaimed, thoroughly confused.

"What Dee says is true," Kat stated. "We have decided to go through with the marriages."

"Marriages!" Eric choked as he glared at Bert. "Listen. I don't know what Bert told you. But there isn't any reason for you to go through with any marriages."

"Bert told us everything," Dee informed him.

"Everything?" Eric looked at Bert angrily.

"Yes. We know all about her unfortunate slip of the tongue in front of the parson," Kat told him. "We also know that now everyone thinks we are your fiancées here from the East to be married. So, you see, Eric, if we do not go through with the marriages your family reputation will be ruined because of us. We can not allow that to happen."

Eric sputtered, unable to say anything. How in the devil his aunt had twisted things around so much that now the girls were insisting on getting married he would never know. And somehow he thought he would much rather not know.

Leif and Sven joined them on the porch and Eric turned to Leif and said, "Congratulate us, baby brother. Sven and I are getting married."

"What!" Leif shouted in surprise.

"We are?" Sven said in astonishment.

Turning to Kat and Dee, Eric said, "I presume that you intend to go through with this as soon as possible?"

Kat took a deep breath and responded, "It would seem the logical thing to do."

"Leif. Saddle a horse and go into town and fetch the parson back here," Eric ordered without looking at him.

"If you say so, Eric," Leif sputtered uncertainly.

"I say so," Eric told him.

As the voice of the parson read the wedding ceremony, Kat could not help but think of the differences between this wedding and the one that never took place. This time there was no large congregation, only Leif and Bert. Dee was also being wed and neither of them had any family present to witness the solemn occasion. She was not gowned in an expensive wedding dress of satin and lace, but a pastel dinner dress of silk. The one difference that she wished for was not there. This time she had agreed to the ceremony knowing that Eric did not love her but that, ironically enough, she might be falling in love with him.

Dee stood nervously by Sven's side, her small hand dwarfed in his much larger one as he placed one of his mother's rings on her finger and the parson said the fateful words, "I now pronounce you man and wife."

How could she be married to Sven? She had only seen him for the first time in her life a few days ago. What had she and Kat done to themselves by agreeing to wed? Dee looked up at Sven as he stood grimly beside her. He doesn't look any happier about this than I am, Dee thought sadly.

She knew that the marriages were for appearances' sake only. Bert had made that quite clear earlier before she would allow Leif to do as Eric had told him and fetch the parson. She and Kat would still occupy their own rooms and everything else would be the same as it was, only now in the eyes of the world she would be Mrs. Sven Thorsen and Kat would be Eric's wife.

Kat's shoulders were drooping with fatigue and Leif was staring solemnly into his coffee cup by the time the parson was ready to return to town. He had insisted on remaining for the bridal dinner and toast to the newly-weds, saying that he was sorry neither bride had recovered enough from her ordeal on the train to have a big wedding with all the townsfolk in attendance, but that he was very honored to have performed the ceremonies.

Dee's head was beginning to spin and her stomach felt queasy after having drunk the toasts the parson kept proposing. She prayed that she would not make a fool of herself and be sick at her own wedding reception.

Eric carried Kat up to her room and tucked her in for the night, remaining only briefly before he returned to see the parson off.

Dee could barely bring herself to look at Sven. He had been staring at her since dinner started and his penetrating observation made her think he could see into her very soul.

Unable to take any more, she rose from her seat, saying, "It has been an unusual day, to say the very least. I hope you will all excuse me when I say I am exhausted. I think it would be better if I retired for the night."

Leif leaned over and placed a chaste kiss on her cheek, saying, "Good night, Dee."

Bert agreed that it had been quite a day and suggested that they all retire and get some rest.

Eric smiled at her and said, "Sleep well, Dee."

Sven rose from his seat and said, "I will see you to your room."

Dee could not refuse his offer without making a scene, so she took his offered arm as he led the way to the staircase.

Neither of them spoke as they climbed the stairs. Dee did not know what to say to this man who was now her husband. Sven did not trust himself to speak at all until they reached Dee's door.

Leaning down, he kissed her gently on the lips and said, "You sleep well, little one." Turning, he left her standing with her fingers on her lips and her eyes wide with surprise.

Chapter Six

IT WAS NEARING MIDDAY AS DEE SLOWLY MADE HER WAY down the stairs. She moved gingerly and with extreme caution, for she was afraid that any sudden move might split her into a thousand pieces.

She could speak only in a controlled whisper as she entered the kitchen in search of some coffee. "Bert, I think my head may explode. Does whiskey always have this side effect?"

"The parson did go on and on with his toasting. That could be the reason you feel under the weather," Bert said as she turned the trout she was frying in the frying pan.

The smell of the frying trout did uncomfortable things to Dee's stomach, making her forego the idea of coffee altogether. "Never mind the coffee, Bert," she grimaced. "I think fresh air might be better."

Dee left the room as the aroma of the fish threatened to make her disgrace herself by being sick.

Wandering down the pathway at the front of the lodge, Dee concentrated on taking deep breaths to calm her churning middle. Paying scant attention to where she was going, she was stunned when she collided with the solid hardness of a man's bare chest.

Terror warred with curiosity as she looked up to apologize. Her mind whirled with impressions and a building scream choked in her throat as she thought wildly, This is not one of the Thorsens!

Gazing down at her intently was the living image of a savage Indian, as though he had stepped right from the pages of one of her books. Adorned in buckskin breeches, bear claw necklace and feather, he was so like one of the illustrations that Dee wondered if she had totally lost her wits.

He lifted a massive hand and, as she stood frozen in shock with flashes of her life passing before her startled eyes, trailed his fingers through one of her blond curls at the side of her cheek. He seemed fascinated with the color and texture of her hair. He is going to scalp me, Dee thought as horrible visions filled her mind.

"Go away!" she stuttered, unable to say more.

The sound of her voice brought his attention back to her face as he stared unblinkingly into her eyes. His dark eyes threatened to swallow her in their depths. His lips parted as though he were going to speak.

Dee's only thought was to try to make it back to the safety of the lodge. Not waiting to hear what he might say, she whirled and ran as fast as she could, all thoughts of her earlier misery forgotten as she raced for her life.

Her headlong flight was seen by Eric and Sven as they were returning from the barn.

"What is she doing?" Sven asked as he saw her run through the open front door as though the devil were at her heels.

Reaching the entryway, Dee spied a shotgun hanging on the wall and grabbed it, praying that it was loaded. The weight told her she was in luck and it was not a mere wall decoration. She returned to the porch and took steady aim at the oncoming savage.

"Good God!" Eric exclaimed as he saw her return.

"The little fool!" Sven cursed as he sprinted onto the porch and grabbed the gun from Dee's grip before she could fire it.

"What the blazes do you think you are doing?" he thundered. "You could have killed someone." He shook the gun menacingly. "This is not a toy!"

Squaring her shoulders and planting her feet, Dee yelled right back at him, "It is a Winchester twelve-gauge repeating shotgun, and it is loaded! So stop shaking it before it does go off!" She saw the Indian as he moved closer to the porch and tried to reclaim the shotgun from Sven.

He brushed her off like a fly, holding the shotgun out of her reach as he picked her up like a sack of meal and held her kicking and fighting on his hip.

Standing at the edge of the steps, the Indian spoke for the first time. "A fine welcome home, I must say."

His cultured voice froze Dee. She stopped struggling to free herself from Sven's steely grip and exclaimed, "He speaks English!"

Acknowledging her attention with a nod of his head, the Indian replied, "French, Swedish and some Latin also."

Sven squeezed Dee, silencing the angry retort that started from her lips as she glared at the newcomer. Still carrying her on his hip, Sven moved toward the doorway, saying over his shoulder, "You certainly set her off. What happened?"

"Nothing! I swear!" was the reply.

This elicited a sharp snort of disagreement from Dee as she tried vainly to pull free of Sven's iron hold on her.

"Nick Clearwater! It's as plain as the nose on your face you scared her almost to death," Sven accused with narrowed eyes. "Next time I'll let her shoot you."

"Nick!" Eric greeted as he clapped him on the back. "Glad to see you. How long will you be staying with us this time?"

"Staying?" Dee gasped as Sven stood her back on her feet but maintained a hold on her arm.

Nick shrugged. "I don't know yet."

Eric viewed Dee's shocked expression and Sven's tense jaw and smiled. "I see you have already met Dee."

"Dee?" Nick questioned as he glanced at Sven.

Sven returned his regard with a slow grin as he said, "Dee Thorsen, my wife."

Nick's next question was cut off as Dee scolded him angrily, "You had no right to frighten me like that, Mr. Clearwater."

"You crashed into me! I was as surprised as you were!" Nick tried to defend himself as he stared at Sven in shock. "Your wife?"

"Crashed into?" Sven eyed Dee coldly. "What is Nick talking about?"

Eric decided that things were starting to get out of hand and said as he ushered everyone inside, "We should tell Bert you are here, Nick."

The sounds of shouting had brought Bert and Leif to the entryway. Seeing Nick, Bert shook her head as she wiped her hands on her apron. "I should have guessed it was you. You never could make a quiet appearance like normal folks." She hugged him briefly and stepped back, still shaking her head.

"Hello to you, too, Bert," Nick grinned as they headed for the parlor.

They were halted as a soft voice called from the stairway, "Leif? Could you please help me the rest of the way down?"

Leif moved to the bottom of the staircase as the others waited. "Kat! You aren't supposed to be up!" He moved up the stairs, placed his arm about her waist and aided her in descending the rest of the way.

Watching their slow progress, Nick looked at Eric in surprise. "There are two of them?"

"If you did not spend all your time working in the hill country, you would know about the train wreck and our . . ."—he hesitated—"guests."

Resting on the sofa, Kat still looked pale to Eric's eyes. Seeing his observation, Kat smiled. "I am fine, Eric. I took it very slowly and you heard me call for Leif. I promise I won't shatter into pieces."

Taking a seat in one of the chairs across from the sofa, Eric replied, "You should have called for someone sooner."

Turning to Leif, Kat asked, "What was all the shouting about?"

Leif sat on the arm of the sofa grinning. "Beats me."

Sven entered the room with a reluctant Dee in tow to hear Kat's question. Eyeing Dee sternly, he said, "This little fool tried to kill Nick and objected when I stopped her from doing so."

Kat looked over at Nick as he relaxed in one of the chairs by the fireplace. "I am not surprised," she said as she took in his fierce appearance.

"I was!" Nick retorted.

"Sven obviously stopped Dee in time. You appear unhurt." Kat smiled. She could see why Dee might react as she had; he looked threatening even as he sat at ease in the chair.

"Sven never gave me a chance to fire!" Dee said as she glared up at Sven.

"Which made you mad." Kat nodded. "That accounts for the shouting that woke me up."

"Made her mad!" Sven declared. "Killing someone is not regarded lightly around here."

"I was not aiming to kill, Sven Thorsen!" Dee stamped her foot.

"If Dee had been aiming to kill, I am afraid she

would have accomplished her goal and your friend would no longer be among the living," Kat told them. "Dee has been a crack shot since the age of thirteen."

"I doubt that!" Sven snorted in disbelief.

"I would rather take the ladies' word for it than have the point proven, Sven." Nick added his opinion.

"I will have you know that I am quite competent with firearms of all types," Dee declared vehemently.

"Sure you are," Sven countered. "And where in the 'wilds' of New York would you be learning all this skill you say you have?" Sven accused her.

Dee seethed with anger at Sven's condescending tone and almost kicked him as she said, "Hunting with my brothers, in case it is any of your business, Mr. Sven Thorsen."

Sven's disbelief was still evident in his lifting of an eyebrow as he said, "Trolley cars?"

"Ohh!" Dee sputtered in exasperation.

"Dee." Kat warned her.

Dee refrained from saying what she wanted to and tilted her head stubbornly, trying to ignore Sven. Damn him, he could make her madder than any man she had ever known, she fumed to herself.

"Kat, will you be dining downstairs with us tonight?" Bert asked.

"I would like to very much," Kat replied. "That is, if my"—she paused slightly—"husband gives his permission."

"Husband?" Nick gasped.

"My wife was injured in the train wreck I mentioned earlier," Eric informed him. "It has been necessary for her recovery that she stay in bed for a period of time."

"Both of you are married?" Nick exclaimed as he stared at Eric and Sven.

"Yes," Eric smiled. "Kat is my wife."

Nick was stunned at this news and turned to Leif,

asking, "I hope you aren't hiding a new wife somewhere?"

Leif shook his head. "There were only two available
ladies and my brothers beat me to the punch."

"Leif!" Bert admonished. "You are too young to get
married and you know it."

Leif cocked a brow at Kat and asked, "Do you have
any eligible friends back East? I am feeling left out."
He laughed, as he enjoyed teasing his aunt and his
brothers.

"You poor boy," Kat chuckled. "I will give some
thought to your question and let you know later."

"So will I," Dee teased him.

The next few days fell into a pattern for Kat and Dee.
Leif became their main companion as Eric and Sven
were either occupied in town or at the newly formed
railroad camp.

Since the day of Nick's arrival, Kat had been allowed
to stay up most of the day with a nap in the late
afternoon.

The absence of Eric and Sven did not bother the
girls. They admitted to each other that they were
relieved not to have to face them except at mealtime.

Dee found it very difficult to know how to act when
she was around Sven. He either ignored her completely
or stared at her as if trying to convince himself she
existed. This made her stutter and stammer whenever
she spoke to him. More than once she had wanted to
scream at him to stop acting like she was some ghost
haunting him.

She had no trouble relating to Eric, which confused
her even more. He treated her as he always had, even
joking with her on occasion.

After a particularly trying day when Sven had almost
bitten her head off for asking him if it was all right for

her to explore around the lodge, she confronted Eric with her anger. "Eric, could you please tell me why your brother is behaving like a bear with a sore head? He is driving me crazy."

Eric smiled. "Sven is always like that when he has a problem. Don't take it personally, Dee."

"Don't take it personally!" Dee exclaimed. "How can I help but take it personally when he yells at me?"

Eric put his arm around her shoulder and they walked back to the parlor. "Give Sven some time, Dee. When he has figured things out, he will probably apologize for the way he has been acting."

Dee looked at him skeptically. "If I don't kick him in the pants first. I hope you know what you are talking about. I do not know how much more of this I can take."

"Trust me," Eric reassured her.

"Eric?" Dee asked. "What is going on with you and Kat?"

"What do you mean?" Eric stalled, not willing to answer her question.

"Do you have a problem where she is concerned?" Dee probed.

"Why do you ask that?" Eric hedged uncomfortably.

Dee hesitated before saying, "I may be getting into something that is none of my business, but I have noticed that you two rarely say anything to each other. When I asked Kat she made up some silly excuse about how I was imagining things. Am I?"

Eric cleared his throat. "I think you are looking for problems that are not there, Dee."

"You are as bad as Kat," Dee told him. "You won't tell me anything either."

It was later that day that Dee became even more confused. She had been on her way to the kitchen to see if Bert needed any help and was startled to see Kat and Sven together in the parlor talking and laughing. Seeing her, they stopped talking and Kat said, "Did you need something, Dee?"

Dee stammered, "No, I was on my way to see if Bert needed any help. I am sorry if I interrupted anything."

Sven sat scowling at her as Kat said, "No, you didn't interrupt anything. Sven and I were just talking, that's all." Kat rose from her chair, adding, "I think I will go with you and see if I can help Bert, too."

Poor Dee! Kat thought to herself as she followed her into the kitchen. I think she might be jealous of my talking to Sven. I had better straighten her out as soon as I can. Things are uncomfortable enough as it is around here without the two of us having problems.

At least, Dee thought to herself the next morning, there isn't any strain where Leif is concerned. She had listened to Kat the night before when she explained that there was no reason for her to be upset that she had been talking with Sven. Dee had ended up denying that she was upset. Kat had looked at her as though she did not believe a word she was saying and Dee had defended herself by telling Kat, "I am no more upset about that than you would be about my talking with Eric."

"You have talked with Eric?" Kat had responded.

Dee had seen the look that passed over Kat's face as she spoke and knew that Kat was disturbed. So were you, she told herself.

"Kat?" Dee had said. "What are we going to do? It's obvious that we both might be letting ourselves get hurt."

Kat had sat on her bed and answered, "I know. We will have to do exactly what we planned on doing from the beginning. We will return to New York and have our marriages quietly annulled and try to forget we ever met the Thorsen brothers."

Dee had thought about what Kat had said and knew she was probably right. But it left an empty feeling inside her that kept her awake most of that night.

Leif tapped her on the arm, saying, "Dee?"

She looked up quickly and laughed self-consciously. "I'm sorry, Leif. I guess I was lost in thought."

"I'll say you were. I called your name twice before you heard me," Leif said. "Is it anything I can help with?"

"No." Dee smiled as she added, "Are we going exploring today or not?"

"Kat is waiting for us outside. I came in to see if you were ready," Leif told her.

"I am as ready as I'll ever be," Dee told him.

Leif enjoyed being with the girls. They treated him as an equal and a friend. They never acted like he was younger than he was like his brothers did.

It was late the next evening that Nick discovered another side to Dee.

He had borrowed a book from Eric's extensive library and was returning to his room when Leif jumped up from his seat in the parlor, calling, "Dee's at it again. The front door just closed."

Sven immediately headed for the back of the lodge as Eric shrugged and followed Leif out the front door. Watching this, Nick called after them, "What in hell is going on?"

Eric called back, "Follow us and you will find out."

Thoroughly puzzled, Nick followed the others out onto the porch, where Eric and Leif split up and moved in separate directions. Nick followed Leif, saying, "Why in heaven's name are we out in the black of night running around like idiots?"

"You will get used to it, Nick. We have." Leif smiled.

"Become used to what?" Nick demanded as he followed Leif down one of the paths.

"Practically since she arrived here, Dee has walked in her sleep. We have grown used to it. In fact, we never know which way she will go next."

"What!" Nick exclaimed.

"She has even crawled into bed with one of us on a few occasions," Leif added as he searched the surrounding bushes for a sign of her.

"She is married to Sven, so I can understand that. But you and Eric? Why didn't I know about any of this?" Nick complained.

"Obviously, she has never tried to join you, or you would have known." Leif clapped Nick on the shoulder, laughing. "You must be slipping."

"Does she ever wake up?" Nick questioned, ignoring Leif's barb.

"Not yet. And she has no recollection of anything the next morning. We haven't said anything to her. It would only embarrass her."

In the star-studded blackness, Sven could be heard calling, "I've found her."

"He usually does," Leif commented to Nick as they moved toward the sound of Sven's voice. Reaching the side of the lodge, they found Sven leading a placid Dee by the hand back toward the front door.

Watching this, Nick shook his head. "Have you tried locking her door?"

"And have her wake up and ask why?" Leif asked. "No, we have only tracked her down and returned her to bed."

Sven led Dee back to her room and tucked her into bed. He joined his brothers and Nick in the parlor, where Nick was full of questions. "Is it always this easy to find her?"

Sven shook his head. "Dee gets herself into places she would never think of going were she awake. Once we hunted for close to thirty minutes before I finally found her in the hayloft of the barn."

"Remember the time we found her on the bench in the garden, sunning herself as though it were broad daylight?" Leif added.

"And what about the time she was in the kitchen?" Eric said.

"The kitchen?" Nick questioned.

"She was cutting up vegetables as though preparing dinner," Leif informed him. "Only she was using the large knife we keep for game."

Looking at Eric, Nick asked, "Have you tried to find out why she sleepwalks?"

"How can we without telling her she does?" Eric returned.

"Besides, we have more serious things to worry about," Sven told him.

"Like what?" Nick asked.

They went on to explain the sabotaged train, the incriminating newspaper article and the talk around town. They also told him what they had heard from New York and why they had agreed to marry Kat and Dee.

"That clears up a lot of questions I have had," Nick told them.

"Questions?" Eric said.

"For instance, why two newly married couples were occupying separate bedrooms. Why the four of you go around each other like cats and dogs ready to start a fight," Nick answered.

"We do not act like that!" Sven protested.

Nick only looked at him and did not say anything more. Sven changed the subject by saying, "We may have even more trouble on our hands."

"How so?" Eric asked.

"Helga sent word from town that two men have been nosing around asking questions about Kat and Dee," Sven informed them. "And one of the men has been trying to pass himself off as Kat's brother from back East."

"Kat's brother!" Leif exploded. "Kat is an only child!"

"I have some men of my own watching for these guys," Sven said in a hard voice.

As the men discussed their courses of action, Kat lay in bed, tossing and turning in her sleep, a fine sheen of perspiration coating her skin as she moaned, "No! No! I can't!"

She threw the bedclothes off her heated body and fought off the demons in her sleep as large tears fell from her closed eyes.

Down the hall, Dee slowly rose from her bed and left her room. The lodge was quiet and dark when she woke and fuzzily wondered why she was in Kat's room and not her own. Leaving Kat's room, still half asleep, Dee made her way down the hall and into a bedroom. She stumbled over to the bed and, lifting the covers, climbed under them to snuggle down and sleep.

Sven stirred, wondering what had caused the sudden cool draft that woke him up. Opening his eyes, he discovered he was not alone. A small curled figure was sharing his bed.

What the hell is she doing here? he wondered. Hadn't Eric said that one sleepwalking episode a night was all they had to be worried about?

Sven barely had time to register his thoughts when Dee rolled over in her sleep and snuggled close to him for warmth. "Oh, no, you don't," he whispered aloud.

Gently disengaging her, he rose and donned his pants. Lifting her into his arms, he had to grit his teeth at the feeling that coursed through his veins as she pressed her breasts into his chest.

He carried her back to her room for what he hoped was the last time that night. Closing her door, he fervently hoped she would not awaken until morning; at least that way one of them would get some sleep.

It was later the next afternoon before Sven and Eric saw either of the girls again. They were returning from a picnic in the woods with Leif. They were laughing as they walked arm in arm.

Nick watched from his vantage point atop his horse. He was ready to return to his work in the hills and Eric and Sven had come out front to send him on his way. But from the looks on their faces as they viewed their wives, it was their brother they would like to send away if they could.

Stopping along the path, Leif bent down, picked one of the wild flowers that grew in such abundance and gave it to Kat. She smiled at him and kissed his cheek in thanks.

Dee pulled on Leif's arm and demanded, "Hey! Where's mine?"

Leif laughed and picked another flower, making a showy production of kissing its petals before handing it to Dee.

She accepted it with a quick curtsey and all three of them began to laugh as they linked arms and made their way to where their audience watched.

Nick decided to push the brothers some and looked down from his horse, saying, "It appears your baby brother is growing up. I would keep an eye on him if I were you."

Sven scowled up at him. "You're not me. They are only playing around."

Eric voiced his opinion. "Nick, quit trying to stir up trouble. They were on a friendly picnic and that's all."

Nick gathered his reins and looked over at the approaching trio. "If you say so. But don't say I didn't warn you."

"Good-bye, Nick," Sven growled.

Eric's eyes widened as if seeing Leif for the first time. "Besides, Leif is still a kid."

"Were you still a kid at his age, Eric?" Nick asked as he headed his mount toward the hill trail.

Both Eric and Sven frowned as they watched Nick's departing figure. "Why do you think he would say something like that?" Eric asked Sven.

"Were you still a kid at Leif's age?" Sven asked him.

Eric's eyes widened slightly. "Were you?"

"Hell, no," Sven returned.

Chapter Seven

THE NEXT DAY DAWNED CLOSE AND HUMID, PREVENTING A person from doing the simplest movements or chores. The air wrapped around everything like a thick cocoon of wool. Distant rumbles of thunder could be heard as the clouds piled higher and higher in towering monoliths in the sky.

The simple act of descending the stairs caused Dee's dress to cling to her back and shoulders as perspiration bled through the light material. Moving into the parlor, she mopped the beaded moisture on her brow and cheeks. Raising her hand to do this caused rivulets of stickiness to trickle between her breasts.

Kat appeared to be faring little better as she perched uneasily on one of the chairs in the room. Seeing Dee, she grimaced. "Who turned the heat up?"

Dee groaned. "If I knew that I would order them to turn it off!"

Unable to bear sitting around idly in the oppressive heat, they made their way to the kitchen to see what Bert was doing.

Entering the kitchen, an aroma fit for kings assailed their nostrils. "What is that, Bert?" Dee asked, sniffing the air.

Bert grinned at them. "Fresh bread."

"Fresh bread!" Kat exclaimed. "How can you bake in this heat?"

"It's the only way we will have any bread," Bert

answered. "We haven't bakeries nearby doing it for us."

Bert opened the oven door to the sight of golden loaves. Taking them out, she thumped the pans to see if they were done. Hearing the hollow sound she was looking for, she placed them near some other loaves cooling on the large counter.

Dee watched with wide eyes, her mouth watering at the tantalizing aroma that permeated the room. "How often do you have to do this?"

"At least once a week," Bert replied as she rubbed freshly churned butter over the tops of the crusts as they cooled.

Kat counted the number of loaves on the counter. "Bert, how many loaves do you have to bake at a time? I have counted over two dozen here."

"Two dozen will last us a week," Bert told them. "The extra ones are for trading with neighbors for fresh eggs and fruit."

"Two dozen!" Dee said.

"Don't forget, I have three Thorsen men to feed," Bert reminded her.

"With Dee and me that makes six people you have to feed," Kat said. "Have we made that much extra work for you, Bert?"

Bert started laughing, "Honey, I have been baking the same amount at a time for over ten years. I haven't needed to add a single loaf for the two of you. And as for your causing me more work, you have helped me more than enough to take care of that."

Placing a pitcher of lemonade and some glasses on the counter, Dee asked, "How hot would you say it is?"

"In here or outside?" Bert asked as she mopped her brow.

"Outside," Dee replied.

"Around ninety, but the air is heavy today and that makes it feel hotter," Bert explained.

Pouring some lemonade, Dee groaned, "Ninety is hot enough by itself. How can you work in such weather, Bert?"

"This weather suits me better than the cold kind. My arthritis doesn't act up quite so badly," Bert told them. "I had better get back to my work here. I still have my garden to water before the weather cooks it."

The thought of Bert hauling the heavy water buckets by herself made Dee say, "Kat and I will do it for you, Bert."

Kat added her voice to Dee's. "The two of us can work faster than you by yourself." She smiled. "Your garden will have less time to cook in this heat if you let us do it for you."

"If you are sure you want to," Bert said as she led them to the back of the lodge.

The porch ran half the length of the backside of the lodge. At one time it had run the full length, but when Bert had come to live with them, the brothers had sectioned off half for a bedroom. With her bedroom next to the kitchen, Bert saved time and effort.

The girls were so anxious to help that Bert shook her head as she let them go their own way and began weeding between her vegetable plants with a secret grin.

Drawing the water from the hand pump to fill the four buckets went quickly at first. But by the time they were refilling for their third load of water, the muscles in Dee's and Kat's arms and shoulders were protesting the unaccustomed effort.

It amazed Dee how quickly the water was soaked up by the parched soil as she tipped her buckets slowly into the furrows on either side of the growing plants.

Stopping on her fourth trip from the pump to the garden, Kat sat her two buckets down and looked at Bert in disbelief. "You were going to do this all by yourself? How do you do it?"

Bert sat back on her heels and twinkled up at Kat. "I usually make one of the boys do the heavy work for me. But seeing as how you and Dee were so anxious to help . . ." She let her voice trail off as she grinned.

Kat did present quite a picture with her sleeves rolled back and the hem of her dress tucked into her belt to ease walking with the sloshing buckets. Her hair clung in damp tendrils around her neck and forehead, where it had come loose from its pins, and she had undone the top few buttons of her shirtwaist to try to cool off.

Dee sloshed her way next to Kat and paused, wondering what the delay was. Kat told her how Bert had worked her wiles on them. Dee's flushed face looked at Bert in mock anger. "Bert! How could you do such a thing?"

Bert grinned back at her. "It was easy."

Kat laughed as she lifted her buckets and went on to the garden. Setting the buckets down, she carefully tipped one into the waiting furrow.

Dee moved beside her and tipped one of her buckets into the adjoining furrow with a mischievous gleam in her eye. Seeing how absorbed Kat was in distributing the water, Dee cupped her hand into the stream from her bucket and playfully flicked it at Kat.

Kat jumped, startled at this unexpected shower. Laughing, she lifted her almost empty bucket and tossed the remaining contents at Dee.

Bert viewed this with growing amusement.

Dee was squealing and laughing as much as Kat as she lifted her full bucket and tried to heave its contents at Kat. She staggered slightly, managing to douse herself more than Kat.

Lifting her skirt away from her, Dee laughed. "I'm wetter than the garden!"

Dropping the soaked material, she eyed her bucket and its lowered water level. Acting before Kat could move, Dee quickly emptied the remaining water on her as she laughed. "And now so are you!"

Ignoring their bedraggled state, they enjoyed the relief from the heat that their impromptu water fight gave them.

Coming from the barn to see what all the noise was about, Eric and Sven rounded the corner of the lodge and were stopped in their tracks as a cascade of water caught both of them full in the face.

Kat had heaved another bucket of water toward Dee in playful enthusiasm, but Dee had dodged the throw, leaving Eric and Sven to feel its full impact.

Kat gasped in dismay as her hand went to her lips to still the unbidden laughter that threatened to escape at the sight of the two.

Dee turned to see what Kat was looking at and exclaimed, "Oh!"

Bert watched it all from her vantage point on the back step. She had no qualms about giving vent to her laughter as she pointed at her nephews with delight.

Leif joined her in unbridled amusement as he came upon the scene from the opposite side of the lodge.

Kat felt the color flow to her face as Eric and Sven shook the water from their eyes and tried to clear their faces with open hands.

"What is going on here!" Eric sputtered as he flicked the remaining moisture from his hands. He looked from Kat to Dee, taking in their total dishevelment.

The swirling dust and clinging mud from their fight had splashed on the girls' dresses and Kat's hair was barely holding onto its former upswept styling. Dee's hair had given up any pretense at neatness and was a soaked curtain about her face and shoulders, its pins lost somewhere in the muddied dirt.

"Well?" Eric asked once again as he tried to hide his surprise at their appearance.

"We are . . ."—Kat hesitated—"watering the garden." She could not suppress a nervous laugh.

"I think my brothers are big enough. You needn't water them anymore," Leif tried to say with a serious tone, but he failed as laughter shook him.

Eric exchanged looks with a soaked Sven. Without a word, they began to advance on the girls. Their intimidating stance caused Kat to take an involuntary step back as Dee nervously watched them through a curtain of wet curls.

They startled both girls with a wink as they lifted their buckets, which still had water in them, and in one motion tossed the contents at Leif.

Leif's laughter ended in a sputter as the unexpected deluge knocked him to his seat in the mud.

The air was alive with laughter as Eric and Sven stood over Leif as he tried to rise from the mud.

Eric looked over his shoulder at Kat and Dee and said, "I hope neither of you regret this. After you've cleaned up I will want to recheck your injuries."

Bert broke things up, saying, "Don't be a spoilsport, Eric. Come on, girls. We will get the two of you cleaned up before that mud dries on you and we have to chip you out of your dresses."

Kat and Dee scurried to Bert's side, not sure what Eric or Sven might decide to do next.

Watching the ladies disappear into the lodge, Eric and Sven helped Leif to his feet and clapped him on the back.

Eric shook his head. "Do you believe those two? They looked half drowned."

"I told you they knew how to have fun," Leif interjected in their defense.

Sven raised his hands. "We were not criticizing them! But they are city raised. We did not expect any of this. That's all."

"We had better clean up ourselves or Bert won't let us inside," Eric said.

The three moved over to the water pump and began sloshing the clinging mud off. Removing their soaked shirts and tossing them to the side, they splashed the cool well water over their chests and shoulders. Sven had a puzzled look on his face as he said, "Why do I think better of them for letting loose like they did?"

Eric was drying himself off with a towel that Bert had tossed from the back steps before returning inside. "Maybe because none of the city ladies we have ever met would be caught dead acting human," he said as he toweled his hair.

"Hey, hold on!" Leif argued. "Don't condemn all eastern females! I have met a few that were fairly nice."

Both his brothers grinned at him. "Have you, now? Care to tell us all about them? We were under the impression that you were back East going to school," Eric teased.

While Eric went on teasing Leif, Sven wondered to himself why Dee's face as she peered up at him through her hair should unsettle him as much as it had. Vigorously toweling his hair, he told himself that it was the heat affecting him and nothing else.

Kat and Dee stood by the doorway to the dining room, not wanting to enter the room and track mud and water all over the highly polished floor. The heaviness of their sodden clothes was becoming uncomfortable as Bert returned from the other room carrying two robes over her arm.

"The boys are busy cleaning up outside. Slip out of those dresses and into these robes and I'll set the dresses aside to be washed," she instructed them as she waited patiently.

Glancing over their shoulders to be certain that nobody would see them, the two girls quickly shed their dresses, kicking them off to the side as Bert handed each of them a robe.

They belted themselves into the large robes and took their muddied clothes to the far side of the porch. Leaving them there, they returned to the dining room and Bert, who then handed each of them a towel to wrap around their heads. "Thank you, Bert." Dee welcomed the towel with a sigh.

Hurrying through the dining room and entryway to the stairs, they hoped to make it to their rooms before any of the men could see them. Luck was not with them as Eric's voice halted them in their tracks. He was coming out of his office, tucking a clean shirt into clean pants and spotted them on the stairs. "Wait right there."

He came over to them and held out his hand, saying, "Dee, let me see your arm."

Dee had to pull the extra long sleeves of her robe back so Eric could see the water-soaked bandage on her wrist.

Eric nodded. "Just as I thought. You go on upstairs and get dressed, then come back here to the office. This will have to be changed."

Dee lost little time in disappearing up the stairs, leaving Kat to face Eric alone.

Kat anticipated Eric's next question and said, "My ribs are fine and so is my head. If I have any trouble with either I will let you know." Having said this, she started up the stairs.

Eric's hand stopped her as he pulled her by the arm.

"Not so fast. I am the doctor, remember? Let me be the judge of what is fine and what is not."

Kat had little choice but to follow him as he held onto her arm and returned to his office. She had never been in his office and liked what she saw. There were bookshelves lining three of the walls and a massive desk near the window with two overstuffed leather chairs placed conveniently for the light. Next to the desk was a flat table that she recognized as an examining table. It was to this table that Eric led her.

"Off with the robe and up on the table, Kat," he ordered her.

Kat felt trapped. She could not refuse to let him examine her; he was her doctor. But she had nothing on under her robe and the thought of him seeing her this way was unthinkable. She tried to convince herself that doctors saw their patients unclothed all the time. After all, it was not the Dark Ages. But she failed to convince herself it was nothing to become upset over because the fact that she was to be the unclothed patient and Eric the doctor overrode common sense.

Eric saw the indecision on her face and could guess what was going through her mind. "If you prefer, you may keep the robe on. Loosen the front, though. I have to check your rib cage."

Kat blushed, wishing that he had been more businesslike and not so knowingly considerate. She climbed onto the table, loosening the tie on the robe before she reclined on the hard surface. She drew in her breath and tried not to flinch as she felt Eric's strong hands slide inside the robe and begin moving about her ribs. She did not have the courage to look at him and kept her eyes tightly closed.

To his surprise, Eric found that he was almost as nervous as Kat when his hands touched the coolness of her skin as he checked for swelling or signs of soreness.

This reaction to her was not one he had expected and he quickly finished his inspection and pulled the front of her robe closed, saying roughly, "You were lucky that carrying those heavy buckets did not irritate anything."

Kat's eyes flew open at the harshness of his voice. She hurriedly climbed off the table, her sides still tingling from his touch, and said, "I was careful, Eric."

"As it would appear," Eric gruffly returned. "You had better get dressed before you catch a chill."

Kat did not need to be told twice and scurried from the office and up to her room, thankful to be away from Eric. He had sounded mad at her for something and she did not want to know what.

After changing, Kat met Dee on the landing and they both went to the kitchen to help Bert. "How did it go?" Dee asked Kat as they descended the stairs.

"I don't want to talk about it," Kat said. She was still too confused herself over what had happened in Eric's office to discuss any of it with Dee.

Dee looked at the worry in her eyes. "You are upset. Did you hurt yourself?"

"No, Dee," Kat reassured her. "Eric said I was lucky that I didn't."

They were nearing the kitchen when Dee could no longer contain her curiosity and asked, "Did you two have a fight or something?"

Kat paused with her hand on the kitchen door and slowly said, "Or something. Now let's not talk about it, all right?"

"If that is what you want," Dee replied, trying to keep the hurt from her voice. Kat had never shut her out like this before. What really did happen? she asked herself.

Joining Bert in the kitchen, Kat scrubbed vegetables Bert had picked and Dee moved to the stove and stirred the contents of a large pot bubbling on one of the burners.

An aching soreness in her side mixed with the lingering feel of Eric's hands and Kat knew that her ribs were protesting. But what they were protesting she did not want to consider.

Dee glanced over at the stiff carriage of Kat's figure by the sink and knew that her throbbing wrist had company in its misery. If Kat was so upset after having seen Eric, Dee hoped he would forget that he wanted to see her. She had no wish to face him.

Bert saw how both girls were quiet and lost in thought as they went about their tasks and wondered if they were regretting what had gone on outside. She hoped not. They had needed to relax and have fun for the sheer enjoyment of it. She did not like the idea that their city upbringing might make them sorry they had enjoyed themselves. This turn in attitudes made her angry and she set the load of plates she was carrying down on the counter with a loud clatter.

Both Kat and Dee jumped as though a shot had been fired and stared at her. "Plates slipped," she told them, refraining from saying what she would really like to have said.

Eric left his office and went into the parlor, where Sven was waiting for the call to eat.

Sven saw the frown on Eric's face and asked, "Catch a chill from your dousing?"

"What?" Eric's thoughts were on other feelings. "Dousing? Oh, I think I will survive that."

"What are you worried about not surviving?" Sven probed.

Eric looked at his brother to see if he was serious and replied, "Being around Kat."

Sven lit one of his infrequent cheroots and mused aloud, "It must be contagious. I seem to be experiencing some of the same symptoms where Dee is concerned."

Eric raised an eyebrow. "What do we do about it?"

"The question is, can we do anything about it?" Sven remarked as he blew smoke toward the ceiling. "Or do we want to do anything about it?"

Eric moved to a chair and sat down. "Things are becoming more and more complicated, aren't they?"

"We never said it would be simple," Sven said. "But I had fun and I think you did, too."

Eric smiled knowingly at him. "I guess you could say I did. Have you ever heard either of them laugh like that before?"

Sven thought back on the past few days. "Only when they were with Leif," he said.

"That's right," Eric nodded. "Sure, they have laughed a few times when they were with us, but not like this afternoon." He looked over at Sven and questioned, "Why do they relax with Leif, but not with us?"

"Because I am so likable?" Leif said as he joined them and heard his name mentioned.

His brothers gave him a look of disbelief. "Don't flatter yourself, baby brother," Sven told him.

Seating himself nonchalantly on the sofa, Leif grinned. "Someone in this family has to be likable. And viewing you two, I see the choice is obvious. It has to be me."

"I think that drenching warped his mind," Sven observed to Eric.

Eric looked over at Leif. "It was already warped. All we may have accomplished was to muddy his thinking even further."

Sven laughed and drew on his cheroot. "I wonder if the damage is permanent? He still looks wet behind the ears."

Leif was accustomed to their teasing and took it in stride. "At least I am not creaky in the joints, eldest brother."

"Watch it!" Sven retorted. "My joints are fine, but yours are in danger of becoming bent if you keep it up."

"No worry. Eric is a famous frontier doctor. He can mend both our joints," Leif shot back at Sven.

"If you are through with your jawing, there is a joint of beef getting cold on the table," Bert told them as she stood in the doorway with her hands on her hips.

The brothers rose to follow her into the dining room. Eric said, "That's one joint I can handle. I'm starved."

Kat and Dee were already at the table when the brothers appeared. Kat voiced a quiet greeting and Dee nodded shyly as the men took their places.

This subdued attitude was a marked change from their earlier exuberance and did not surprise Sven. Eric noticed it at once and said to Dee, "When are you going to allow me to change that bandage?"

Dee's face reddened under Eric's scrutiny. "I can manage it myself."

Eric saw the flushed glance she exchanged with Kat. "Did you two get too much sun this afternoon? You are both awfully quiet this evening."

"Quit badgering them and carve the meat!" Bert ordered him.

Sven saw the play of emotions on Dee's face and Kat's suddenly downcast eyes and could have kicked Eric under the table for his unthinking questions.

Leif saw that things were starting out on an uneasy note and said, "Don't pay any attention to Eric. He and Sven were just discussing the fact that they think I appear to be the one most damaged, and at their own hands."

"Damaged?" Dee gasped.

"They are of the opinion that the shower they gave me may have muddied my thinking." He passed her the bowl of vegetables before adding, "Although if what they say is true, I have no idea what their excuses are for their own muddled thinking."

He returned his brothers' warning looks with a knowing smile.

The heat still rested heavily in the evening air and Kat found she had little appetite. She looked around the table and saw that Dee was picking at her food. But the heat appeared to have little effect on the others as they enjoyed the meal.

Dee shuddered as a loud rumble of thunder sounded nearby. "Will it storm?" she asked the table in general.

"We might have some rumbling and a few flashes. But I doubt if any moisture will come from it," Bert replied.

Dee furrowed her brow. "Flashes?"

"Heat lightning," Leif explained. "New York has thunderstorms, if I remember."

"Of course we have thunderstorms!" Dee defended her curiosity. "I know what they are like." She hesitated and then clarified her statement. "In New York, that is." Having said this she decided she had better be quiet before she made an even bigger fool of herself.

"City storms are different," Sven commented as he cut his meat. "They are tamer than our Montana storms."

"Tamer?" Dee could have kicked herself for speaking and revealing her ignorance.

"I experienced one of your storms when I went back for Eric's graduation," Sven explained. "The rain did pour down and the sky did rumble, but it was restrained, like the clouds knew it wouldn't be polite or civilized to do any more than that."

Resenting this condescending attitude, Kat said, "I

would think a thunderstorm is a thunderstorm, no matter where it occurs."

"No, ma'am. The storms out here know the land is still pretty wild and unsettled, and they can let it rip without offending too many people," Sven told her. "The weather out here is a lot like the people out here, Kat—honest, hard-working and natural."

"I take it, then, that you did not find the people back East any different from the weather?" Kat said defensively.

Leif glared at Sven, wondering how the conversation had drifted so quickly into personalities from Dee's simple question.

Sven thought a moment before answering Kat. "The people have the same potential, but how they use this potential differs."

"In what ways do you feel they differ?" Kat asked, interested to hear what he would say.

Eric watched Sven with narrowed eyes, trying to guess how he would answer Kat's question as the lodge was buffeted with rolling thunderclaps.

Sven looked up at the ceiling and smiled. "For one thing, a New York storm would never be so rude as to interrupt a dinner conversation."

"And the people?" Kat persisted as Dee stared at her in surprise at her pushing Sven as she was.

"I admit that I have limited experience with Easterners, and what experience I do have does not give me the authority to judge all Easterners. But the ones I have met did not make me overly anxious to cultivate further experiences," Sven told her.

"Why is that?" Dee could not help asking.

"When I was back there, I was surprised to see how people were judged on what they had or who their relatives were and not on their own individual merits. I also saw a stifling set of rules governing behavior."

"Oh, you disagree with law and order?" Kat noted sarcastically. Sven was saying aloud things she had thought to herself for years, but even so she felt impelled to defend New York and its people.

Sven looked over at her with an indulgent expression as if he had not really heard what she had said. "I did not say that. You are reading that into what I said," he informed her. "Everyone knows we have had our problems here with law and order. That is one of the reasons the vigilante groups were formed." Sven stared across the table at Kat and Dee as though speaking to the both of them and not merely replying to a question from Kat. "Your saying what you did is a good example. Here we speak plainly, saying what we think. Easterners say many things, and rarely are they what they really would like to say. Especially if their true feelings conflict with the prevalent opinions of a select few."

Dee gasped as Kat was swift to disagree. "We do speak plainly, as do you. Easterners may not be as rough in their manner of speech as you are accustomed to hearing, but we speak our minds nonetheless," she insisted.

Seeing the rising color on Kat's face, Eric put his hand on Sven's arm and said, "I think this discussion has gone far enough for now."

"No, Eric," Kat interrupted him. "I would like to hear what else Sven has to say about Easterners. I am finding this conversation very educational."

Sven looked at Eric before replying to Kat's statement. Eric removed his hand from Sven's arm and, shrugging, said, "She wants to hear what you have to say."

Sven used care as he countered Kat's last statement by saying, "I am glad to see you are interested in what I have to say. It is not too very different from the way most Montanans feel. Rough or smooth speaking has nothing to do with what you are saying. In the East, I saw a few control the many. Call it social censure if you like. I call it snobbery. And in business a man will clasp your hand in friendship and plan on stabbing you in the back. No matter if it is in the business or social world, they live by their own code of dishonor and think nothing is wrong as they laugh with their cronies over how they put another one over on some poor fool who believed them."

"Kat's grandfather is not like that!" Dee exclaimed heatedly.

"That's why we do business with him." Sven smiled at her. "We know where we stand with Patrick Gwyn and need never watch over our shoulders for that hidden knife ready to stab us."

Unbidden visions of J. P. Morgan, Edward Harriman and a few other men she had met through the years crossed Kat's mind as she listened to Sven's words.

"Your grandfather is an honest man." Sven's voice broke into Kat's troubled memories.

"I have always thought so," she replied. "I am happy to see that we can agree on one thing."

Sven laughed. "You started asking the questions, not me."

"No, I did," Dee contradicted him, adding, "And I never knew there would be so many answers."

The ingenuousness of her last statement brought smiles to everyone's faces as Dee blushed furiously in embarrassment.

Eric tried to ease her embarrassment by saying, "Sven may not say much often, but when he does, he says a lot."

"Sometimes more than we want to hear." Leif grinned.

The room was shaken again by loud thunder as if the

storm agreed with Leif's opinion. Kat and Dee joined with the general laughter caused by this punctuation mark of nature.

"Bert," Eric said, changing the subject, "could you answer a question for me?"

"Everyone seems all-fired curious tonight," Bert said as she frowned at Eric. "Besides, I thought you already knew all the answers."

"Far from it." Eric smiled. "But one thing has been puzzling me since this afternoon."

"And what is that?" Bert asked cautiously.

Looking from Dee and Kat to Bert, Eric went on, "Why didn't you show the girls how to use the irrigation ditches to water the garden?"

"Irrigation ditches?" Dee frowned.

"You mean we did not have to haul those heavy buckets?" Kat said in surprise.

Bert grinned sheepishly. "They were enjoying themselves so much that I didn't have the heart to tell them there was an easier way."

"Bert! How could you!" Dee exclaimed.

Bert twinkled at them in a fashion they were beginning to recognize. "It was easy."

Chapter Eight

THE CONSISTENT FLASHES OF LIGHTNING ADDED TO THE earthshaking claps of thunder had made sleep a sometime thing for Kat and Dee. They were awakened numerous times during the night wondering if the lodge would collapse about them.

This intermittent slumber proved to be a boon for the brothers. They had not looked forward to the possibility of having to try to locate Dee should she decide to venture outside on one of her nocturnal rambles.

At breakfast, only the men were refreshed and alert. They had not been bothered by the storm. Eric saw the tired droop to Kat's shoulders and the dull look in Dee's eyes and suggested that they return to bed and try to catch up on their sleep.

His considerate suggestion was almost completely drowned out by the continuing storm, and the girls knew it would be an exercise in futility if they tried to do as he suggested.

As the day lengthened, the heat increased and the unbelievable humidity felt even more oppressive than the day before.

"This is decidedly not a civilized storm," Dee said to Kat as the wind picked up and the sound of tree branches crashing against each other could be heard between the claps of thunder.

"Welcome to Montana." Kat grimaced at the sound of a bone-shaking thunderclap. "Sven was right. Could

you see what the reaction would be to something like
this if it hit New York?" Kat shook her head.

Dee waved a hand dramatically in the air, saying,
"There would be ladies swooning all over the place.
Mrs. Astor would not be pleased at all!" She giggled. "I
can even think of a few prominent gentlemen that
might pale should something like this strike near any of
their grand estates."

Kat laughed. "I bet I could name a few who would
turn tail and run."

Dee grinned. "I won't take that bet."

"We had better not throw stones, Dee." Kat so-
bered. "Some would say what we did was turning tail
and running."

"I don't think it was an act of cowardice for us to
leave!" Dee defended their actions. "I would call it an
act of self-preservation."

"There are those who would disagree with you on
that definition," Kat commented wryly.

Dee snapped her fingers. "That's what I think of
them. Let them find someone else to pick on."

Kat smiled. "No one can say you don't have an
opinion, can they?"

"And I will give it to anyone I think needs it," Dee
stated firmly.

"I have no doubt you will." Kat laughed softly.

"I guess we had better find something to do today or
I might end up in trouble, with my big mouth." Dee
blushed.

Kat ran her hand over her hair. "What I would love
to do is shampoo my hair. This heat has made it a sticky
mess."

"Mine feels full of grit from yesterday," Dee admitted. "We could ask Bert if it would be all right. Maybe
she has a special place reserved for shampooing."

"Why should there be a special place?" Kat asked.

"I haven't the slightest idea," Dee replied. "But, after not being told about the irrigation ditches for the garden, I am not going to take any chances."

Having consulted Bert, they found they could use the back porch and the very same buckets that they had toted the day before. Bert smilingly offered to heat some of the water they hauled.

Having carried as much water as they thought they would need, Dee knew she would have to swallow her pride and visit Eric sometime that day. Her wrist was protesting strongly at the strain she had put it under.

"Dee, I'll wash your hair for you," Kat volunteered. "You won't have to get your wrist wet that way."

"Only if you let me comb your hair out for you after you wash it. I know what a strain that is on your side," Dee agreed.

"But that would hurt your wrist as much as toting buckets!" Kat protested.

Bert joined the conversation uninvited. "I think if you use this shampoo you will find it much easier to comb your hair afterward." She held up a jar of golden liquid.

"What kind of shampoo is it?" Dee asked.

"It's one Sven makes up for me from roots and herbs," Bert said. "And before you stick your city noses in the air, let me tell you it is better than any store-bought shampoo I have ever used."

"Bert!" Kat cried. "We would not think of making fun of you or your shampoo."

Having shampooed their hair, the girls raved at how clean it felt and how easy it had been to comb. "Bert, you have to give us the recipe! My hair has never felt like this before," Dee badgered her.

"If you bottled this and sold it back East, you would be rich overnight," Kat told her, amazed at the silkiness of her hair.

Bert threw her hands up and exclaimed, "Hold it! You will have to ask Sven. He is the one who makes it up for me."

"Fine, we will ask him," Kat said.

"Where is he?" Dee asked, noticing for the first time that she had not seen him since breakfast.

"He is gone," Bert answered them. "And before you start badgering me on where he's gone, I'll tell you I don't know and I don't know when he will be back, neither."

The disappointment in their faces made Bert relent a bit and she added, "Why not take a walk in the woods and let the fresh air dry your hair."

"But what about the storm?" Dee asked her. "Isn't it dangerous to be near trees in weather like this?"

"What storm?" Bert asked her.

Bert's question hung in the air. Neither Kat nor Dee had noticed the quiet. It was as if the heavens had never growled and complained. The storm had abated and no longer was the day rent by flashes of lightning or claps of thunder. "Does it always end like this?" Dee asked in surprise.

"Sometimes." Bert shrugged. "The storm has probably moved to the next county. Storms out here are choosy about where they will stay." Bert smiled. "Why, some storms may even decide to water your backyard and not your front."

"What?" Dee found it hard to believe such a fantastic claim.

"I said they could be choosy, didn't I?" Bert grinned at her. "Now go on and take your walk. And don't come back until your hair is dry. I don't want it dripping on my clean floors." Bert scolded them just as she did the brothers.

Moving down the path toward a stand of trees, Kat

looked at Dee and smiled. "I think we have been banished."

Dee walked a short distance ahead, saying, "I know we have."

The trees formed a roof reaching to the sky. The two knew they could never tire of such beauty and grace or the delight of strolling through the majestic setting.

As they moved deeper and deeper into the trees, they could hear what sounded like gurgling water. Dee forged ahead to see what was making the sound. Finding the source, she called excitedly, "Kat! Come see what I've found."

Kat hurried to join Dee and found her on the banks of a beautiful pool set in the midst of the trees like a gem in a jeweler's setting.

The water looked so cool and inviting as it lapped gently at the banks of the secluded pool. The canopy of tree branches overhead filtered the sunlight to slim fingers of radiance that dappled the quiet scene with a caress.

Kat knelt on the grassy bank and cupped her palm into the crystal water to bathe her hot forehead. The relief it gave her was wonderful. "Dee! Come try some," she called.

Dee moved from where she had been resting on a nearby rock. "Is it clean?" she asked dubiously.

"Of course, silly," Kat admonished her. "You remember Sven telling us how all the streams and pools around here were either natural springs or mountain fed from melted snow."

Dee had forgotten that conversation, but Kat's reminder brought it all back. Sven's voice had painted a lovely picture of gurgling brooks and placid pools that had made Dee want to see some of these wondrous things for herself. She cupped both her hands and lifted enough water to rinse her face. "Ohh!" she gasped, not prepared for the temperature to be as cool as it was.

Kat chuckled at Dee's reaction. "Feels good, doesn't it?"

"Delicious!" Dee exclaimed as she rinsed her heated face a second time. "I bet it would be heavenly to swim," she murmured wistfully.

A slight breeze in the treetops brought a shaft of sunlight down on the pool and spotlighted a small sandbar in the center with eddies of current licking at its edges. The presence of current, however slight, meant that the pool's supply of water was constantly being replaced by an underground spring.

Dee looked at Kat with pleading in her eyes. "Come on, let's swim."

Kat scanned the surrounding area pensively. "I guess we are private here."

Dee did not wait to hear another word and began to remove her clothing. "Wait!" Kat said. "We can't stay here too long, Dee. Someone might come looking for us."

Dee discarded the rest of her clothes and laughed as she dove into the water to come up sputtering, "Let them look. This is bliss!"

A small pile of Kat's clothing joined Dee's on the bank as she hurried to take advantage of the cooling water.

Reveling in the feeling of the water, Dee rolled onto her back as she glided through the silvery expanse with small kicks. "Kat, remember the last time we did this?"

Kat's reply was warmly reminiscent. "Do I? Yes, I doubt if I will ever forget. Your mother was furious when she found out."

"If my brother hadn't spilled the beans about it, we would have never ended up in as much trouble as we did." Dee chuckled. "I thought I would be locked in my room forever!"

"Two days is not forever!" Kat remonstrated. "You know she was only doing what she thought best for you."

"You didn't say that when she told your grandfather what we had been doing." Dee relaxed, losing herself to the sylvan luxury.

"We have managed to upset a few people, haven't we?" Kat laughed.

"Kat? How long do you suppose we will be here?" Dee asked.

Kat felt the languor in her limbs as the caressing water cooled them. "I already told you, we shouldn't stay here too long," she called back at Dee.

"Not here in the water," Dee corrected as she splashed at her. "Here in Montana is what I meant."

"I don't know. I expected to hear something from Grandad by now." Kat shrugged and almost went under water.

"Why do you think we haven't heard anything?" Dee asked as she drifted slowly past Kat's relaxed form.

"I don't know. And I am beginning to worry that I don't know," Kat replied. "When did you send the wires to New York?"

"Oh! I thought you knew. I didn't send the wires. Eric did," Dee informed her.

"Eric?" Kat questioned in surprise.

"When he and Bert went into town shortly after we arrived. He sent word to our families," Dee went on.

"Why didn't you go into town with them?" Kat asked as she swam over to where Dee had drifted.

Dee wrinkled her brow thoughtfully. "I wasn't asked to go. Eric said something about how I needed to rest as much as you did."

"Hmm," Kat murmured. "Has anything been said to you about why the train derailed?"

"No. I still now as much as before, which is nothing," Dee answered. "Have you heard anything?"

"No, I haven't," Kat said. "In fact, I have a few questions that I would like to have answered."

Dee steadied herself in the water and eyed Kat carefully. "Do you think we are in any danger?"

"I think we had better be careful. Keep our eyes and ears open as always. I want to find out exactly what is going on around here that the Thorsens are not telling us," Kat said as she moved toward the far bank, nearer to their clothes.

"What if we can't find out what we want to know?" Dee asked quietly.

"We will decide what to do when the time comes," Kat replied. "Ohh!" She shivered suddenly and dropped under water to her chin.

"What's wrong?" Dee whispered as she followed Kat's example and hid herself as much as she could.

"I thought I saw someone in those bushes." Kat pointed to the thick shrubbery to their right.

"Could you see who it was?" Dee asked as she sidled next to Kat and peered in the direction she had pointed.

"I can't even be sure I saw someone," Kat replied. "It was so sudden and such a shock."

"Maybe it was nerves?" Dee suggested hopefully. "We haven't been discussing the most relaxing of subjects."

"Maybe you're right," Kat agreed as she nervously scanned the bank.

"I think we had better head back before someone does come looking for us," Dee decided. The carefree feeling had evaporated, leaving a feeling of unsafe isolation.

As they quickly dried off with their petticoats, the girls kept a watchful eye on the surrounding bank. Reaching the open sunlight on the journey back, they breathed a sigh. Kat could not shake the feeling that they had been watched and Dee knew Kat was not normally upset over nothing.

The bushes returned to their normal position and the mean-eyed stranger moved back to his horse. He had moved off the trail to investigate when he had heard feminine laughter. He had discovered the secluded pond and its occupants. He had watched them and was pleased when he identified the two as Katherine Gwyn and Aphrodite Higgins. His boss would be glad to hear that their suspicions regarding the Thorsen brothers and their unusual weddings had proved correct.

He mounted his horse and urged it into a fast trot. The sooner he left the area, the less chance of his being discovered.

Uncomfortable with the way she was feeling, Dee tried to lighten the mood as they returned to the lodge. "Kat, maybe all you saw was a small animal?"

Kat shook her head. "What small animal would stare like that?"

"A gentleman raccoon? A thirsty fox?" Dee replied. "I can think of any number of animals that would be curious to see us in their waterhole."

Kat eyed Dee slowly as though saying she did not believe a word that she was saying.

Seeing her disbelief, Dee launched into a descriptive

account of a leering raccoon overcome by the sight of them in his waterhole.

Kat could not help but laugh at Dee's imaginative description. "Dee! Please!" she gasped as she grabbed her sides. "I can't take anymore!"

"That's what the raccoon said," Dee dimpled back at her.

Chapter Nine

SVEN COULD HEAR LAUGHTER FILTERING THROUGH THE AIR and left the barn to see what was happening. He saw Kat and Dee coming across the yard from the path leading to the woods. Kat was squeezing excess water from her hair and Dee was plaiting hers into long braids as they walked. They must have found the swimming hole, he thought to himself with a grin.

Seeing him, Kat waved as they came over to where he stood watching them. "I think your country inhabitants were shocked today by us city folk." Kat smiled.

Smiling back at her, he asked, "Did you try to sell them something?"

"It was more along the line of an unintentionally free show," Dee explained as she finished braiding her hair.

"I take it you are referring to the four-legged creatures down by the swimming hole?" Sven inquired with a chuckle.

His lighthearted inquiry was met by an uncomfortable hesitation on the part of Kat and Dee. His smile was replaced by a look of concern as he said, "What's wrong?"

"Do you know if anyone else was down by the pool today?" Dee asked him.

"None of us were, if that is what you are asking," Sven replied.

Kat put her hand on Dee's arm and shook her head. Dee ignored her and said to Sven, "I am asking because

Kat thought she saw someone while we were swimming."

"What!" Sven commented, not liking what he was hearing.

"I said, Kat thought she saw someone watching us while we were swimming," Dee repeated.

"What did they look like, Kat?" Sven questioned her.

Kat had not wanted to say anything to Sven about the incident at the pool, but now that Dee had said what she had, she felt she had little choice but to answer Sven's question. "I only caught a glimpse of dark hair and hard eyes staring at us through some bushes," she told Sven, ready for him to say she was imagining things.

Sven's eyes narrowed as she told him what she had seen and his mouth hardened. "Maybe it would be a good idea if the two of you stayed around here until we can check this out," he said. "It might have been a drifter on his way to the rail camp, but I don't like the idea of some stranger roaming around on our land."

"Well, we didn't like being spied on, either," Dee declared, angry that Sven appeared more concerned with the thought of someone trespassing than on any danger they may have been in.

Sven saw the anger in her eyes and chose to ignore it as he crisply ordered both of them, "Go on up to the house and get changed. I'll handle this."

Dee's eyes flashed at his tone of command and she started to snap back at him. Kat grabbed her arm and pulled her toward the lodge, hissing in her ear, "Not now!"

Dee fumed all the way to her room, mad at Sven for his bossy ways and angry with Kat for not letting her tell him what she thought of him. Reaching the privacy of the bedroom, Dee turned on Kat and nearly exploded. "Why did you stop me! There is no reason for Sven to order us around like that and he should be told so."

Kat moved to her wardrobe and took out a pale blue gown of linen before answering Dee's outburst. "Dee, calm down. We have to be careful what we say."

"Why?" Dee demanded. "Are you saying that we can't even trust Leif or his brothers?"

"We can trust them," Kat replied, "but I am not sure if we can trust them completely."

Dee sat on the foot of her bed in shock. "Do you realize what you are saying? You are saying that the men we are married to can't be totally trusted!"

"Dee," Kat said, trying to calm her down. "I do not mean that they might harm us in some way. What I meant was that I think they know something we don't."

"Do you mean about the man you saw at the pool?" Dee asked as she slid off the bed and headed toward the door.

"That, maybe," Kat answered her. "I have a feeling that it is more than that."

Dee shivered. "I am beginning not to like these feelings you keep having. Do you have any other reason for suspecting them of keeping secrets from us?"

"Only the fact that we have not heard from Grandad or been allowed into town," Kat responded.

"Try and come up with something better than that while I go and change," Dee said. "Neither of those are that strong as reasons go."

After changing into a dress of buttercup linen, Dee rejoined Kat in her room, hoping that she had thought of some other reasons for her suspicions.

Kat sat at the dressing table and brushed her hair up onto her head, securing it in place with hairpins, as Dee moved to the window and gazed out at the tall pines and rugged mountain vista. "I could never have dreamed anything like this existed," Dee said.

Placing her brush on the small table by the dresser, Kat agreed. "You are right. It is unlike anything we have ever seen."

"Kat, come here," Dee called softly.

Kat went to her side at the window and looked down at where Dee was staring. Sven was speaking with Eric and Leif and none of them looked happy with what he was saying.

"What do you think all that is about?" Dee asked uneasily.

Leif headed in the direction of the pool as his brothers moved toward the lodge, still lost in discussion. As they passed under the open window, the girls heard Sven say, "I don't think we should leave them alone. It's no longer safe."

Dee looked at Kat and whispered in a frightened voice, "Leave who alone? What's not safe?"

Kat moved away from the window. "I don't have to guess twice who they are discussing. It's us."

Dee sat on the edge of the bed and nibbled at her thumbnail thoughtfully. "Maybe Sven wants to know who was spying on us as badly as we do."

Kat crossed her arms in self-protection. "I hope you're right. I don't even want to consider what it means if you're not."

Dee's head snapped up and her eyes widened with anguish. "You think they had something to do with the train derailment?"

Kat walked across the room. "I am not sure anymore what to think."

"I can't stand not knowing," Dee said. "I am going to ask them tonight."

"What?" Kat wasn't sure Dee had said what she thought she had.

"You heard me correctly. I hate this feeling of being left in the dark," Dee told her.

"I don't like it any more than you do," Kat agreed.

The air was crackling with heat and tension. The mood at dinner had been strained and conversation had consisted of polite requests that serving bowls be passed.

Bert felt sorry for the girls as she watched Kat pick at her food and Dee jump any time someone spoke.

The Thorsen men had been unusually terse and cold. Something was giving them fits; Bert recognized the signs. She knew that the night was far from over.

Having retired to the parlor after Bert had shooed them from the kitchen, Kat sat stiffly on the edge of the sofa while Dee roamed around the room, pretending an interest in the bric-a-brac that Bert had collected over the years.

Sven watched Dee with careful eyes. She was agitated to a point he had never seen, and he had to resist the urge to take her into his arms and ease her worries by telling her the whole story.

Eric could feel the tension heighten as time passed and hated the position that Gwyn had placed them in by instructing that the girls know nothing about what was going on. Kat scored a hit on him every time she raked him with her eyes cold as ice. Things were fast becoming ugly and Eric disliked his role more with every second. Finally, he spoke, exasperation lacing his words. "What is the matter with the two of you?"

Kat eyed him coldly. "Nothing that a few answers to a few questions could not cure."

Dee moved to stand behind Kat, but Sven blocked her way. She was forced to stand at his side as she waited for a reaction to what Kat had said.

"Answers?" Eric raised his hand questioningly.

Kat lowered her eyes, unable to look at Eric. His

gray eyes bored into her, baring her very soul to his inspection.

Seeing Kat's withdrawal, Dee leaped to her defense. "To some questions we feel we should have asked a long time ago."

Sven stared at her, his gaze watching her like a hawk. "Ask them," he said in a soft voice that carried hidden steel.

Dee looked at him and tendrils of ice coursed through her veins. She had to drag her eyes from his before she became frozen to the floor. Fear tried to raise its ugly head in her heart and she crushed it down with a deep breath and a glare of defiance at Sven. How dare he look at her like that! She nursed her anger to keep her fear at bay. Her hand unconsciously took hold of his arm as she fought her fear.

Kat looked over at her, saw the flare of Dee's nostrils and knew that she was fighting to maintain her control.

"We're waiting," Eric reminded them.

"I have heard it said that patience is a virtue you might consider cultivating," Kat snapped at him defensively.

Eric rose from his seat and took a step toward her, his face tight with anger. "Woman, you would try the patience of a saint!"

"Stop blustering, Eric. We know we are being held as your prisoners," Kat said in a voice sheathed with steel.

"Prisoners!" Leif choked.

Sven growled in his throat and snorted in disgust at what he heard. Eric stopped him from saying anything by raising his hand again and stating in a calm voice, "Have you been locked in your rooms or denied any freedom of movement? Have we tortured or abused you?"

"No," came Kat's hard reply.

"Then what gives you the gall to state that we are holding you prisoners!" his voice lashed at them.

"We have been kept ignorant of things that could closely affect us. You have, for reasons of your own, kept us from going into town. And treat us like we are children whenever we come close to something you do not want us to know," Kat answered his demand for an explanation.

"I have no doubt your ignorance is great. But why expect us to remedy such a gap in your knowledge?" Eric said cuttingly. "And there has not been any reason for you to go to town. As to your last comment, I will not even bother to answer that, as it sounds like the hysterical ramblings of a female mind."

"What caused the train to derail?" Dee asked Sven point-blank, no longer able to watch Kat be the sole brunt of his anger.

"The couplings on your car had been tampered with and the brakes on the car ahead of you failed," he answered flatly.

"Have there been other incidents against the line?" Dee pushed.

This question brought Sven's head up and Eric's eyes flashed with surprise.

"What does that have to do with you?" Sven returned carefully.

"So, there have been other incidents," Dee stated calmly. Now that she had started asking questions it was a relief to bring all her doubts into the open and confront the men with her fears.

"From what you have said, and especially from what you have not said, I would guess that there is a power play of some sort going on that Kat's grandfather has warned you not to tell us about."

"You have a very active imagination for such a little

female," Sven told her casually, as though he were enjoying every minute of their conversation.

"We have found out what it is we wished to know." Kat sighed softly as she rose from the sofa. "Why all men think women are incapable of taking care of themselves I will never know." She smiled sadly. "Come, Dee. We will retire now and allow the men to decide how they are going to tell Grandad that we are wise to his game."

Leif moved as though to intercept them, but Eric waved him off as he shook his head. The girls departed in silence and moved up the staircase to their rooms.

"Damn females!" Sven swore as he stomped to a seat on the sofa.

"What now?" Leif asked as he stared after them.

"Gwyn was right," Eric said. "Now we have a choice of telling them everything that has happened or protecting them in spite of themselves."

Sven ran a massive hand through his thick hair. "If you ask me, we have another problem on our hands."

"And what is that?" Eric asked him.

"Now that those two think they know what is going on they might try to handle it by themselves," Sven answered him grimly.

"You think they would?" Leif asked him doubtfully.

"I know they would," Sven returned.

Eric sank back in his seat, saying, "I think so, too. But how do we stop them?"

"Either we tell them everything so they don't go off half-cocked or we lock them in their rooms." Sven voiced the only alternatives he could think of.

"Lock them in their rooms!" Leif was shocked. "It can't be as serious as you are saying."

"It could mean their lives," Eric told him softly.

"Do you think they will try anything tonight?" Sven asked Eric.

"They might," Eric replied.

"Good grief!" Leif exclaimed. "All they will do tonight is try to get some sleep. Something I think we all need. Things are sounding crazy around here."

Reaching their rooms, the girls found that solitude was not what they wanted. It gave each of them too much time to think, thoughts that did not help their situation but revolved around Eric and Sven. With these thoughts came unbidden feelings that neither girl was ready to face.

Leaving her room, Dee checked to be sure she would not meet any of the men on the landing and silently glided to Kat's room, her dress a soft whisper against the highly polished floor.

Rapping softly on the door, Dee waited for Kat to let her in, praying that she would not have to face anyone else that night. Her nerves were strung as tightly as a bow and the slightest tremor could shatter them. Kat let her into the darkened room and closed the door.

Dee moved to the center of the room and waited for Kat to speak. "I guess we found out what we wanted to find out," Kat said softly.

"I want to leave, Kat," Dee told her.

Kat moved to the bed and sat down as Dee paced the short distance to the window and looked out at the star-studded blackness.

"We can't leave tonight. We haven't any place to go," Kat told her.

Dee turned and faced her. "We can camp out if we have to. We have both done it with my brothers. I don't think I can stay here any longer."

Kat frowned. "Camping with your brothers is a far cry from what you are suggesting we do now, Dee. We don't know the area, haven't any supplies or weapons for protection."

"I can make snares to catch rabbits and squirrels for

food. We can take the blankets from our beds and I am willing to fight tooth and nail to defend myself if I have to," Dee told her in desperation.

Kat put her arm around Dee as she moved to her. "You have fallen pretty hard, haven't you?"

"I don't know what you are talking about," Dee bluffed uneasily.

"I think you do," Kat laughed softly. "Don't try to deny it, Dee."

"Kat, all I know is that I won't be responsible if we stay here a minute longer than we have to," Dee pleaded with her.

"All right, we will leave. But first, let's plan on what we need to take with us," Kat urged.

Dawn was tinting the horizon as an exhausted Dee crept silently back to her room, tumbled onto her bed and slept.

Chapter Ten

PATRICK SAT AT HIS DESK AND REREAD THE PAPERS IN front of him. What he read made his eyebrows bristle for the second time that day.

He had ordered an investigation immediately after the first incident of sabotage against the Great Northern. During this investigation threads of a far more complex web of larceny and deceit began to surface. With each report his suspicions had grown and he had intensified his investigation after the death of Paul Forbes.

The report he read for the second time that morning held proof confirming his suspicions.

It detailed the activities of the three men he most suspected of somehow being involved in the troubles that had plagued the Great Northern over the past months.

One part of the report had surprised him. It had become increasingly clear there was a connection between the sabotage of the Great Northern and Paul Forbes's death. A death that looked more and more like murder.

He ran his hand through his hair as he rose from his desk and paced across the oak-paneled office to stand at the tall, glass-paned doors leading out onto a small terrace.

So, Paul was a blackmailer, Patrick thought as he crossed his arms behind his back. He had been using his

149

power at the insurance company to find out things he could hold over the heads of clients.

Apparently, the report stated, Paul had been quite successful with his blackmail schemes over the years. That is, until he became overconfident and picked the wrong people to threaten.

Patrick frowned deeply as he thought, Kat almost married the man!

A knock on the office door pulled his attention back to the problems at hand and he called, "Yes? Come in."

The door opened and a heavyset man dressed in a rumpled tweed coat and pants with a battered felt hat atop flaming red hair entered the room, flanked by a uniformed policeman.

"Inspector O'Shea?" Patrick greeted him. "Brian, what may I do for you?"

Patrick resumed his seat at his desk and motioned to the chairs in front of him. "Do sit down, Brian."

"Thank you, Patrick," Inspector O'Shea replied as he took a seat.

Patrick watched his two visitors a moment before speaking. "I take it this is not a social call?"

Brian removed his hat and cleared his throat. "I wish it were, Patrick. I have a warrant for the arrest of Elias Spencer."

"On what charge, Brian?" Patrick was stunned.

"On the charge of murder," the inspector answered. "He is to be charged in connection with the murder of a Mr. Paul Forbes."

With Brian's words, the last pieces of the puzzle fell into place for Patrick. He had decided that Paul had been murdered by someone he was blackmailing but could not place the blame on any one victim. "But of course," Patrick muttered aloud as the picture became clearer and clearer.

"What did you say, Patrick?" Brian asked.

"Nothing, Brian. I was merely telling myself how stupid I have been," Patrick replied.

"Stupid?"

"Yes. All the facts have been staring me in the face for days and I was too blind to see them." Patrick shook his head in disgust.

"What facts, sir?" Brian's tone became official.

Patrick lifted the papers from the desk in front of him and handed them to the inspector. "It is all in there, Brian. Paul Forbes was a blackmailer. He picked the wrong person to blackmail and was murdered for his error."

Brian scanned the papers and looked up. "May I have a copy of these, Patrick? They contain some background evidence the department has not uncovered to date."

"Keep those, I have others," Patrick said. "But I doubt if they will be of any use to you."

"Why?"

"Elias Spencer disappeared over a week ago, leaving no trace," Patrick informed him.

"Why didn't you notify the police?" Brian asked curiously.

"Because at the time, I did not know he was involved in Paul Forbes's murder," Patrick returned. "I had reasons of my own to suspect him of selling me out to rival business interests."

"I suppose you wouldn't care to enlarge upon that, Patrick?" Brian said.

"No, I would not," was Patrick's response.

Brian O'Shea knew he would not get any more from Patrick Gwyn. They had known each other for many years, and as monied people went, Patrick had always been the most cooperative. But his cooperation was only to a point.

As with most of the rich and powerful, Patrick preferred handling certain matters "in house," as he always called it.

Watching him as he sat at his desk with that closed look in his eyes, Brian could not help but feel Spencer would have had an easier time of it if he'd stayed in New York and faced the police.

After O'Shea left to return to police headquarters with the papers Patrick had given him, Patrick busily made plans of his own.

Scribbling a few quick messages, he had wires dispatched and began to solidify his plans for leaving New York as soon as possible.

What he had not told Brian was that now he had a good idea of where Elias Spencer had run.

Lifting the telephone by his side, Patrick began making the many calls necessary to clear his calendar and give him the freedom to leave New York and not have to worry about an attack from the rear.

Telegraph wires hummed, messages were received and sent, while Kat and Dee stumbled upon an unexpected pool.

Reining his horse to a walk, Robert Grebe made slow progress as he headed through the crowded street toward the livery stable.

Since the erection of the new rail camp for repairs to the line damaged in the recent derailment, the population of the area had grown. Though temporary in its intended life span, the rail camp housed large repair crews. These crews drew a heavy influx of gamblers, con men, pimps and whores, all eager to help the men part with their hard-earned money.

This mingling of fast-dollar types and the normal hard-working residents led to overcrowded streets. The mixture made Grebe laugh as he observed a dowdy farm wife draw away from a garish redhead who strutted brazenly across the street and into one of the many new tent saloons that had appeared overnight to cater to any number of thirsts the rail crews might have.

The sight of the livery stable brought Grebe's mind away from the overblown whore and the thirst he'd love to quench with her. He dismounted, handing the reins to a freckled-faced stable boy with orders to feed and groom his mount.

Slapping the trail dust from his clothes, he pushed his way through the raucous street people and moved up the stairs to the town's one permanent hotel.

Entering the lobby, he ignored the desk clerk and took the stairs leading up. Mounting the stairs two at a time, he mulled over in his mind the news he had to report. Reaching the room he wanted, he knocked twice and a muted voice called for him to enter.

Closing the door behind him, Grebe moved toward the seated figure at the table in the center of the sitting room of the suite. A muffled giggle could be heard from behind the partially opened bedroom door to his right. Wondering if he had interrupted something, he waited until the man at the table looked up from the papers he was reading.

Elias Spencer eyed the dirt-stained man in front of him. "Well?" he questioned.

"They're out at the Thorsen place, all right," was the curt reply.

Spencer's eyes glinted at the news and a scowl twisted his face as a nasal voice from the bedroom whined, "Are you coming, honey?"

"Shut up!" Spencer snapped harshly in reply.

"But baby's getting lonely," the voice continued to whine.

Seeing the amused look on Grebe's face, Spencer

rose from his seat and closed the bedroom door with a loud click as he snarled at the other man, "Wipe that look off your face and tell me how you know for sure they are at the Thorsen place."

Grebe stiffened with anger at Spencer's treatment of him and filed it away for future action as he related how he had stumbled upon the girls swimming in the woods.

"Did anyone see you?" Spencer questioned sharply.

"No."

"Are you sure?" Elias pushed.

Grebe's face contorted maliciously. "I ain't a fool."

Spencer ignored the venom in Grebe's voice and lifted a wire from the stack of papers before him. "We haven't much time," he said, waving the telegram in the air. "Gwyn is on his way out here. And we have to get to those two before he does."

Pushing his hat to the back of his head with a dirty forefinger, Grebe asked, "How long until he gets here?"

"Two days, maybe three and he should be here," Spencer said.

"What do you expect me to do?" Grebe waited for his orders with an expectant air.

"Continue with the rail camp as we planned," Elias ordered.

"What about the females?" Grebe's eyes gleamed.

"Grab both of them when you have the chance. Keep them out of sight until we can find out how much Forbes may have told them about our operation," Spencer directed.

"Then do I kill them?" Grebe asked in a flat tone.

"Not until we find out what we want to know."

"When we know?" Grebe pressed.

"Greenhorns are getting lost out here all the time," Elias grinned.

Grebe's face was split by an evil smile.

Chapter Eleven

DEE'S HEAD THROBBED FROM LACK OF SLEEP AS SHE
joined an equally weary Kat for breakfast. Anxious to
continue planning their departure, Dee struggled to
maintain an attitude of patience as she watched Bert
pour coffee from a large coffee pot and hand a cup to
Kat.

I wish she would hurry up and leave, Dee thought. I
want to speak to Kat before anyone else comes in. The
hairs on the back of her neck tingled and her heart
pounded as she knew her chance was lost and the men
approached.

Glancing over at Kat, she wished she could be as
calm. Kat was sipping her coffee as though she hadn't a
thing on her mind.

Dee almost jumped out of her chair when the seat
next to her scraped the floor as it was pulled out from
the table. Her pulse settled as she scolded herself that it
was only Leif taking his seat. Turning to greet him, her
smile froze in place as Sven's ice-blue gaze stunned her.

"Good morning," she said, unable to tear away from
his penetrating regard.

Kat watched as Sven usurped Leif's usual spot at the
table and her brow creased thoughtfully. Her curiosity
was short-lived as Eric claimed her attention by asking,
"Did you sleep well?" as he took his place.

Confusion whipped through Dee's thoughts as she

saw Eric engage Kat in a softly worded conversation. Looking around the table, she saw Leif's smiling face across from her in Sven's usual seat. She smiled at him, relieved to see at least one friendly face. "Good day, Leif."

"Morning, Dee," he returned with one eye on his older brother sitting next to her.

Dee's eyes widened; even Leif was acting strangely this morning. Why? Dee blinked and tried to organize her thoughts. Was it because of last night? Do they know that we are planning on leaving?

Bert had to repeat her question twice before Dee heard her. "How are you planning on spending today, Dee?"

"Pardon me?" Dee faltered. "Oh, my day? I haven't any plans, Bert."

I'll bet you don't, Sven said to himself as he watched the hastily concealed guilt in Dee's eyes.

Kat barely tasted the food in front of her. Her insides were a knot that she forced the food past. Why would Eric ask her to accompany him to the rail camp? He had never asked before; why now? He had taken her by surprise when he asked, and she had been trapped into accepting his invitation.

Having secured Kat's agreement to go with him to the rail camp, Eric contented himself with finishing his meal.

Kat found that for some unknown reason she dreaded the journey ahead. She would be alone with Eric, something that she did not want to be.

Dee pushed her plate away from her, unable to eat another bite. She began to excuse herself and retreat to her room when Sven's hand covered hers on the linen tablecloth.

"You haven't any appetite this morning? What you need is a change of scenery and some fresh air. I'm going into town this morning. I'll take you with me," he said.

Dee gasped at this. He hadn't even asked if she wanted to go. He had informed her that she was going! She could not believe the arrogance of the man!

Sven pulled her chair out for her and held his hand out to aid her in rising as he added with a steady look, "Don't dawdle if you plan on changing. We leave in half an hour."

Dee hurried by him, not trusting herself not to slap his face. How dare he!

His next words sent her temper soaring. "If you're not ready when I am, I will come up and get you."

Keeping a tight hold on her rage, Dee returned to her room, where she slammed the door, uncaring of who heard it. Pacing the floor, she fumed. He infuriated her beyond belief. She'd show him! She deliberately sat on her bed and silently dared him to come and get her.

Eric left Kat at the table finishing her coffee and went to his office. He saw Sven sitting in one of the overstuffed chairs as he entered and smiled. "I think you made Dee mad at you."

The sound of her bedroom door slamming echoed throughout the lodge and Sven grinned. "I know I did."

"Are you sure you want to take her to town with you?" Eric asked as he sat in the other chair.

"The farther apart we can keep Dee from Kat the less chance they will have to plan anything foolish," Sven answered. "She will wear herself out being mad before we reach town. I think I can handle her."

"What if she refuses to come down when it's time for you to leave," Eric questioned with a grin. "Will you go up and get her?"

"I fully expect to," Sven replied as he looked up at

the ceiling. "I'd say about now she has stubbornly decided that I will have to come and get her because she won't go any other way."

Eric shook his head. "I wish I could read Kat as easily as you read Dee. Kat is still a mystery to me. Every time I think I am making progress in figuring her out, she does something I don't understand."

Sven laughed. "I may be able to 'read' Dee, as you call it, but that doesn't mean I understand her. Can any man really understand a woman?"

"Patrick Gwyn seems to understand Kat," Eric stated as he remembered the instructions Gwyn had sent telling them not to say anything to Kat or Dee about the problems on the Great Northern.

"I disagree, Eric," Sven told him. "I think Gwyn is acting on knowledge of past behavior and not on any true understanding of Kat."

"Maybe—" Eric started to say and stopped.

Sven looked at the clock on the wall. "Maybe what? I haven't too much time left before I have to make my appearance upstairs, so say what you want to say."

"Nothing," Eric said. "I was thinking that with the way things have been going lately, I will probably end up dragging Kat to the rail camp while you drag Dee into town."

"So?" Sven asked.

"I'm not sure either of them will forgive us," Eric said.

"Quit imagining things, Eric," Sven admonished. "Sure they'll be mad. Wouldn't you be if someone ordered you around?"

"I certainly would be mad," Eric agreed. "But you don't understand, Sven. Kat makes me so mad sometimes I could throttle her."

"Why? What has she done?" Sven asked.

"You've seen her. She erects that icy shell around herself that holds everyone at a distance," Eric said. "I'll tell you, Sven, sometimes she frustrates the hell out of me when she does that."

"Did you ever think she might be doing it as a form of self-protection?" Sven suggested. "Like a porcupine bristling up when threatened."

Eric's eyes opened wide and he smiled. "You know, you're right."

Kat finished her coffee and went upstairs to knock on Dee's door. "Dee? It's Kat," she said as she knocked on the door.

The door opened a crack and Dee peeked out at her. Seeing that it was her, Dee grabbed her by the wrist and pulled her into the room quickly, shutting the door behind them.

"I thought you might be Sven," Dee explained as Kat stared at her in surprise.

"You haven't changed? Aren't you going into town with Sven?" Kat asked.

Dee sat down on the bed, a stubborn look on her face as she said, "If he wants me to go that badly, he can come and get me."

"Dee!" Kat exclaimed. "He will, you know."

Dee hesitated a second, then repeated firmly, "He can come up here like he said he would and get me."

"Don't you want to go to town?" Kat asked as she sat next to Dee on the bed.

"Of course I do," Dee replied.

"Then why are you acting like this?" Kat inquired. "Is it because Sven is the one who asked you to go?"

"No," Dee admitted. "Not really."

"I don't understand." Kat frowned.

"I would rather be asked than ordered," Dee whispered.

"Oh, Dee!" Kat hugged her. "You silly goose! I'm afraid that the only way either of us will get into town is if you go with Sven, ordered or not."

"But—" Dee started to protest.

"But, nothing. How else will we be able to find out what we want to know about the Great Northern?"

"My going to town with Sven will tell us that?" Dee said in disbelief.

"No. But once you are in town, you might overhear something that can answer some of our questions," Kat explained.

Dee still resisted the idea and parried Kat's logic with a question of her own. "Is that why you are going to the rail camp with Eric?"

"Why else would I go?" Kat asked.

"You tell me." Dee stared at her.

"This is pointless, Dee. Now hurry and change," Kat said as she left the room.

Standing in the hallway, Kat sighed. She had not wanted to answer Dee's pointed question because she did not know the answer herself. She hoped to find an answer soon.

Dee glared at the door as Kat closed it behind her. Why should I change? she thought stubbornly, unwilling to admit even to herself that she was frightened of being alone with Sven.

The heavy tread of Sven's boots on the staircase made her hold her breath, as she knew it was too late for second thoughts.

A loud knock on her door announced Sven's presence as he called, "It's time to leave."

Berating herself for cowardice, she replied, "I will be ready in a minute."

She wasted no time in stripping off her housedress and flinging it in the direction of the bed as she reached into the wardrobe and grabbed a sturdy poplin skirt and tailored shirtwaist. Her fingers were clumsy as she tried to fasten the many buttons on her shirtwaist and she cursed softly.

Sven's voice startled her as he said, "If you needed help, why didn't you say so?"

Her eyes flew up at him as he stood not three feet away. He had entered the room so silently that she had no idea he was there. Her tumbled thoughts registered the contradiction this made with his noisy ascent of the stairs and she stared at him blankly in confusion.

Ignoring her surprise, Sven moved in front of her and swiftly fastened the remaining buttons on her shirtwaist, saying, "Time is wasting."

Dee turned red with embarrassment; she could have finished dressing without his help. She turned to tell him as much and saw his departing back as he headed for the door.

Grabbing a hat and gloves, Dee hastened to follow him, grateful that she had at least donned her skirt before he entered or he might have dressed her in that as well.

Following his silent figure down the staircase, she remembered that she was furious with him. As they went out the front to the waiting buckboard, Dee had worked herself into a fine rage.

She considered refusing his help in mounting the high wagon, but common sense said she would be a fool if she did. Stiffly accepting his outstretched hand, she seated herself on the edge of the hard seat and gathered her skirt about her, trying to leave as much room between them as possible.

Sven was not blind to her actions and smiled as he moved to his side of the wagon and climbed aboard, grasping the reins and clucking to the team to move out. He knew Dee had wanted to defy him and now was regretting that she had not.

Dee tried to pin her hat on without sticking herself as the wagon jolted and rocked over the rutted roadway. Throwing a disgusted look at her companion, she briefly considered sticking him with one of the long, vicious pins that held her hat in place. There was no reason for him to be going so fast. She was convinced he was doing it deliberately to punish her. Pulling her gloves on with quick motions, she grabbed onto the edge of her seat to keep from falling off the wagon as they bounced over the hard ground.

Seeing Dee's precarious perch, Sven slowed the team, saying, "You had better sit all the way back on the seat or you'll be bounced off. I don't have time to stop and pick you up."

Dee glared at him as she scooted back on the hard board seat and found that it did feel more secure. Damn him, she thought.

The journey into town was completed in silence. As they approached the outskirts of town, Dee felt relief flow over her that their destination was not far off. Every bone in her body was bruised and battered from Sven's rough driving. She felt a small measure of satisfaction when he was forced to slow the team to a walk in the crowded streets.

Sven glanced at his passenger from the corner of his eye and saw that she was staring intently about her. The sounds filtering from ahead warned him that she might see more than she had bargained on seeing. They reached the source of angry noises and Dee's green eyes mirrored her shock.

Two men were trying to beat the daylights out of each other in the street and the rest of the populace appeared intent on continuing on their own business, ignoring them as they wrestled in the dirt. A few onlookers called encouragement to one of the men, but for the most part, the scene went apparently unnoticed.

Dee grabbed Sven's arm. "Can't you stop them? They're trying to kill each other!"

"It's none of our business," was his short reply.

"What!" Dee was horrified at what she heard. "You are going to sit there and let them kill each other?"

Sven stared down at her steadily. "They won't kill each other."

Dee could not believe what she was seeing. The dust swirled from the street as the two men grappled with one another, intent on bashing each other as hard as they could.

One man had blood trickling from his nose and the other had one eye almost swollen shut. Dee knew one of them was going to end up dead if someone did not put a stop to it.

Tightening the grip she had on Sven's arm, Dee gasped, certain she was about to witness the end. Alarm raced up her spine as one of the men suddenly began to laugh loudly and his opponent joined him. Confusion replaced alarm as she saw the two clap each other on the back and depart for a nearby building with swinging doors and a sign that read, "Best Whiskey West of the Missouri."

"But . . ." she stammered.

"They were only horsing around," Sven explained to her as he headed the team to the side of the street and stopped.

"They were playing?" Dee repeated in disbelief. "It looked too rough for that."

"This is rough country," Sven said as he jumped down and walked around to her side of the wagon.

Dee could not believe what she had seen nor Sven's easy explanation and sat unmoving. The feel of his hands around her waist, lifting her down from the wagon, brought her back to reality with a jolt. "Ohh!" she gasped.

His hands left her waist slowly as he said, "We're here."

Here was a covered walkway fronting a large building proclaiming itself Jensen's General Store. Dee viewed this imposing structure with curiosity as she followed Sven into its dim interior.

When her eyes had adjusted to the change in light, her senses were assailed by the sights and aromas that filled the establishment.

One whole wall was covered with tack of all types and she could feel the biting tang of its aroma in her nose. Across from that wall was an array of farming tools so varied in number that she could not begin to guess half their uses. Her skirt rustled over the rough plank flooring as she followed Sven to the back of the store, passing tables piled high with colorful dress goods and oilcloths.

The fragrance of soap and perfumed talc wafted by her as she saw a counter displaying a myriad of toiletries for both men and women.

Her observations were interrupted as a pleasant-looking man, the proprietor by his dress, approached Sven. "Good day to you, Sven. What can I do for you?"

Sven shook the outstretched hand offered him and said, "Karl. Bert needs what's on this list." He handed Karl a piece of paper.

Karl scanned the list and nodded. "Looks as though she plans on baking and canning. Give me a few minutes and I'll have your order loaded."

"Fine, Karl," Sven said as he startled Dee by putting his arm around her and continuing, "My wife and I will look around."

Karl noticed Dee for the first time. "Mrs. Thorsen, allow me to welcome you to my store."

"Please call me Dee," she stammered, unable to hear herself referred to as Sven's wife.

"Dee it is. Excuse me a moment and I will tell my wife Helga that you are here. She may be able to help you with anything you may need."

Going to the very back of the store, Karl called, "Helga."

His wife came to the curtain that separated their living quarters from the store and said, "What is it, Karl?"

"Sven is here with his bride. I have an order to fill for Bert. I thought you could wait on her while Sven and I load the wagon," Karl told her.

Helga looked across the store at Dee as she and Sven strolled by the display of dress goods. "She is young and very pretty, Karl," Helga said with a smile.

Sven had seen the quiet conversation between Karl and Helga and knew they were talking about Dee.

Dee was oblivious to the attention her presence attracted and was fingering a bolt of pale yellow cotton that she found tempting. She wished she could purchase it. It would make up into a comfortable day dress, more attuned to the climate than her eastern dresses. Her eyes moved to a nearby bolt of the same cotton in a fresh shade of blue. That would be ideal for Kat, she thought. Shrugging, she moved to the next section of goods. She knew she had no money to make any purchases and contented herself with looking.

Sven noticed her contemplating the material and her resigned shrug before she moved away. Motioning to the approaching Helga, he asked that the two bolts of cloth and any necessary additions be added to his bill.

Helga smiled in agreement at his request and hurried

to gather threads and needles as Dee looked at Sven in dismay.

"I can't let you buy that for me," she protested.

"Why not?" he asked. "Since when can't a husband buy things for his wife?"

Helga rejoined them and Dee was unable to say more without creating a scene. Sven knew he had won and, feeling generous, said to Helga, "Anything else my wife needs, Helga, put on the bill."

He moved away to help Karl carry the heavy sacks of flour and sugar that Bert had ordered out to the wagon.

Dee watched him leave, a feeling of consternation making her stare after him. "Men!" she muttered.

"I heartily agree!" Helga jovially chuckled. "They can be so exasperating at times, but what would we do without them?"

She gave Dee such a knowing look that she could not say anything in return. Placing a plump hand on Dee's arm, Helga quietly but firmly directed her over to the toiletry counter. Moving behind the counter, Helga reached for a package of bath crystals and handed them to Dee. "Give these to Bert for me, please? I always try to save a few special items for dear friends."

Dee accepted the small package. "I'd be more than happy to, Mrs. Jensen."

"Call me Helga."

"Only if you will call me Dee." Dee smiled at the warm and caring woman with the golden coronet of braids on her head.

Helga leaned across the counter and whispered, "Between us women, is there anything you need that would put your husband to the blush to order for you?"

Dee had no idea at all what might make Sven blush as she had never seen him do so and answered, "I could use some soap and tooth powder, Helga."

Helga took a sheet of brown wrapping paper from under the counter and laid it on top as she placed tooth powder and some bars of soap on top. "Now. What else will you need?" Helga asked with a smile.

"That's all, thank you," Dee replied.

Helga looked down at the brown paper and clicked her tongue. "This will not last you any time at all. You go and look around the store and leave it to me. I will package enough to last you a decent length of time."

Dee started to protest, but Helga shooed her away and she had no other choice but to obey her.

It was only a few minutes later that Helga handed her a large brown paper bundle tied with triple lengths of twine, saying, "We women must stick together, no?"

"Yes." Dee laughed in reply. "Thank you so much, Helga."

"What are you two plotting?" Sven asked from behind Dee.

Dee spun, grabbing her bundle tightly to her chest. "Don't sneak up on me like that!" she exclaimed.

"What's in the package?" Sven asked with a pointed look.

"It's between us women, Mr. Nosy Thorsen," Helga scolded him with a teasing twinkle in her eye. "Unless you like perfumed soap and skin cream for yourself?"

Sven threw his hands up in defeat. "I give up. Never try to pry a secret out of a woman who has been shopping."

"That's the truth," Karl agreed. "You might find out she bought a bear trap for your bed."

"Are you ready to go?" Sven asked Dee as he laughed at Karl's wit.

"Oh, yes. Anytime you are," Dee quickly replied. She had been unable to find out anything concerning the Great Northern and Kat would be disappointed when she told her, but Dee wanted to leave and return to the lodge.

"The wagon's loaded, so we had better head back," Sven told her. "Good day to you, Helga. Karl, watch out for bear traps in your bed."

"I always do," Karl returned as he and Helga walked them out to the wagon.

Chapter Twelve

KAT WAS SUSPICIOUS OF ERIC'S MOTIVES AS THEY PULLED
up at the rail camp. Coupling her suspicions with the
unusual invitations of Eric and Sven to escort her and
Dee to places that until this morning had been off limits
to them, Kat was on her guard. Something was wrong
with this sudden change in attitude and until she could
find out what, she could not trust anyone.

The rail camp itself was vastly different from the rail
camps used during the original construction of the line.
There were no long, three-deck bunk cars with their
attached dining and cooking car.

As the camp was mainly a repair camp for a short
section of the line, it could be based in a permanent
position. Two lines of tents had been set roughly in
military fashion with one large tent set aside for
cooking at the far edge of the camp and a first-aid tent
stationed near it.

The sounds of hammering and shouted orders echoed through the now deserted camp.

Eric and Kat moved through the camp to a hitching
line near the first-aid tent, where they dismounted and
tethered their horses. Kat noticed with interest the
apparent order and unusual cleanliness of the camp. It
was obvious that Eric's medical hand had dictated the
placement of the latrine facilities at a sensible distance
from the cook and sleeping tents to avoid any contami-

nation. She stored all she saw to report to her grandfather.

She saw the stacks of new rails waiting placement and the damaged rails discarded with their broken ties in a pile next to them.

Eric stood by his mount and waited as he watched Kat survey the camp. "How do you find things? Are they the way you imagined they would be?"

Kat removed her riding gloves as she said, "I find it interesting. You have added some touches of your own that would please my grandfather."

Turning to face him, she smiled. "But looks can sometimes be deceiving, as we both know. How goes the repair work?"

Eric frowned. "On schedule." Moving in the direction of the cook tent, he added, "Why do you ask? I thought you came to visit, not check up on things."

Kat followed him, secretly pleased that she had irritated him with her question. He was too smug for her liking and acted as if he was doing her a favor by speaking to her.

"Would you care for some coffee?" Eric asked politely. "The cook usually has a pot on the boil."

Kat knew from the stories she had heard that rail camp coffee was legendary in its strength. It was brewed that way to keep the rough railmen happy, and according to her grandfather it could eat through rock. She accepted Eric's offer with a secret smile. "Thank you, that sounds good."

She knew that Eric thought of her as a complete greenhorn and decided to play the part. He would not be as careful to keep things hidden from someone he thought would not know the difference. Maybe she would be able to find out more about the sabotage the line had sustained and clues as to who was responsible.

Entering the cook tent, Eric called out, "Soo Lin?"

A wiry Chinese man with a pigtail trailing halfway down his back answered Eric's call and bowed deeply when he saw who it was that had summoned him.

"Stop that, Soo Lin," Eric told him. "We are helping ourselves to some coffee and will be out of your way in a few minutes."

The dark eyes of the cook darted from Eric to Kat as he stood with his hands folded in front of him. At Eric's mention of coffee, his eyes had widened slightly and quickly moved to the floor. He kept them downcast as he shuffled across the tent to the heavy metal stove resting atop large flat stones to prevent its heat from burning through the wooden floor of the tent. A large metal coffee pot sat bubbling atop the stove, and Soo Lin lifted its lid and looked inside the pot as he muttered something in his own language. Replacing the lid, he bowed once more in Eric's direction and shuffled back to his chopping board to work.

Kat watched him curiously. She was surprised to see a Chinaman as head cook. She knew that the many Chinese work crews used in the original construction had maintained their own Chinese cooks, but to see one in charge of an entire camp was unusual.

Eric noticed her look of surprise as he poured two cups of coffee. "Soo Lin has been a rail cook since he came to this country. It's all he knows and the men like his cooking. Some used to complain that he served too many vegetables, but now they have come to expect them."

He handed her a cup and motioned that they go outside to drink their coffee. The singsong voice of Soo Lin could be heard as they left the tent, crooning a rhythm to pace his chopping.

Standing near the first-aid tent, Eric politely waited for Kat to take a sip of her coffee. She obliged him by lifting her tin cup and taking a swallow. Even though she was prepared for its strength, the acrid bitterness almost took her breath away as she swallowed.

Eric watched her with veiled amusement in his eyes as he sipped from his own cup. "How is it?"

"As camp coffee goes, I find it rather mild," Kat returned steadily.

Eric frowned; nothing was going as he had planned. He had deliberately offered her the coffee as an example of how life in a rail camp was no place for a lady.

"Could we see the work site?" Kat asked, as she calmly took another sip from her cup.

"If you insist," Eric said as he tossed the remainder of his coffee back in one swallow and waited for Kat to do the same.

She accepted his silent challenge and finished hers in the same way, wondering as she did so if she would survive the effects. She handed Eric her empty cup, pleased that she was still able to breathe. "Thank you," she smiled at him.

Eric set their cups on a nearby rock and said, "Shall we be going?"

"Lead the way."

Eric moved through the thick trees, holding back his frustration. That show of bravado on Kat's part had rubbed him raw. What was she trying to prove?

Reaching the rail bed, Kat saw how everything had been systematically set up to ease the repair work. Crews of five men to a rail were pulling new rails from lightweight carts and moving them to where another group with a notched wooden gauge would space each rail precisely at the necessary four feet eight and a half inches apart before the spike men could begin swinging their mauls, securing the new rails to the already laid new ties.

Eric was even more frustrated as he saw that the

noise and clamor did not seem to bother Kat in the least. She viewed the repairs as though they were exactly what she had expected to see.

One of the crew foremen came over to them and respectfully doffed his hat to Kat as he spoke to Eric. "Two more days and we should be finished here, Mr. Thorsen."

"Any trouble with the men?" Eric inquired.

"No more than usual," was the foreman's reply.

"Oh?" Kat said interestedly.

The foreman looked to Eric to see if he could reply to Kat. Seeing Eric's nod, he cleared his throat and said in a rumbling voice, "It isn't much, ma'am. The men lead a rough life and always enjoy complaining about something."

"What you mean is it is normal for them to get drunk and fight, generally enjoying their payday sprees?" Kat said with a chuckle.

The foreman's eyebrows shot up and he chuckled in reply. "Yes, ma'am." He knew she was not a camp woman from her appearance, but how did she know so much about camp life?

Eric stepped in, saying, "Ben, this is my wife, Kat Gwyn Thorsen. Her grandfather is Patrick Gwyn. She was on the train when it derailed."

Now he recognized her. She was the unconscious lady he had carried to Sven's wagon. "I'm happy to see you are recovered, ma'am."

"Ben was one of the men who helped pull you and Dee from the wreck," Eric told Kat.

Kat stretched out her hand, saying, "Allow me to thank you, Ben. We owe you a debt of gratitude for our rescue."

Ben looked down at her small white hand and rubbed his calloused palm against his pant leg before taking her soft one in his grip. "There's no need for thanks. We were just doing our job."

A shout from up the rails halted further conversation as Ben and Eric went to see what was wrong.

Kat trailed in their wake, not wanting to be left behind and in ignorance. A small crowd of workmen was gathered next to a new section of ties. One of the workmen was crouched down on his haunches looking at something by one of the ties. Kat tried to move closer and see what he was pointing to as Ben and Eric bent down next to him.

Kat inched her way forward and the hovering workmen parted their ranks on seeing her. Reaching the front of the group, she could clearly see what the shouting had been all about. Protruding like the tail of a rat was what she recognized as a fuse, which led to the gravel beneath the new tie. Its implications made her wonder if she was so lucky to know what it was or not. If her grandfather had not taken her with him on that construction trip, she would not be as frightened as she was now.

Eric carefully scooped the gravel surrounding the fuse into a small pile behind his left leg. Visible now was a recently dug up section of earth the size of a dinner plate, with the fuse centered in the repacked soil.

Seeing this, Ben motioned for everyone else to stand clear. The workmen did not need to be told twice. They withdrew to a hopefully safe distance, leaving Kat to stand alone as she watched.

Eric turned to say something to Ben and saw her standing behind him. "What are you doing here? Move back with the men," he barked at her tersely.

"I am well aware of the danger, Eric," she replied.

He rose to his feet and grabbed her by the arms. "Which should be more than enough to tell you that it is safer somewhere else. Go on back to where we first met Ben, until I say it is safe," he ordered.

Kat pulled her arms free of his punishing grasp and glared at him. "I am not one of your workmen, Eric," she told him.

"Go now or so help me, I'll carry you there myself," he threatened.

Silence fell over the men as they watched this battle of wills. Feeling their silent eyes, Kat conceded to Eric for the moment and made her way slowly down the line to where she had been ordered.

Watching her departing form to see that she was obeying him, Eric knelt down in the gravel and dirt of the roadbed, his sole attention aimed at the fuse and its hidden power. "Where's Flynn?" he asked Ben.

"I'm right here, Eric," came the reply from a lilting voice.

"You're a powder monkey. What do you make of this?" Eric asked him.

Joining Eric in the dirt, Flynn examined the fuse and traced his finger slowly around the perimeter of the exposed area. "It could be a dummy or filled with blasting powder," he explained in a thick Irish brogue. "There be no way of telling for sure. We will have to play the odds and dig it up."

"Are the odds in our favor?" Eric asked grimly.

"Do we have another choice?" was Flynn's calm rejoinder.

Slowly scooping the loosely packed earth from around the fuse, exposing its length, Flynn's touch was as gentle as a mother with a newborn babe.

As Flynn removed the soil, Eric pushed it away from them and kept the area clear to work. Both men moved with slow, careful actions, knowing the instability of blasting powder, should that be what they were dealing with.

When the last of the dirt was loosened, a small keg with the fuse leading into it lay exposed. "I think it would be wise for me to remove any temptation from whatever is in this wee barrel," Flynn observed wryly.

The workmen moved even farther back into the trees. They did not want curiosity to get their heads blown off for them.

Flynn gently grasped the fuse where it entered the keg and crooning softly as beads of sweat covered his brow spoke to the keg. "Easy now, my powerful friend. It is only your mate Flynn that's playing with your tail. Don't bite me now." He carefully tugged and the fuse popped out into his hand.

Flynn rasied his eyes with a knowing look to Eric. "I do believe there is more to this little game."

Eric took the harmless fuse and laid it in the dirt as Flynn ran knowing hands over the surface of the small keg. A smile of triumph lit up his face as his hands ceased their inspection and he crooned once more, "Ahh, Flynn is wise to your tricks, ole friend."

Eric watched as Flynn carefully parted the keg in half lengthwise. A seam that was invisible to the naked eye had not eluded Flynn's searching touch. Nestled on a bed of raw cotton was a bottle filled with a clear liquid.

"Nitroglycerin?" Eric questioned the powder monkey.

"I be doubting that it was holy water," Flynn replied. "I will take this sweat of the devil and dispose of it before it can make any trouble." He closed the keg and raised it like a fine piece of china, saying to Eric, "Will you be wanting its bed after I've settled it elsewhere?"

"Yes," Eric replied as he refilled the now empty hole.

Flynn moved away from the work site and was lost in the trees. All the workers sighed as they saw him disappear. They knew that Flynn was the best powder monkey in the state and he would handle things from now on.

Eric motioned for Ben. "Have the men search the rest of the roadbed. I don't want any more surprises or anyone getting hurt."

Ben moved among the workmen and relayed Eric's order, cautioning everyone to go carefully and lightly.

Kat fumed as she watched from so far away she had no idea what was happening. How dare Eric order her around like that. She was not a fool and knew the risks she was taking by staying there with him. How dare he treat her as though she were stupid.

She saw the workmen disperse along the railbed and knew that they were searching for more fuses. She wished she knew what it was that Eric had found under the gravel.

Time passed and she was still being left alone as everyone else searched. Unable to wait idly for Eric to notice her and probably start another argument over her behavior, she walked over to the roadbed next to her and began searching on her own.

She had rounded a bend and was out of sight of the others when she saw the fuse sticking up like a bent twig of deadwood. This time it was not on the edge of the roadbed but square in the middle, where it would go unnoticed unless you looked hard.

Kat looked back toward where she had started, to see if there was anyone she could call. The track was empty. She did not want to leave the fuse like it was and go for help because she didn't trust herself to be able to locate it again.

Rolling up her sleeves and kneeling in the dirt, she slowly removed the top layer of soil as she had seen Eric do. Having cleared that away, she sat back on her heels and looked at what she had uncovered. The worked section of earth was half again as big as the one

Eric had cleared. A cold sweat bathed her as she thought of the disastrous havoc it would cause if it blew up.

Kat knew she could not deal with something like this alone and looked back down the track again, hoping to see help. The track was still empty. *Where is everyone? I haven't gone that far away, have I?* Kat scanned her position and realized that she was on a section of track that had not been damaged in the derailment. A chill gripped her as she thought, *If I had not been searching this way . . .* She put a stop to her thoughts. She had to get help.

Dusting her hands on her skirt, she made her way back toward the work site. She was within hailing distance when one of the men saw her and called over his shoulder to someone. Ben and Eric appeared at his call.

"Eric!" she called.

He looked at her and started toward her, his pace quickly closing the gap between them. She could see from the expression on his face that he was furious.

Reaching her, he gave her no chance to speak as he exploded. "I have enough problems right now without you adding to them. What do you think you were doing wandering off like that? Any idiot knows that now is not the time to go sight-seeing!"

Kat was aghast at his attack and lost her temper completely as she yelled at him, "My sight-seeing, as you call it, found something you would not have even looked for, Eric Thorsen! There is a nice surprise package buried back there that would have gone unnoticed if it weren't for me! You are the idiot, not me. Not everyone is a fool like you." She turned her back on him and retraced her steps, not caring if he followed her or not.

Viewing her discovery, Eric saw the size and the fact

that Kat had cleared it. He grabbed her arm and shook her roughly. "You could have been blown to pieces doing that! Why didn't you call for help!"

"Let go of me!" Kat wrested her arm free and rubbed it with her other hand as she retorted, "I was on my way to get help when you started shouting and carrying on like a madman."

Eric's fists opened and closed at his sides. "You haven't seen me really mad. And you better hope you never do, Kat Thorsen! Now get back to the horses and wait there until it's time to leave!" Eric snapped the words at her.

Kat wanted to hit him, she was so mad. Instead, she eyed him as though he had climbed from under some rock and said, "At least the horses have more brains than you do." She pointed at the same area he had been gesturing toward so wildly. "I know enough to know that that is not the way to run a railroad."

Her teeth were chattering uncontrollably with rage as she pushed by him and ran back to the horses.

Hot tears scalded her eyes as she reached the horses. No one had ever made her as mad as Eric did. He took more power upon himself than he was entitled to as a doctor in the employ of the Great Northern.

Her mind said, Wait a minute! Was Eric an employee of the Great Northern? He had never said he was.

Kat's chin trembled in anger. The Thorsen influence and power had been taken for granted by her and Dee and they had not questioned it. But where did they get the right to order rail crews and oversee repairs? Thinking back, Kat recalled that the only business they had ever mentioned was their logging and lumber company.

Kat felt fear chill her and she wanted to run. The Thorsens could be responsible for all the trouble as well as anyone else! Was there a better way to insure business for their company? Kat shook her head in disbelief. No, she told herself. If they had wanted to ruin the Great Northern, why derail a train and rescue the passengers? Too many thoughts raced through Kat's mind and confusion made her cry. For every reason she could find to say the Thorsens were the ones responsible for the trouble on the Great Northern, she also found a reason why they were not the guilty ones.

She had to get back to the lodge and talk to Dee. Maybe together they could find out the truth.

Chapter Thirteen

HEARING THE SOUND OF RIDERS, DEE WENT TO THE window and looked out. Eric and Kat were returning from the rail camp and Kat was upset. Dee hurriedly put the rest of her toiletries away and made her way downstairs to meet Kat.

The sight of Kat's face still flushed with anger startled Dee. Eric's grim expression, when she looked at him, did nothing to comfort her, either.

After throwing a black look at Eric's departing figure as he went into his office, slamming the door behind him, Kat moved past Dee and went straight upstairs.

Dee stood in the entryway, looking from Eric's door to the stairs in shock. She rushed to Kat's room to find out what had happened.

Kat was throwing a change of clothing onto her bed and ruthlessly pulling off her clothes and tossing them across the room.

"Kat? What happened?" Dee asked worriedly. "You look as though you could chew nails."

Kat turned, sparks flying from her eyes. "That is the understatement of the decade! Eric Thorsen is the most pig-headed, overbearing man I have ever had the misfortune to meet!"

"You had a fight?" Dee asked uneasily.

"It stopped short of blows if that is what you mean," Kat replied. "Next time, if there is a next time, I plan on delivering the first blow!"

"Kat!"

Kat went on to relate everything that had happened from the time she and Eric had arrived at the rail camp until the time they left. At this point in her tale, she stomped her foot and rubbed the back of her hand over her mouth in disgust.

"You aren't telling me everything," Dee accused her. "What happened at the rail camp is horrible, but the expression on your face tells me that something worse happened after that. Now tell me!"

Kat paced the room in agitation. "After treating me like he did, insulting me in front of the entire camp, questioning my intelligence and bullying me beyond belief"—she took a breath—"Eric had the nerve and unmitigated arrogance to try to kiss me!"

"He what!" Dee exclaimed. "When did he try that?" Dee asked as she watched Kat pull on fresh clothing.

"On the way back here," Kat said in a clipped voice. "We had stopped because he said he wanted to talk. He said he wanted to apologize for his behavior at the rail camp!"

"So, what is so terrible about that?" Dee asked, not understanding why Kat was overreacting like this.

Kat stopped dressing and stared at her. "What is so terrible! Besides the fact that no apology could make amends for the way he acted? He no sooner said that and he leaned over and tried to kiss me!"

"Oh." Dee frowned. "Did you let him?"

"Dee!" Kat exclaimed in horror. "I did not! I pushed him away from me and kicked my horse into a gallop."

"What did Eric do?" Dee asked.

Kat grabbed her hairbrush and began to pull at her hair with it, sending the pins cascading to the floor. "That is not important," she said to Dee.

"I would like to know, Kat," Dee cajoled. "It

shouldn't matter if it isn't important. So why not tell me?"

Kat laid her hairbrush down in front of her and hung her head, her hair covering her face. "If you must know, he chased after me and grabbed the bridle of my horse."

"Did he say anything, Kat?" Dee questioned softly.

Kat lifted a tear-streaked face and looked at her. "He said he was sorry for me."

"Sorry for you?" Dee repeated, trying to understand.

"Yes. He said he felt sorry for anyone that frightened of feeling any emotion but anger," Kat said in a choked voice.

"Oh, Kat!" Dee said as she put her arms around her. "That was a horrible thing for him to say."

"What if he's right?" Kat whispered.

"Shh!" Dee stroked Kat's hair as she tried to comfort her. "It doesn't matter what Eric said. You have to try to not let him upset you so much. You'll make yourself sick this way."

Kat drew away from her and dried her face. "Dee, I am not staying here another minute longer than I must."

"I'm going with you," Dee replied. "When are we leaving? Where are we going? How are we going to get there? And will they let us go?" she asked in one rush of breath.

Kat could not hold back a smile. "That's what I love about you. You get to the heart of the matter after you agree to doing it."

"I can't let you leave here without me," Dee insisted. "Do you think I want to be left here alone when they find out you have gone? I'm not crazy."

"No, you're not," Kat agreed. "Enough about my

disastrous day; I don't even want to think about it. How did your trip into town go?"

Dee told her about the fight she had seen and the kindness of Helga Jensen as she showed her the things she had brought back with her. "I'm sorry I didn't find out anything about the train wreck."

Kat looked at her sideways. "Do you think Mrs. Jensen would help us if we asked her?"

"You're not mad at me?" Dee asked.

"Why should I be? The chances of finding out anything in town were slim to start with, but you tried," Kat replied. "Now, what about Mrs. Jensen?"

"It would depend on what we asked her," Dee said. "She is a very close friend of Bert's. She might tell them where we are."

"Not if we are careful not to make her suspicious," Kat said. "Do you think she would send a wire to New York for us?"

Dee's eyes narrowed in thought and her forehead crinkled as she said, "Why New York?"

Kat explained her suspicions about Eric's control of the rail camp and added, "I want to check with Grandad to see if he has any authority to act like he does."

"When do we try to leave?" Dee asked as she walked to the window.

"I thought we could try to sneak away tonight after everyone is asleep," Kat answered as she repinned her hair.

Looking out the window toward the barn, Dee suggested, "Maybe we could borrow the wagon?"

"Do you know how to hitch a team?" Kat asked her.

Dee moved away from the window and shrugged. "I watched Sven do it one day. It looks simple enough."

"Dee?" Kat asked. "I can't face going down to eat

tonight. Could you say I'm too tired to eat and have gone to bed?"

"If you are sure that's what you want to do," Dee replied.

"I'm sure."

"I'll make your excuses for you," Dee told her. "Why not try to get some rest while I'm gone?"

"I think I will," Kat said as she moved over to the bed and lay down on top of the quilt.

Dee was not surprised to see Eric's empty seat as she and the others sat down to dine. She told Bert all about her trip to town and gave her the package that Helga had sent out for her.

Bert was happy to receive it, saying, "Helga is a dear friend."

No one seemed inclined to linger over coffee very long and Dee was rising to say good night when she remembered she wanted to speak with Sven. Going over to where he sat smoking his pipe, she asked, "How much were the material and things you bought today? I'd like to know so I can repay you."

Removing the pipe from his mouth, Sven looked at her and answered, "Don't worry about it."

"But I do and will worry about it," Dee explained. "I am not accustomed to having a man buy things for me. Please tell me how much I owe you."

Sven tapped the dottle from his pipe into a nearby ashtray. "I am not accustomed to buying things for a woman. Consider it as my way of keeping you busy and out of trouble."

"I beg your pardon?" Dee was not sure she had heard him correctly.

"If you think you need my pardon for something, I forgive you. But I don't want to hear any more about you repaying me."

Dee knew he was trying to make her mad and refused to take his bait. Bidding Bert and Leif a good night, she went up to her room.

Sven was surprised that Dee had not snapped back at him and wondered what she was scheming to do this time.

He knew what had happened at the rail camp because Eric had told him before leaving for town to send a wire to Patrick Gwyn informing him about the recent attempted sabotage.

Could it be that both Kat and Dee were up to something? He knew that Eric had scared the hell out of Kat by trying to kiss her and was kicking himself for trying. Was Kat really too tired to eat or were they planning something they didn't want anyone to know about? Sven looked at the clock on the mantel and saw that Eric should be back soon. He would talk to him about this and see what he thought.

Dee thought the house would never settle for the night. She had been waiting under the covers for hours for everyone to go to bed. She had heard a rider and had peeked out her window to see Eric dismounting and leading his horse to the barn. I wonder where he went, she murmured.

Climbing back under the covers, Dee waited for Kat's signal that it was time to leave. It was much later when she was awakened by Kat shaking her. "Come on, now. Wake up."

"Sorry, I must have dozed off there for a second or two," Dee apologized as she left the warmth of her bed.

"I have been tapping at your door for almost five minutes with no answer. I think you were sound asleep," Kat told her.

"Oh," was Dee's quiet reply as she followed Kat to

the door and waited for her to see if it was clear in the hallway.

Nodding that it was safe, Kat led the way out onto the landing as Dee closed the door quietly behind her.

They crept down the staircase, ready to bolt at the slightest noise. Reaching the main floor, they edged their way to the front door and out onto the porch.

Kat closed the heavy door behind them as Dee took the lead across the porch to the stairs. Stepping carefully, they still found one of the weather-worn planks, which groaned under Dee's slight weight. The sound reverberated in the still night air. Panicked, they made a wild dash for the barn and, they hoped, safety.

They huddled in the barn's moonlight shadow, waiting to see if anyone had heard the noise and come to investigate. Time moved at a snail's pace. They waited close to five minutes, too afraid to move until they were sure no one had heard the porch groan.

Sneaking into the barn, they ran into their first snag. It was almost impossible to hitch a wagon for the first time in pitch dark. Kat kept watch at the door as Dee struggled to remember how she had seen Sven harness the horses. She managed to do it with only minor scrapes and cuts and one sore foot from one of the horses stepping on her.

She motioned for Kat to open the barn doors wider and she led the team out. With the aid of the moonlight she hitched them to the wagon. She pulled herself up onto the seat and gathered the reins, calling softly to Kat, "Come on."

Kat closed the barn doors and hurried up onto the wagon next to Dee. "Let's go," she whispered urgently.

Dee looked nervously toward the lodge. "What if they hear the wagon pull out?"

"Now's a fine time to worry about that!" Kat hissed

at her. "We can't stop now. We will have to take our chances and make a run for it."

Dee gritted her teeth and slapped the reins on the backs of the horses as she had seen Sven do. They just stood there.

"Come on! Make them go!" Kat urged.

Dee slapped the reins a second time and clicked her tongue for good measure and the team started moving forward. She held her breath, praying that they wouldn't stop.

They moved at a steady but slow speed away from the lodge, and neither Kat nor Dee felt secure until they were out of sight around a turn in the road.

"We almost messed that up," Kat exclaimed, exhaling in relief. "I thought the team would never start moving."

"So did I," Dee replied. "If they hadn't started when they did, I don't know what I would have done next."

"Did you have to tell me that?" Kat complained as she tried to find a comfortable spot on the hard seat. "I thought you knew how to drive a wagon."

"I never said I did!" Dee defended herself.

"You never said you didn't!" Kat accused in return.

Dee tried to keep the team on the roadway as she replied, "You never asked me!"

Kat folded as much of her skirt as she could under her to try to give herself a padded seat before saying, "I figured you knew. After all, you were always doing things with your brothers. Didn't they teach you how to drive a wagon?"

"No! They would only let me clean and groom their horses, and you know as well as I do that we didn't have a wagon!" Dee protested.

"Oh." Kat sighed.

"I think we may have an even bigger problem on our hands," Dee said as they continued down the roadway.

"I don't want to hear it," Kat declared. "Nothing could be worse than it is now."

Dee found that she was beginning to gain some confidence the farther they traveled. Maybe she had learned something by watching Sven as closely as she had that morning on their way to town. "I think you will have to hear it," Dee informed Kat. "If we don't do something about it fairly soon, we will be sorry."

Kat squinted at Dee in the moonlight. "We will?"

Dee nodded vigorously. "We will."

They had come about a mile and a half from the lodge and the moon was starting to set, making it harder to see the roadway ahead of them. Dee wanted to talk to Kat before it set altogether.

Kat took a deep breath and steeled herself for the worst possible thing Dee could say and muttered, "Tell me."

"We never decided where we were going," Dee explained in a quiet voice.

"I was afraid that might be what you were referring to," Kat replied. "Drive on and I'll try to come up with an answer."

Dee drove for another two miles and halted the team completely, saying to Kat, "I hope you have come up with something. If we keep heading the way we are going we will be in the middle of town."

"The best I can do is suggest we pull off the road and try to hide the wagon in the trees until morning. Then we will have sunlight to see where we are going," Kat informed her. "I thought about town and dismissed that idea because of the time of night. And we would be crazy to take off on some side trail not knowing where it led."

"Are you saying that we aren't crazy now?" Dee asked. "I have my doubts about that. Here it is the middle of the night and we are sitting in a borrowed wagon alone in the middle of nowhere calmly discussing what we should do next." Dee shook her head. "Sounds crazy to me."

"We are not in the middle of nowhere," Kat protested. "We are on the road to town."

"And likely to remain here until doomsday if we don't make a decision pretty soon," Dee chided.

Kat turned in her seat and scanned the surrounding darkness. "Do you remember if there is a clear area anywhere between here and town?" she asked Dee.

"There is one. But it is fairly close to town. Why?" Dee was anxious to move somewhere; anywhere was preferable to sitting like ducks in the road.

"Right," Kat stated firmly. "We move there and turn off into the trees and wait for morning."

Dee eyed her skeptically. "I think our planning leaves something to be desired."

"What planning?" Kat replied.

Slapping the reins once again, Dee started the team forward, saying, "Exactly."

"Now, if you had asked me how to get to any of the major department stores in New York or the opera or Carnegie Hall, I could tell you in a minute," Kat tried to explain her problem to Dee. "Out here, it's another thing altogether. Besides, I haven't heard you coming up with any bright ideas. And you have been to town and I haven't." Kat quieted.

"Are you through?" Dee asked.

"Yes."

"Fine. Now as to my having to come up with a bright idea, not likely. You are forgetting that I come from New York, just like you. You are also forgetting that you are older than me, and, being the elder, you have always made our decisions and led the way," Dee explained carefully.

"I make all our decisions!" Kat exclaimed. "I will

agree with you on every point but that one. You have been as responsible as I have for the many times we ended up in trouble. Don't try to lay all the blame at my door."

They broke free of the trees and were in an area where the road was bordered by soft grasses and wild flowers. "Here we are. What now?" Dee asked Kat.

Kat put her hand on Dee's arm, shushing her. "Wait a minute. Do you hear anything?"

Dee listened carefully and groaned. "Tell me I am not hearing the sounds of a rider heading this way."

"If you aren't, then neither am I," Kat muttered. "But I think our unheard rider is coming from town."

"I think you're right," Dee said. "I guess we try to bluff our way out of this somehow."

"I know." Kat straightened her posture and smoothed her skirt. "Try to act natural," she instructed Dee.

"At this time of night? Who would believe us?" Dee shot back at her.

"Hopefully, he will," Kat murmured under her breath to Dee as a rider came into view from the direction of town.

"I don't like the looks of him," Dee whispered as she pulled the team to a halt.

"How can you see that far in the dark?" Kat whispered back.

"Fear does wonderful things for my eyesight," Dee replied.

"Hush!" Kat warned her. "He's going to stop."

"I was afraid of that," Dee groaned quietly.

The moonlight must be playing tricks on him, Grebe thought as he broke through the trees and saw a wagon stopped ahead on the road.

He slowed to a walk as he neared the wagon. He couldn't be that lucky, he said under his breath. He recognized the occupants of the wagon and wondered what the hell they were doing out there at that time of night.

But he wasn't a fool not to take advantage of the situation. He formulated a quick plan in his head as he came abreast of the wagon and reined in his horse. "Evening, ladies. Do you need any assistance?" Grebe drawled smoothly.

A germ of an idea began to form in Kat's mind as she replied, "Thank you, sir. Maybe you could aid us? We were on our way to visit our sick aunt and I am afraid we have lost our direction," Kat lied sweetly.

Dee shuddered as she heard what Kat said. She shuddered again on seeing the rider up close. She did not like the looks of him at all.

"This is the road to town, ma'am. But, if I may say so, it is not a very wise idea for young women to travel it alone at night," Grebe returned with false sincerity as he tried to figure out the real reason for their being there.

"Normally, we would not have dreamed of undertaking such a journey as this, but our aunt is so sick we felt it necessary to go to her as soon as possible," Kat embellished her tale.

Dee had to cough to cover her snort at the outrageousness of Kat's story. If this man believed them, he was as crazy as they were, as far as Dee was concerned.

Kat dug her elbow into Dee's side warningly under the pretext of straightening her skirt as she awaited the stranger's reply.

"If you would allow me, ma'am, I would be willing to act as an escort into town," Grebe intoned politely as his mind raced ahead to how he would take them to Spencer.

"We would be most grateful for your protection,

sir," Kat answered with heartfelt relief that he had bought her story.

Suddenly the rider's head snapped up and he looked behind them. Turning his horse with a quick motion, he cursed under his breath and galloped back the way he had come.

"Why did he do that?" Kat asked in disbelief.

The sound of hoofbeats pounding on the road behind them answered her question as three riders came into view. "Damn," Kat said, echoing the stranger's curse.

Dee slapped the reins as hard as she could on the back of the horses, trying to make them run. The wagon jolted ahead, gathering speed as the team raced to full stride.

The three riders increased their speed of pursuit and began to overtake the wagon. One of the riders moved to the front of the team and, leaning down, grabbed their bridle straps as one of the others came abreast of the wagon and leaped from his horse onto the back of the wagon. Rising up behind the seat like an avenging angel, Sven reached over and grabbed the reins from Dee's hands and pulled as he called, "Hold onto their heads, Eric."

The wagon slowed to a halt and the night was deadly still as Eric rode back and broke the silence. "Head them home, Sven."

Turning the wagon in the tight roadway was no trouble for Sven and soon he had them headed back to the lodge. Eric rode on one side of the wagon and Leif rode on the other, with Sven's horse in tow.

None of the men said a word to either Kat or Dee.

Chapter Fourteen

Dawn was tinting the horizon as the wagon pulled up to the lodge. Sven halted the team by the front porch and barked his first words at Kat and Dee. "Get down."

They hurriedly scrambled down from the wagon as best as they could without help and stood waiting by the steps to the porch.

Dee saw the vivid pinks and golds of the sunrise and whispered to Kat, "Enjoy the sunrise while you can. It might be our last."

Kat stiffened and looked over at Dee. "They wouldn't dare."

Dee looked at the men as they tethered the horses and unhooked the team. She could feel the anger radiating from them. "I would not be too sure about that, if I were you," she whispered to Kat.

Kat felt so tired she could cry. Her entire body ached and her hands felt stiff from hanging onto the seat of the wagon. The last thing she wanted now was a confrontation, but seeing the expression on Eric's face as he joined them, she knew there was going to be one.

Eric stared at them, his eyes like storm clouds of gray. He motioned for them to go into the lodge and followed them as they moved up the stairs.

As they passed through the front door, Kat's tiredness was replaced by anger. There was no reason for them to be treated like criminals. Instead of taking heed from the storm clouds of anger in Eric's eyes, she felt her own anger rising to respond. She would tell them exactly what she thought of their high-handedness.

Dee winced as she saw Kat's shoulders straighten and her chin go up. It meant Kat was preparing to battle with the men. Dee knew that it could be a battle that might lose them the war.

When they had entered the parlor, Kat eyed the men coldly and said, "You realize this is kidnapping in addition to false imprisonment."

Eric slapped his hand down on the table next to him and said in a cutting voice, "Shut up. I do not want to hear another word out of either of you. What you did tonight makes you both guilty of horse theft, if you want to levy charges against someone."

Kat drew her breath in sharply, ready to retort, when Sven's voice cut her off. "We do not particularly give a damn what you say we are guilty of doing. You are in no position to accuse anyone of anything. I would listen to Eric's warning if I were you."

Dee's nostrils flared in defiance as she said, "You are not me."

Sven took a step toward her and was stopped by Leif grabbing his arm and saying to Dee, "If you won't listen to Eric, maybe you'll listen to me. We hang horse thieves in Montana."

"Leif!" Dee paled, as she had thought he was on their side and their friend.

"Threatening women? My, what big men you all are," Kat said sarcastically.

"Not threatening, just stating some hard facts," Eric returned.

"You will regret it. When my grandfather hears about this he will make sure you all get what you deserve," Kat shot back at him.

"We have a few things of our own to speak to him about," Eric informed her. "For one thing, when he asked us to keep an eye on you two until he could come out here, he forgot to tell us you were given to fits of irrationality."

"What do you mean my grandfather asked you to keep an eye on us?" Kat exclaimed in surprise.

Ignoring her question, Sven said, "Riding around the countryside in the dead of night could have gotten you both killed. Don't either of you realize that this is not New York, with its police force to watch over society's darlings should they decide to take a midnight ride through town!" He turned his back on them, not trusting himself to continue.

"Any number of very unpleasant things could have happened out there," Leif tried to explain to them. "Two women alone like that are prime targets for trouble."

"But we were not alone!" Dee protested angrily. "Until the three of you came rushing up like madmen, we had someone who'd agreed to escort us the remaining way into town!"

The men looked at each other and Eric ran a hand through his hair in frustration. "I suppose it never occurred to either of you to ask what he was doing on the road at that time of night?"

"It was none of our business!" Kat replied hotly.

"It was your business to do what you did?" Eric grated at her.

"Where was your escort when we arrived?" Sven questioned coldly.

"You scared him off!" Dee told him. "He probably thought it wasn't safe to hang around when he heard you galloping toward us."

"If this escort was as harmless as you insist he was,

why didn't he stay and protect you if he thought there was going to be trouble?" Sven demanded.

Neither girl could answer him. They knew that what they had done was extremely foolish and the more the brothers said, the more they began to realize how dangerous.

"When did my grandfather ask you to keep an eye on us?" Kat insisted on knowing.

"When I sent him news of what had happened. He replied that he preferred that we keep you here until he arrived," Eric answered calmly.

"Why didn't you tell us about any of this?" Dee asked with a frown.

"We decided it was better if you didn't know there might still be some danger to you," Leif explained carefully.

"But we had a right to know!" Kat protested.

Eric paced the floor in front of her, then turned to face her, his eyes boring into her. "Would it have changed anything if you had known?" he asked her.

"Kat wouldn't have thought you were responsible for the sabotage on the Great Northern," Dee blurted without thinking.

Eric's eyes widened as he glanced at Dee and back to Kat. "You thought we were responsible?" he asked with tones of ice.

Kat thrust her chin up and replied, "What else was I to think? You wield a lot of power with no apparent authority to do so. You control the repairs on the line. You order everyone around like you have the right to do so. You conveniently own a logging and lumber company that happens to be the only one around to provide the necessary materials to complete repairs on the line."

"Are you finished?" Eric demanded.

Kat glared at him but remained silent. She had said what she wanted to say. Let him deny her accusations if he could.

"Oh, Kat." Leif shook his head in disbelief.

"Did it ever occur to you to ask me where my authority came from?" Eric questioned.

"No. We were in no position to ask questions like that after your family had taken us in and cared for us like they had," Dee told him as Kat remained stubbornly silent.

"Now you are in a position to say such things?" Sven said.

Dee looked over at him and responded, "Eric asked us. Kat gave him an answer."

Sven's jaw tightened. "She made accusations that are very serious. She did not simply answer a question."

"That is a chance you take when you ask a serious question," Dee defended.

"Eric is the regional representative for the Great Northern." Leif's words cut through the air like a knife.

"What?" Kat stammered. "Why didn't I know about that? I know the names of my grandfather's agents and Eric's name is not one of them."

"You expect your grandfather to tell you everything?" Sven questioned.

"Of course not!" Kat declared. "But, as we were traveling through this area, I would assume he would tell me in case there was anything he wanted me to discuss with his local representative."

"You spend most of your time assuming things," Eric observed. "Why not try spending more time finding out for certain before you act?"

Kat lowered her eyes and murmured, "Why don't you try trusting people and not keeping secrets from them?"

Eric frowned at hearing this and moved away from her to stand by one of the chairs. She had scored with that and he had nothing more to say as he asked himself the same question.

"What happens now?" Dee asked softly.

"Since none of us appears to trust each other that much, one of us will be with you whenever you leave the lodge," Sven replied.

"We are to be allowed to leave?" Dee asked in surprise.

"Not if I am with you," Sven answered her.

The thought of Sven following her around watching her every movement unsettled her to the core. Her reaction was a mixture of resentment and, oddly enough, pleasure at this news.

"And who is Kat's watchdog?" she asked.

Eric cleared his throat and said, "That will be my job."

Kat lifted her eyes and looked at him as he answered Dee's question. No! I can't have him looking over my shoulder all the time, she thought. He makes me feel threatened.

Leif had been watching his brothers closely since the time they had discovered the girls were gone. He wondered who they were trying to fool. Eric had been more concerned than angry on finding out they had disappeared. And Sven had acted as though he had expected something like that to happen all the time. Now they were behaving out of character.

Listening to the angry words the four were throwing at one another, Leif had to laugh. If they only could see how ridiculous they all looked.

"What do you find so amusing, Leif?" Sven asked suspiciously. "You think what Kat and Dee did was funny?"

"You know better than that, Sven," Leif returned in a hard voice that made his brother's eyebrows rise in surprise.

"Then what is it you find so funny?" Sven demanded.

"You would not find it as amusing as I do," Leif told him cryptically.

"Maybe I would," Eric interjected.

"I doubt that, Eric," Leif replied steadily. "I seem to be the only one left around here with a sense of humor. The irony of the situation has obviously escaped all of you."

This had four pairs of eyes staring at him as he shrugged his shoulders and continued. "By setting up all these rules and guards, you are doing exactly what you have denied having done in the past. Guests do not require watchdogs."

His brothers scowled at his words and Dee smiled in satisfaction that Leif had proved their point for them. But her smile faded and she and Kat gasped in shock as Leif looked at them and said, "And guests do not repay hospitality by sneaking away in the middle of the night and then throwing temper tantrums when they are brought back for their own safety." Leif shook his head and took all of them in with a look. "What happened here tonight is the result of a series of misconceptions and misunderstandings."

Silence filled the room as they all looked at him in disbelief. His words were not what anyone had expected or wanted to hear.

"Misconceptions! Misunderstandings!" Sven spit out. "That is your explanation of why these two"—he pointed at Kat and Dee—"took off in the middle of the night risking life and limb!"

"I haven't heard any of you asking why? All I have heard is charges and countercharges and ultimatums by both sides. If any of you took the time to talk to each other and not at each other, you might discover that you are all on the same side," Leif retorted as he viewed the stubborn faces around him. "But as emotion rules and not reason, I hardly expect any of you to understand what I am saying. None of you have any objectivity left."

"And I suppose you do?" Eric commented sarcastically.

"More than you'll ever know, Eric," Leif laughed as he shook his head at them. Taking one last look around as would an indulgent adult viewing children bickering over a bag of candy, he left the parlor and went upstairs.

His parting words hung in the air and none of the remaining four said a word. Kat found that she could not bring herself to look at Eric. Dee looked over at Sven, but he was staring at the parlor doorway with a look of consternation on his face.

Eric was terse as he broke the heavy silence by saying, "I think enough has been said by everyone tonight. We will discuss this again in the morning when we have all had time to rest."

Sven nodded his agreement as he thought of Leif's parting words. Leif had never spoken that way before in his life. He had sounded fed up with them all. Why? What was it that he saw that none of them could see?

Kat and Dee left the parlor without saying a word. They were too exhausted to think of anything else to say. Leif's outburst disturbed both of them. He had been their friend from the day they had arrived. Why did he turn on them now? Was it possible that he was right? Were they all victims of misconception and misunderstanding?

These and other thoughts plagued them as they went to their rooms and tried to sleep.

Chapter Fifteen

IT WAS LATE AFTERNOON AND LEIF WAS PLEASED WITH
what he saw and heard. His airing of the way he saw
things was bearing some results.

The mood this afternoon was one of forgotten anger
and harsh words. Eric and Sven had gone out of their
way to explain to Kat and Dee everything that had
happened leading up to the previous night's fiasco.

Kat and Dee had surprised and pleased him with the
calm way they had listened to his brothers. They had
asked intelligent questions that showed his brothers
had been mistaken in judging them unable to handle
hard truths of a situation. They had even admitted
candidly their own reasons for leaving as they had.
Although, Leif could not help but feel, Kat was not as
forthcoming on that as was Dee.

By evening, Leif was almost sorry he had said
anything at all. Dee had made plans with Sven to return
to town in the morning and Kat was anxious to go over
all of Eric's records with him, hunting for possible clues
to the sabotage on the line.

This left Leif alone with Bert, his law books and a
distinct feeling of being left out by the others.

Sven and Dee were the focus of sidelong looks and
hurried conversations as they made their way down the
covered walkway to Jensen's General Store.

Neither of them said anything, wary of upsetting

their newfound truce. But when they entered Jensen's Dee was close to tears and Sven's lips were thin with anger.

Karl saw them enter and called to Helga that they were there as he left the counter and went to welcome them. His eyes widened with curiosity as he saw Sven's tight-lipped anger and Dee's obvious distress. "What's wrong, Sven?" he asked.

Sven put his arm around Dee's shoulders and said, "Karl, would it be all right if Dee sat in the back for a few minutes?"

Helga joined them and hearing Sven's request and seeing Dee's white face, she answered, "Certainly she can. Come, dear. We will go and have a cup of coffee and leave the men to take care of business."

Dee smiled weakly at Helga. "Thank you, that would be nice."

Sven released Dee into Helga's care, saying, "We appreciate this, Helga."

Helga escorted Dee to the privacy of their living quarters and made her sit down at the table. Watching her with concern in her eyes, Helga bustled about pouring them some coffee and placing the cups on the table as she sat in the chair across from Dee. It was obvious to her that something had happened that had greatly upset both Sven and Dee. She left Dee alone and did not badger her with questions as she sipped her coffee and watched the girl try to regain her composure.

They were on their second cup of coffee before Dee poured out her story to Helga. It had happened as she and Sven were entering the store. Two townswomen had been leaving the store, and when they saw Dee, they had drawn their skirts away from her in disapproval and sniffed audibly. "Obviously the Jensens are not picky who they sell to."

Upon hearing the self-righteousness in their voices, Sven had tipped his hat in their direction and said, "Yes. Isn't it generous of them to do business with you."

The townswomen had gasped in outrage and quickly hurried away, one of them saying to the other, "What else could you expect from a man who would take a whore for his wife?"

Sven had started to walk after them, but Dee had stopped him by putting her hand on his arm and saying, "Things are bad enough now. Please don't make them any worse."

As Dee related all this to Helga, she began to feel a little better. It helped to be able to talk to someone.

Helga was outraged at what Dee told her but refrained from making any comment, letting Dee get it out of her system. When Dee's voice trailed off, Helga patted her hand and suggested something to take Dee's mind off the hurtful incident. "Come with me and see what came in with my latest shipment of goods. You might see something you like."

They went back out into the store and Dee remembered. "Oh, Helga." She reached into her reticule and withdrew a small handful of bills. "Bert sent this in with me to cover her last order."

Helga took the money and grinned. "Bert never has trusted the boys to remember to pay her bill. I'll bring you her change. Why not look around?"

Dee watched her move across the store to the cash box, and she was surprised when a group of brightly colored fabrics caught her eye. Looking around the store, she saw Sven was with Karl and they were busily inspecting some tack that Karl had removed from a hook on the wall.

Dee's practical nature began to assert itself, telling

her that she should think more about replenishing her meager wardrobe. She moved over to the pile of colorful fabrics and started to look through it. She found three different materials and some matching thread that should keep her occupied plying her needle.

Looking over her shoulder to see if Helga was returning, she saw that two ladies had stopped her and were busily talking to her. Dee threw her a smile as she watched Helga deal with their needs. Helga returned her expression with a warm smile of her own.

Dee was content to browse and explore as the earlier incident began to fade from her mind. She found a few more items to add to her collection of purchases, looking up as the not-so-quiet voices of the two women Helga was waiting on ruined all the pleasure she had gained. She heard one of them say to Helga, "Surely business is not so bad that you are forced to deal with people"—the woman paused—"like her?"

The insult was aimed at her and Dee cringed as she heard the other woman say, "Is it true? What the newspaper said about that man in New York killing himself over one of them? I think it is quite dreadful. What woman of good character would be involved in such a sordid affair?"

Dee felt anger rising at the maliciousness directed at her and Kat by these total strangers. They had been tried, convicted and branded as not fit to be seen in public on the viciousness of one newspaper article! She stiffened her shoulders and held her head high, refusing to let them see that they had upset her.

The first woman spoke again. "And living out there with those men! Poor Bertal must be at her wit's end! Such goings on! Under her own roof, yet!"

Helga's voice cut the woman off, saying, "Bert is very fond of both her nephews' wives. She told me herself that she could not be more pleased than when they joined her family. Will that be all, ladies?" Helga's hard tone and level stare dared either of them to say another word. They quickly completed their transactions and with a show of injured dignity left the store.

Helga moved to Dee and told her, "Now don't you let their narrow minds hurt you."

"I'm fine, Helga," Dee tried to reassure her.

Helga did not believe her and continued. "They are part of a small group of sanctimonious biddies, suffering from a bad case of sour grapes."

"What?" Dee looked at her in confusion.

Helga smiled warmly. "There was bound to be some jealousy no matter who the Thorsens married. They were considered to be private property by some of the more ambitious mothers here in town. They had decided among themselves that their daughters were the only ones worthy of Thorsen notice."

"They are jealous of me?" Dee said in wonder.

"Green as apples!" Helga smiled broadly.

If Helga and those women knew the true reason for our marriages, they would all be shocked, Dee thought as she could not resist a small laugh. What would they think if they knew about the separate bedrooms!

Sven had finished his business with Karl and joined Dee as Helga handed her a neat bundle containing her purchases. He had seen part of what had happened and asked, "What was all that about?"

Dee gave Helga a glance of warning before saying to Sven, "It would seem that I have put a few noses out of joint by marrying you."

"What?" Sven asked in surprise.

"Helga has been telling me what a prize you were considered to be by other hopeful ladies of the community. I never dreamed I had married such a popular man," Dee teased him, hoping that he would not ask exactly what the two women had said.

"Hogwash!" Sven dismissed what she told him. He stared at her, trying to read by her expression if she were hiding something else from him.

Dee withstood his gaze, praying he would not ask any more questions she might have trouble answering.

Helga thought it was wrong for Dee not to tell Sven what had been said. She hoped that Dee knew what she was doing. She should not have to deal with such hurtful talk by herself. Mind your own business, Helga Jensen, she told herself sternly as she watched the young couple in front of her.

Breaking the spell that Sven's look held her in, Dee said, "Hogwash? That's what you say. But I think I should warn Leif, in any case."

"Leif?" Sven questioned.

Dee picked up her packages and started to the door with a smile of good-bye for Helga as she answered him. "Now that you and Eric are married, Leif is the only eligible Thorsen left." Dee's bubbling laugh punctuated their departure and Helga was the only one to catch its strained undertones.

They had traveled halfway home when Sven pulled the wagon to a stop off the side of the road. He didn't give Dee a chance to ask why as he reached under the seat and withdrew a basket, saying, "I had Bert pack us a lunch. I thought we would stop here and rest while we eat."

He hopped down from the wagon and came over to her side to lift Dee down before she could utter the protest that rushed to her lips.

Setting her down next to the wagon, he rummaged around behind the seat and pulled out a blanket with a triumphant grin. "Here we go. Now pick a spot you would like to rest."

Dee looked around her at the towering trees with the wind ruffling their tops and saw a spot near a group of three trees not far from the wagon. "Over there?" She pointed.

Sven carried the blanket and basket to where she pointed and spread the blanket on the ground, saying, "Come on, I'm hungry."

She hurried to join him, her thoughts a mass of confusion. Why was he being so nice to her? The last time they had gone to town, he had raced there and back as though he could not stand being with her any longer than he had to.

She had been startled enough at his invitation last night, but now a picnic? She sat down on the blanket and automatically began to distribute food from the basket that Sven placed beside her.

She was amazed at the quantity of food Bert had packed. There was fried chicken wrapped in a cloth to keep it fresh, wedges of cheese, melon and, at the bottom of the basket, a beautiful fruit pie with a flaky golden crust.

Having set out the food, Dee searched for the plates and utensils. There was nothing else but some cloth napkins. Not finding what she was hunting for, she said, "We may have a problem. I can't find anything to put the food on or cutlery."

Sven laughed, startling her. "My dear Dee. You have a lot to learn. This is a western picnic. We use our laps, our hands and napkins."

He showed her what he meant by picking up a crisp chicken leg and biting into it as he held it with his fingers.

"I didn't know." She could feel herself blushing with embarrassment.

"Don't apologize. You had no way of knowing,"

Sven said. "Here, I'll teach you. Take a piece of chicken."

She looked at the pile of chicken. She had never eaten it without the proper utensils before and wasn't sure how to go about it.

"Go on, now. Pick up a piece before I eat it all," Sven instructed her.

She settled for the remaining leg and lifted it gingerly between two fingers.

"Not like that," Sven told her easily as he showed her how to grasp the leg. "Like this."

Dee watched how he did it and tried to copy him. Having mastered that much, she took a bite. It was delicious! She had no idea she was so hungry. She quickly finished the chicken leg and reached for a second piece.

"That's more like it," Sven commented as he took his third piece. "But you had better take bigger bites or I'll eat it all," he teased her.

"Oh, no, you won't!" Dee laughed as she grabbed two more pieces and put them on the napkin in her lap. "These are mine!"

Sven was glad to see her smile. Watching her as she nibbled on her chicken, he saw how the sun reflected itself in the shining highlights of her hair and the rosy glow the fresh air had brought to her cheeks.

Seeing him stare at her, Dee felt flustered and laid down the piece of chicken she was eating, saying, "I must look a mess! You've got me feeling like a child caught stealing cookies from the cookie jar." She tried to wipe her mouth and chin with the corner of the napkin in her lap.

"You look fine," Sven told her. "Don't worry about that now. We'll wash up with water from the canteen when we're finished."

Dee felt a warm glow not caused by the sun spread through her at his words. She was enjoying this time together and hoped Sven was, too.

Having demolished the chicken between them, Dee refused any of the cheese, saying she wanted to save room for some of the pie as she handed a wedge of the rich-smelling cheddar to Sven.

He looked at her with a twinkle in his eye and opened his mouth, waiting for her to feed him the cheese.

After a moment's hesitation she did and was shocked at the thrill of feeling that raced through her fingers as he nibbled at them. To cover her reaction, she quickly withdrew her hand and pulled the fruit pie closer, saying in what she hoped was not a shaky voice, "How do we serve this?"

Sven watched her with a glint in his eye. She had not fooled him in the least. He did have an effect on her. "Hand it over here. I'll wait on you this time," he said in a tone that sent shivers up Dee's spine.

She lifted the pie to hand it to him and froze when his hands covered hers as she held the pie plate. Their eyes locked with unspoken words as time came to a standstill.

When she thought she would faint from holding her breath, Sven moved one of his hands under the pie plate and took it, letting her withdraw hers to safety.

The air was heavy with feeling as she watched him slice the pie with his knife and remove a piece. Oh, God, she thought, why am I feeling like this? All her senses were on edge. The air had never looked so clear, the sky so blue or the birds as they sang their songs so beautiful.

Dee sighed a prayer of thanks as Sven placed the first piece on his napkin and, cutting another piece, told her to hold out her hand. She did so and he placed the pie in it.

The vulnerability mirrored in her eyes had given Sven second thoughts. She was his wife by law, and he wanted to touch her and love her. But he was more concerned with frightening her and maybe doing something that they both would regret later.

Dee ate her pie even though it tasted like dust in her mouth. Since handing it to her, Sven had been ignoring her completely. Why? What had she done?

She finished her pie and looked over at him. He was reclining on the blanket with his hat tilted over his eyes and looked like he was asleep.

She cleared the remnants of their meal and repacked the basket as he dozed. Finishing, Dee found herself watching Sven as he slept. After awhile, her own eyelids felt heavy as the afternoon sun warmed her with its caress. She decided that a short nap would do her some good as well.

She awakened later to something tickling her nose. She tried to brush it away without opening her eyes, but it kept coming back. She opened her eyes and saw Sven leaning over her with a long blade of grass in his hand. He smiled down at her and tickled her nose. "Time to wake up, sleepyhead."

Before she could move or say a word, he followed his words by leaning even closer and placing a soft kiss on her lips.

"Wife, you tempt me greatly. I would like nothing better than to spend the rest of the day out here with you in my arms." He kissed her again, coaxingly this time.

Dee returned his kiss as he gathered her into his arms and held her. The feel of his body next to hers was so heady that she unconsciously tried to mold herself even closer to him.

Breaking away from the kiss, Sven smiled at her. "Sorely tempted, indeed," he murmured, his lips bare-

ly touching hers. "You have bewitched me, woman."
He kissed her as though he could not get enough of her.

Dee's world became one of feeling and reaction as
her body responded to Sven's touch. Her mind was
whirling with confusion as he finally pulled away from
her and lifted her to her feet. She stood with her hands
still clasped in his and looked at him, a question in her
eyes. She felt an aching emptiness replacing the warmth
of his embrace and her lips tingled from his kisses.

He kissed her one last time, saying, "Don't look at
me like that. You have no idea how desirable you are at
this moment or the effort it's taking for me to resist
you."

He put his arm around her and directed her back to
the wagon, where he lifted her onto the seat with a
lingering promise in his touch.

Leaving her, he gathered the blanket and basket,
trying to regain his control. He could have taken Dee
right then and there. She would not have stopped him.
He knew that. He had stopped himself; when he made
love to her, it would be because they both knew what
was happening and not because he had taken advantage
of her vulnerability.

Slipping the blanket and basket into the back of the
wagon, Sven climbed up front next to Dee and picked
up the reins. He turned the wagon back onto the road,
glancing over at Dee, who looked at him with confusion
in her eyes.

He knew she did not understand what was happening. He could see from the way she was holding her
body that she was fighting back tears. He tried to smile
at her reassuringly, but when she timidly returned his
smile, he felt desire race through him.

He slapped the reins on the backs of the team,
hurrying them forward. The sooner they got back to the
lodge, the less time he would have to change his mind.

As the team speeded up, Dee was forced to grab onto the edge of the seat to keep from falling off the wagon. Why was Sven acting the way he was? What had she done that made him so anxious to get home? Hot tears burned the backs of her eyes as she tried to understand. Her throat closed and misery engulfed her as she thought, He's sorry he kissed me!

She stole a look at him as they neared the lodge and saw how stiffly he held himself and the tense set of his jaw. He had withdrawn from her completely. She choked back her tears as an aching emptiness filled her.

If he felt that way about her, she decided, then she had made a complete fool of herself back there. She gathered the remnants of her tattered pride about her like a cloak, swearing that she would never let him know how crushing his rejection of her was. She would never give him the satisfaction. If he felt the way he did, then she would do her best to stay out of his way.

Pulling up in front of the lodge, Sven climbed down from the wagon and moved to Dee's side. He reached up to help her down and cursed at her quick withdrawal from his touch. He watched her as he put his hands around her waist and lifted her to the ground. She kept her eyes lowered and would not look him in the face. Removing his hold on her, he stood and watched her move slowly up the steps to the porch. He mentally kicked himself for handling things so badly as he called softly after her, "Dee?"

She stopped partway up the steps and straightened her shoulders before turning slowly to look at him. Her eyes were cold and her face closed. All the vibrancy of earlier had disappeared as though it never existed. She was like marble as she stared at him wordlessly.

He took a step toward her, holding his hand out to her. When she ignored it, he let it drop to his side as he spoke. "You don't understand. We have to talk."

"Sven? Is that you?" Eric's voice could be heard as he called from the doorway.

"Yes," Sven called back as he continued to look at Dee.

"Come to my office, there's something I want to show you," Eric told him.

"Damn!" Sven muttered softly. "Dee, we do have to talk."

"Hurry up, Sven!" Eric's voice called impatiently.

"Later tonight, I promise you, we will talk," Sven told Dee as she stared at him, unmoving.

"We have nothing to say to one another, Sven," Dee told him through stiff lips. She turned around and went inside.

Sven slapped his hand against his leg in frustration. He had to make her understand. She was wrong; they had a lot to say to each other. He would make certain that they talked.

What could we possibly have to say to each other now, Dee told herself as she made her way to her room. Sven's actions had said more than any words.

Eric and Sven were absent at dinner that night. They had been closeted in Eric's office since Sven and Dee had returned. Dee was glad Sven was not there; she was not ready to face him again so soon.

Kat noticed Dee's unusual quietness and asked, "Are you feeling all right, Dee?"

"I'm tired," Dee lied. "I think today wore me out." Looking at the others at the table, Dee continued, "If you will all excuse me, I think I will go up to my room and go to bed."

Leif nodded, a concerned look on his face. "That sounds like a good idea. Why not sleep in tomorrow morning? You look as if you could use the extra rest."

Bert added, "You go on, dear. I hope you feel better in the morning."

Dee laid her napkin next to her untouched plate and rose from her seat, saying, "I hope I will, too, Bert."

The lodge was quiet as Sven made his silent way up to his room. He tried to flex the fatigue from his aching shoulders as he rubbed a hand over the back of his neck. Eric had retired hours ago. But he wanted to go over the reports Eric and Kat had unearthed one last time before retiring. What they held was a possible key to the sabotage they had been experiencing on the line.

He'd read and reread the report until his eyes ached but still couldn't find what it was he was searching for. He knew it was there somewhere, but it eluded him.

Deciding that he'd try to clear his mind by working on the backlog of paperwork he had for the company, he set the reports to the side. Maybe something would come to him when he wasn't worrying at it like a dog with a bone.

Time passed as he became enmeshed in shipping orders, systematic scheduling of tree harvesting and routine. When he'd cleared up the backlog, he once again tried to go over the reports. But his mind refused to concentrate. He kept thinking of Dee and the look of her pain-filled eyes as she'd said they had nothing to say to each other.

Finally, deciding that it was a waste of time to try to do any more that night, he had filed everything away and started up to his room.

Reaching the upstairs landing, a frown creased his brow as he saw Dee's bedroom door ajar. He had not had a chance to speak with her all evening and he wondered if the afternoon's events had upset her to the point of triggering her sleepwalking. Moving to her half-open door, he looked inside, calling softly, "Dee?"

Her bed was empty and she was nowhere in sight. The air in the room was chill, as was the indentation left in the feather mattress by her small form. He lifted his hand from the vacant bed and returned to the landing. He was tired enough to feel irritation as he viewed the closed doors surrounding him with their unanswering blankness and worried enough to hope she had not done anything foolish because of him.

As his mind ran through the many places and circumstances he had found her in the past, he checked his own room on the chance that she might have wandered in there. Not expecting to be so lucky as to find her the first place he looked, he was not surprised to find his room empty.

He could hear the chiming of the parlor clock as it announced the late hour and muttered a curse under his breath. The task of checking all the other rooms like a peeping Tom was not what he wanted to do at that time of night.

His hand was on Leif's doorknob, about to open the door, when a sound from downstairs halted him. All his senses came alert as he recognized the sound of the hammer being pulled back on a gun.

He moved to the edge of the stairs and peered into the darkness below, straining his eyes and ears to try to pinpoint the sound. Time was meaningless as he stood immobile and listened.

The rustle of material sliding across the floor told him that Dee was downstairs. Adding that to the first sound he'd heard made him start down the stairs to the main floor.

The sound of a door opening and closing made him move faster. The sound had come from the dining room and he moved in that direction, pausing at the entrance of the room to listen for the sound of movement.

Hearing none, he moved near the door to the kitchen. He stopped cold as the door opened and the barrel of a gun pointed straight at his chest as a voice said coldly, "That is as far as you go."

"Put the gun down, Dee," Sven said as calmly as he could. He did not want to startle her awake, causing her to pull the trigger.

"Sven? You almost scared me to death!" was her unexpected reply.

"I what?" he said as it dawned on him that she was wide awake. "Why are you wandering around at this time of night with a gun?"

Dee lowered the gun barrel and moved through the doorway to one of the chairs in the dining room. She leaned against it as she replied in a shaky voice, "I could have shot you!"

Taking the gun from her nerveless hand, he said, "I know. Now tell me why?"

Dee strained to see his face in the darkened room. Failing to see more than his outline, she shivered and said, "I was in bed and couldn't sleep. I came down to get a glass of water and heard someone moving near the front of the house. I was sure everyone else had gone to bed and thought it was a prowler."

Sven interrupted her, saying, "That's when you picked up the gun?"

She nodded, then remembering he couldn't see her in the dark, replied, "I heard slow, sneaky footsteps on the stairs and took the gun from the entryway."

"What you heard was me trying to haul my tired body to bed," Sven told her. "Why did you come back to the kitchen?"

She turned and faced him, trying to see his expression. She couldn't tell from the sound of his voice if he was mad at her or not, and not knowing bothered her. "I thought I heard another noise and went to check on Bert," she answered him dispiritedly.

"Let's go to bed. I think we both have had enough excitement for one day." He put his arm around her and drew her to him in a comforting embrace.

Dee found herself burrowing closer to him as tears ran down her cheeks and she choked, "I'm sorry."

He enfolded her shaking form in his arms. "So am I. I didn't mean to frighten you."

The comforting warmth of Sven's arms as he held her made Dee realize that this was where she wanted to always be. She never wanted to leave him. He was too important to her life; how and when he had become so she could not say. But the thought of nearly shooting him made her face what she had been avoiding for days: she loved him.

After she had calmed down, Sven escorted her back to her room and left her at her door with a soft kiss on her forehead. She went into her room and gazed down at the cold, empty bed and knew she could not face its lonely isolation. She moved to the window and stared out at the night sky with her arms wrapped around her chest to hold back the urge to cry.

Sven tossed and turned, finding sleep an elusive thing even as tired as he was. His mind kept returning to how he had felt when Dee had sought comfort in his arms. He hadn't wanted to let her go. His feelings had been crystallizing into something he never thought he would feel for a woman. He knew now that he loved her.

Frustration flowed over him as he wrestled with his thoughts. After this afternoon, the chances of her ever loving him were slim. What reason could make her love him, now that he had rejected her so cruelly? He knew he had only done what he felt was right at the time, but Dee saw it as a refusal to accept what she had so lovingly offered him. Pounding the pillows, he tried to force her from his thoughts and sleep.

Dee made a painful decision as she stared out at the

stars through silent tears. She had to speak to Sven, she had to tell him how she felt. After that she would leave Montana; she knew she could not bear to be around the man she loved when he did not love her.

Throwing the covers off, Sven rose from his bed and walked to the door. There was no way he was going to get any rest until he spoke with Dee. He had to make her understand.

Opening his door, he was shocked to see her standing there with her hand up ready to knock. She opened her hand and put it to her heart, as surprised to see him as he was to see her.

She bit her lip nervously before saying, "Can we talk?"

Sven moved back from the door and let her enter the room as he replied, "I think we better."

Chapter Sixteen

DAWN WAS CRESTING THE HORIZON AS SVEN WOKE. HE looked down at the curly head nestled against his chest. Dee had not moved away from him even in her sleep. He smiled to himself. He liked the feel of her cuddled next to him in the crisp morning air. He gently kissed the top of her head and whispered, "I love you."

She snuggled closer to him in her sleep as though she had heard him. He could feel the soft contours of her body through the thinness of her nightdress. He slowly caressed her back with his hand as he remembered what they had said to each other only a few hours earlier.

Dee had come into his room and stood facing him, her face a ghostly white. She spoke barely above a whisper and he had to strain to hear what she said. She told him that she was leaving Montana but could not go until she had told him something that he might not want to hear. She had paused and looked at him with tears glistening in her eyes and said, "I love you, Sven."

He could not trust himself to speak at first he was so overcome with his love for her. She had misunderstood his silence and started to leave, saying, "I know you don't love me. That's why I have decided to leave. I—"

He had found his voice and stopped her from saying any more. "No."

She had become confused and repeated, "No?"

He had moved closer to her and stopped as she

started to back away from him. "No, you aren't going anywhere."

"I'm not?" she barely whispered.

"I love you too much to lose you now," he'd told her.

"But this afternoon . . . ?" she stammered.

"This afternoon I did not trust myself not to make love to you."

"Oh," she whispered softly as she looked at him. "Sven? Will you hold me?"

He had held his arms out to her and she had come to him with a sigh. He drew her close to him as she rested her head on his shoulder. He asked her, "Are you sure?"

"Yes," had come her soft reply.

Dee moved her head and her breath stirred the golden mat of hair on his chest, sending a tingle of sensation through him. She had stayed in his arms for the rest of the night.

As Sven caressed her back, she stirred again, bringing her bare silken thighs against his strong legs. Her nightdress had drifted upward during the night and little of it remained between them.

Slowly waking, her small hand moved across his flat stomach. He drew his breath in sharply as he felt his desire for her grow.

Dee was floating on a cloud of warm sensation. She felt a sensuous glow as a hand moved slowly over her back. She wondered fuzzily if she could be dreaming. Raising her head slightly, she opened her eyes and saw Sven. If she was dreaming, she never wanted to wake up.

He lowered his lips to hers and gently caressed them with a soft kiss. She returned his kiss, reveling in her newfound love.

His lips moved across her cheek and over her eyes before returning to her lips. Her entire body felt alive

with his touch as a growing ache filled her and a soft
moan sprang from her lips.

He held her so he could trail kisses over her neck and
throat. His strong hands burned her skin through the
material of her nightdress as he moved her slightly
away from him and undid the ribbons at her throat with
his teeth. She felt her breasts swell against his muscular
chest and a gasp of pleasure escaped her as his warm
breath floated over them as he nuzzled at the opening
of her gown. She shivered, lost in a world of feeling as
he lifted her and pressed his lips to the valley between
her breasts. Her hands moved of their own accord to
brace themselves on his wide shoulders, her fingers
curving to support her weight.

Sven's hands released their grip on her upper arms
and, reaching down, found the hem of her nightdress.
He stared into her eyes as he drew the gown up and her
bare skin lay next to his.

Dee had never felt anything like this. She offered no
resistance as Sven pulled her gown the rest of the way
off and tossed it out of sight. The feeling of their bodies
touching one another sent waves of delight coursing
through her veins. Sven's exploring kisses traced a path
of fire across her skin.

Her breath caught in her throat as he teased the rosy
tip of her breast with gentle kisses. Her arms began to
shake as they tried to hold her weight. Turning, Sven
moved her to his side, where he could stroke the curve
of her hip as he took possession of her lips, kissing her
slowly and tenderly. She felt drugged with emotion as
his kisses deepened and he molded her to his side. He
buried his head in her hair and his lips found the
sensitive chord in her neck.

Shudders of delight coursed through her again and
she trembled in his arms as his hand moved sensuously

over her and he parted her thighs with a gentle touch. She barely felt the pain of her maidenhood surrendering to his presence as wave after wave of pleasure carried her higher and higher until she cried out his name and was engulfed in a cloud of pure joy that carried both of them to fulfillment.

As their breathing quieted and they rested in each other's arms, Sven gazed down at her with a look of love in his eyes that deepened as he said softly, "Good morning, Mrs. Thorsen."

Secure in his love, she smiled shyly, saying, "Do you wake up like this every morning?"

Sven laughed. "I might from now on." He looked beyond her to the window and saw that it was still very early. Smiling down at her, he said, "We still have some time to sleep, little one."

The security of his embrace and the languor of her senses lulled her and she drifted into sleep.

Kat moved back to her room and closed the door. She had wakened early and, unable to sleep, had started worrying about Dee. She had been so unlike herself at dinner the night before. Wanting to reassure herself that Dee was all right, Kat had quietly left her room and gone to Dee's. Finding her room empty, she had become frightened and hurried to Sven's door to wake him and tell him Dee was gone.

Reaching Sven's door, she stopped suddenly, as she could hear the murmur of voices inside the room. One of the voices was Sven's and the other was Dee's. Kat sat on her bed and prayed that Dee knew what she was doing.

It was late when Sven and Dee joined the others at breakfast. Sven exchanged a secret look of reassurance with Dee as he seated her at the table. She had been nervous about facing everyone, knowing that they had probably guessed why they were so late in coming down.

Sven seated himself and was greeted by Leif, who said, "We were about to send out search parties. Breakfast is almost over and we were wondering if you had decided to skip it this morning."

"Did you leave us anything to eat?" Sven asked as he looked around the table.

"Dee?" Kat looked at her anxiously. "Are you all right?"

"I'm fine." Dee laughed nervously as she grabbed Sven's hand under cover of the tablecloth. "I slept in like Leif suggested and came close to missing the entire day."

Eric caught the twinkle in Sven's eye as Dee answered Kat and contemplated his brother closely. Sven had not risen to Leif's banter and appeared more intent on watching Dee than eating. What was going on with those two? Eric's contemplation was noticed by Sven, who returned his look boldly. Lowering his eyes to his plate, Eric finished his meal, determined to speak with Sven the first chance he had.

Sven had seen Eric's speculative look drift from Dee to him and back and had purposely stared him down to keep him from asking any questions that might embarrass Dee.

Leif smiled inwardly. He knew the real reason Sven and Dee had been late joining them. He had seen Dee's partially open door when he had risen and closed it before coming downstairs. As far as he was concerned, he wished Sven and Dee all the best in the world and hoped that the same might prove true for Eric and Kat.

He covered his thoughts by teasing Bert. "I do believe that you are without a doubt the best cook in the state of Montana."

Bert huffed at him, "I don't know how much of a compliment that is. You will eat almost anything."

After breakfast, Kat and Dee went with Bert to clean the kitchen and do the dishes. Eric disappeared into his office and Sven went out back to the woodpile to chop firewood. Leif followed him.

Going out back, Leif saw Sven rolling up the sleeves of his blue work shirt and pick up the axe. Taking a seat nearby, Leif watched as Sven made short work of some logs, cutting them as though they were made of butter.

Sven paused in his labors and rested on the long handle of his axe, asking, "You got a problem, Leif?"

"That depends," Leif replied cryptically.

"On what?" Sven asked as he stacked the cut logs.

"Do you love her?"

Sven did not pretend that he didn't know what Leif was talking about and answered him, "Yes."

Rising from his position, Leif smiled. "Then there's no problem."

Sven smiled in return as Leif casually walked back inside and could be heard teasing the women as they worked.

The morning had turned into afternoon when the sound of a rider approaching brought the men out onto the porch.

It was Ben from the rail camp. He had ridden over to tell them that the repairs to the line should be finished by nightfall and to ask for further orders.

Eric thought a few moments and then, turning, he called into the lodge. "Kat? Would you mind coming out here a moment?"

She rose from the chair in his office and moved out onto the porch. "What is it, Eric? Has there been more trouble?" she asked as she saw Ben still astride his horse.

"No. Ben came by to tell us the repairs are almost

complete," Eric told her. "What I called you for was to see what you thought our next move should be?"

Kat moved down the stairs and stood by him, trying to hide her surprise at his asking for her opinion. "What do you think?" she asked, hoping to get some idea of what he had in mind.

"I thought we could split the crew and send half the men back to work on the spur line to the mill and leave the other half to guard the mainline. What do you think?" Eric said evenly.

Kat thought about what he suggested and asked, "Will doing it that way leave enough men to do either job efficiently?"

"It should," Eric nodded. "We have that deadline to meet on the completion of the spur line and we can't leave the mainline unguarded. It would be an open invitation for trouble if we did."

"I'll be glad when we find out who is behind all this trouble," Kat said half to herself. "That sounds like the best way for us to go," she added, loud enough for Eric to hear her.

Eric turned to the waiting horseman. "You heard the lady, Ben. Split the crew and send half to the spur line and arrange guard schedules for the rest."

Ben nodded that he'd heard and understood and headed back toward the rail camp.

Kat looked over at Eric before she started back inside and could not help saying, "I'm surprised that you asked me for my opinion."

"Why? You know as much about what has been going on around here as I do," Eric replied.

Kat found it hard to accept the change in their relationship. The change had started on the day they had spent hours together going over reports. Eric was nice to her. He no longer acted arrogant or superior.

She had discovered to her surprise that she liked this new side of his personality very much.

Eric smiled at her. "Do you have to go back inside? It's a beautiful day. The fresh air might do us both some good. We have been cooped up inside too long already these past few days. Why not take a break? We can go for a walk and clear the cobwebs."

Kat was torn. Part of her wanted to go with Eric and part of her was afraid to go. She knew the walk would do her good, but the thought of walking with Eric troubled her. He had been so much easier to deal with when he ordered and yelled at her. She had been justified in lashing back at him in defense. Now he was threatening her in an entirely different way and she could not lash out without exposing her true fears.

Eric saw the indecision in her face and held out his hand, saying, "Come on. Is it such a hard choice to make?"

Kat placed her hand in his and followed as he strolled slowly toward the trees. They walked together hand in hand down a path leading to a quiet glade. Kat's nervousness eased slightly as Eric appeared content to remain silent and enjoy their quiet stroll.

If only he would let go of her hand, she might be able to think more clearly. She could feel the strength that lay hidden in his grip and it sent odd feelings up her arm.

Her reaction to his holding her hand confused her, as did he. She stole a glance at him from the corner of her eye and thought, Why is he being so nice? What does he want from me? He must want something or why would he be so nice? Agitation swept over her as her thoughts went in circles. She pulled her hand from his and walked a few paces ahead. She did not like the way she was feeling.

Hadn't she learned at an early age to control her

thoughts and her actions as she watched others closely? She had always been in control of her life until she had met Eric. But could she trust him? Grandad and Dee were the only two people she had ever trusted completely. Everyone else had always wanted something from her and she had discovered painfully how they would use her if they could.

She was brought up short as a tight grasp on her arm halted her and Eric's voice warned, "Careful. You almost went off the path."

She looked at her surroundings. She had been so lost in thought she hadn't noticed how far they had come. She was at a bend in the path that bordered a thickly wooded area. If Eric had not stopped her, she could have been hurt had she fallen on the rugged terrain.

"Oh!" she gasped. "I wasn't watching where I was going."

Eric's hand held her arm still and he turned her to face him. "You were lost in thought." He looked about them. "These woods often have the same effect on me."

"They do?" she said in surprise.

He let go of her arm and motioned for her to continue around the bend of the path toward a small group of boulders. Once there, he made her wait as he checked the piles of rocks carefully before allowing her to rest on the natural seat of one of them.

Seeing her puzzled look, he explained, "I was checking for snakes. They like to sun themselves on rocks like these."

He sat next to her and Kat found she did not feel threatened as much by him as she had before. He was relaxed and untroubled as he leaned back and looked about them. His continued silence was something that Kat found oddly relaxing to her frayed nerves. She felt the tension flow out of her as she rested in the sun and relaxed her shoulders with a sigh.

"Feeling better?" Eric asked quietly.

"Yes, I am," she answered truthfully.

"Good," was his only comment.

Kat had no idea how much time had passed when Eric spoke again. "We should start back. They will be wondering where we are."

Kat stood up and found she had to stretch the laziness from her limbs. She had come very close to falling asleep where she sat, it was so peaceful.

Eric waited with an indulgent smile for Kat to shake her lethargy. Take all the time you need, he thought, I am in no hurry to leave here.

He had watched how the tenseness in Kat's eyes had cleared and the rigid way she held her body had softened to a natural posture. This new Kat with all her barriers down was one Eric enjoyed. If returning to the lodge meant that she would again don her shell of self-sufficient touch-me-not, Eric was prepared not to return at all. He was seeing the real Kat for the first time: carefree, fresh and beautiful as she twirled about letting the sunlight play across her upturned face.

He laughed with her as dizziness made her grab his arm for support and she quipped, "I think all this fresh air has gone to my head."

Eric hesitated before pulling her into his arms and kissing her smiling lips. He did not want another episode like the return from the rail camp, when she had run from him in panic. He held her gently and kept his kiss light and gentle, breaking it off as he felt her stiffen in surprise. He ignored her wide-eyed look of shock and said, "Fresh air has that effect on some people."

Kat's body was surprised by Eric's sudden kiss; her

mind was a wild mixture of surprise, pleasure and fear. She had no time to think clearly as Eric's gray eyes stared into hers, making clear thinking impossible.

"Why?" she murmured, meaning why had he kissed her like that.

Taking her hand in his, Eric headed back the way they had come, saying, "Why not?"

Kat could not answer him; she did not have an answer that made any sense.

Nearing the lodge, they saw a rider leaving and Sven standing at the foot of the porch with a hard look on his face.

They walked over to him and Eric asked, "What now?"

Kat could feel all her old anxiety flood over her, erasing the peace she had found in the woods and masking the turmoil of Eric's kiss. She unconsciously tightened her hold on his hand.

He looked over at her and saw the lines of strain reappearing in the way she held her body and cursed under his breath.

Sven saw the way Kat held onto Eric's hand and filed this observation for future reference. Now he had things of more importance on his mind. "That was a wire from your grandfather, Kat. He is leaving today from New York and should arrive here by the end of the week."

Her grandfather was coming! The news was something she had been expecting, but she felt none of the joy she thought she would when it did. "I will go and tell Dee," was all she could say as she brushed past Sven and went inside.

The brothers watched as she disappeared and Eric said, "There is more, isn't there?"

"Yes," Sven nodded. "Karl sent word that there are rumors floating around town that someone is planning on making certain that Patrick Gwyn never makes it this far."

"Who?" Eric demanded.

"Karl could not find that out," Sven said. "You know how rumors spread, and their source is never uncovered."

"What now?" Eric asked.

"I've sent word to Ben at the camp to be on the alert," Sven told him as they started back inside.

Eric's expression was grim as he asked, "Do you think the trouble will come from there?"

"I don't know," Sven shook his head. "Like most rumors, these were not specific."

"I wouldn't say anything to Kat," Eric warned as they neared the parlor.

"I had no intention of doing so." Sven gave him an icy look.

"Is it true? Is Kat's grandfather on his way here?" Dee asked as she joined them, placing a hand on Sven's arm.

"Yes." Sven's face softened as he looked at her.

"That means he will be here soon," Dee said to no one in particular as she squeezed Sven's arm nervously. She did not want to go back to New York unless Sven went with her. She wanted her family to meet the man she loved and had married. But she was afraid that Patrick Gwyn's coming to Montana could cause problems; she was not ready for anything like that. She wanted some time with Sven and their newfound love before the world tried to pull them apart.

Sven covered her hand with his and tried to calm the agitation he felt in her. "Don't worry, little one. Everything will be fine."

"I hope you are right," she answered him as they moved to the sofa.

Chapter Seventeen

BERT WAS DRYING THE MORNING'S DISHES AS KAT WASHED them. Dee could see there was nothing for her to do here. Picking up the garden basket, she said, "Bert, I'll go pick some vegetables for tonight if you want me to."

Bert smiled over at her. "Why don't you, Dee. I'll let you decide what we are having tonight. Pick whatever is ready."

Dee was pleased that Bert trusted her judgment enough to know she would harvest only the ripe vegetables. She had learned a lot since her first try in the garden; now she knew better than to pick the cabbage one leaf at a time. Moving out onto the back porch, she saw Sven and Eric. She called out, "I'm off to the garden" as she held up the empty basket.

Eric looked at her with a smile and Sven opened the porch door for her. She wondered what she had interrupted. They had been in deep conversation when she approached but stopped talking the minute they saw her. What was going on?

The porch door closed behind her and her curiosity flared even higher as she heard the rumble of their voices resume. I'll have to speak with Kat and see if she knows what is going on, she thought as she picked some of the vegetables. I hope she knows, was her final thought as Leif breezed around the corner of the house and moved to join her.

"What are we having?" he asked as he peered into

the basket she carried on her arm. "Carrots and squash, hmm," he said as he slyly snatched a fresh carrot from the basket and, rubbing the excess soil off on his pants leg, bit into it.

"Hey!" Dee swatted his arm. "Stop that!" She watched him devour his plunder. "There won't be enough to cook if you insist on eating them now."

She could not help but laugh at the unrepentant grin on his face. "I would ask you to hold the basket for me while I harvest, but"—she paused, shaking her head at him with an expression of mock rebuke on her face—"that would put too much temptation in your way."

Leif put his hand to his chest in surprise. "Would I do something like that?"

Eyeing him and his feigned look of innocence, Dee replied, "Yes, you would." She tugged on an especially stubborn carrot that released its hold on the ground and almost upended her in the dirt.

Leif whisked the basket from her arm, smiling. "I promise I'll behave myself."

With his aid it did go faster, and Dee had picked more than enough in a matter of minutes. Placing the last of her selections in the basket, Dee brushed her hands together and surveyed her harvest. "That is enough," she commented with a twinkle in her eye.

She reached into the basket and plucked a fat carrot from the hoard of vegetables. Holding it out to Leif, she smiled. "Sir, your payment for services rendered."

He handed her the basket and accepted the carrot, saying, "How generous of you, madame."

"Generosity has nothing to do with it. Prudence tells me that if I wish to recover the fruits of my labor, I would be wise to offer a small bribe to their captor," Dee said with a laugh as she headed toward the house.

Eric and Sven had viewed the byplay between Dee and their brother. Nodding to Dee as she passed them on her way to the kitchen, Eric commented, "Our country life-style seems to agree with her."

Sven watched his wife disappear into the kitchen and replied, "It is still new to her. The glow has not faded from the rose."

"You talk as though you expect it to," Eric said with a frown.

"I am hoping it doesn't," Sven replied. "But I can't say I will be surprised if it does."

"I think you are selling her short," Eric told him.

"Dee is used to a life filled with beautiful people, parties and the socially elite," Sven explained. "Our world and hers could not be more different."

"Has she ever complained? Does she expect people to wait on her? Has she had attacks of homesickness?" Eric demanded, not liking the way Sven was talking.

"Why, I think you like her!" Sven said in surprise.

"What's wrong with that? She is married to my brother," Eric defended. "Don't create problems for yourself where none exist, Sven."

Leif came in on the last of their conversation and furrowed his brow as he heard Eric defending Dee to Sven. "I have the feeling I've missed something," he told them. "Why all the serious faces?"

Seeing him for the first time, Eric frowned. "No reason. I am trying to tell Sven what a fool he is, that's all." With this Eric walked into the house, leaving Leif alone with Sven.

"What did he mean by that?" Leif asked Sven.

"Nothing," Sven said. "If anything comes up, I'll be in the office doing paperwork."

Leif was left standing alone, no wiser than before he'd started asking his questions. Brothers, he thought; who can figure them?

Bert went out onto the porch and saw him standing

there. "So, you have nothing better to do than stand around?"

Dee could hear Bert and Leif talking on the back porch as she washed the vegetables she had picked. Finishing, she dried her hands and hung the towel made from flour sacking on its hook, thinking, I wonder what else Bert has for me to do? She walked over to the doorway leading to the back porch and saw Leif nod his head at something Bert said to him.

"Bert? Pardon me, but is there anything else you would like me to do?" Dee asked.

"Ahh! You are just the person I wanted to see." Leif grinned. "I was telling Bert what a great team we made harvesting her vegetables and she has another job for us."

"Did Leif tell you that it took bribery on my part to force him to leave any vegetables for the rest of us?" Dee asked Bert with a chuckle.

"No, he didn't," Bert returned. "But I know how he is and I am not surprised." She eyed Leif with a twinkle. "That is one of the reasons I suggested he take you with him. Maybe that way he won't stuff himself completely."

"Take me where with him?" Dee asked curiously. "And stuff himself with what? I don't understand."

"Berries," Leif answered her, licking his lips. "Bert wants us to pick some berries for her." Looking at Bert, he said, "I promise to restrain myself and not eat everything I pick."

"See that you do," Bert warned him. "Dee, keep an eye on him to see he keeps his word."

"Yes, ma'am," Dee laughed.

"Help! They are ganging up on me!" Leif threw his hands up in defense.

"Go on with you!" Bert chuckled at his antics.

"Dee. Go and change into something you won't mind getting stained and dirty and meet me back here in half an hour. I'll gather the gear we will need," Leif ordered quickly.

"On my way." Dee laughed as she rushed upstairs to change.

Right on time, she descended the stairs ready to leave. She had tried to talk Kat into going with them, but Kat had demurred, saying she wanted to finish some mending.

Returning to the back porch, Dee saw Eric bending over some pails near the back steps. Joining him, she saw gloves and rope next to the pails and asked, "Is this the gear we'll need?"

He straightened at hearing her voice. "We?"

"Leif and I," Dee answered as she looked around, trying to locate him.

"I was wondering," Eric said. "I came out and saw this stuff and knew someone was planning on picking berries."

"Where is he?" Dee muttered, anxious to start.

Eric heard her and shrugged. "Who knows? He probably forgot something and went to get it."

"What's holding you up?" Bert called from the back porch.

"Leif," Dee called back. "I can't find him."

Bert snorted. "Time's wasting. Eric, you and Dee go. I can't wait for Leif to show up; I need those berries."

"Do you mind?" Eric asked Dee.

"Why should I?" Dee responded. "Shall we go?"

Eric lifted the pails and Dee gathered the rope and gloves and they headed down the path behind the barn.

An hour and a half later, Dee was hot, tired and stuffed. She had not been able to resist the sweet-looking berries and had almost gorged herself on them as she picked. She looked over at Eric and saw his face showed evidence of having enjoyed the berries as much as she had. She laughed. "Poor Leif!"

Eric looked up from placing a handful of berries in his pail. "Why do you say that?"

Dee reached into the thorny vine, glad that she was wearing gloves, and plucked a group of fat, juicy berries as she replied, "Bert had been warning him not to eat everything he picked. I think we have come close to doing that ourselves."

Eric smiled. "It's his own fault for not showing up when it was time to leave."

A loud rustling came through the thicket nearby and Dee jumped. "What is that?"

Eric listened for a few seconds and replied, "We are not the only ones berry-picking today." He bent and lifted the full buckets by his side and carried them over to where Dee stood with a perplexed look on her face. "It sounds like we are sharing our berry patch with a bear," Eric explained.

"A bear!" Dee gasped. "What if he sees us?"

"Hey, it's okay. As long as we keep our distance there's plenty of berries to share," Eric told her.

Dee swallowed nervously. "If you say so." But she hoped he knew what he was doing. She had seen bears only at the zoo or at the circus and had no desire to meet one face to face.

The rustling grew louder and Dee could hear the bear's movements as he foraged closer. "I don't think our friend wants to share," she told Eric in a tight voice.

"You might be right," he agreed. "Let's move farther that way." He pointed in the opposite direction from the rustling noises.

Dee didn't need to be told twice. Picking up her buckets, she hurried down the path with Eric right behind her. The more distance she could put between her and their unexpected company the better she would feel.

A sudden loud crashing from behind them and Eric's yell of "Run!" added wings to Dee's feet.

She careened down the path, her buckets banging against her legs. Rounding a corner, she didn't see a protruding root sticking up from the ground and caught her foot on it to tumble off the side of the path and down an embankment, coming to a halt in a pile of pine needles at the base of a group of trees. Her buckets came rolling down the hill after her, spilling some of their contents along the way.

Frightened and trying to catch her breath, she yelled back up at Eric, "Watch out for the—"

But her warning came too late and she watched helplessly as she saw him come tumbling down the embankment to a stop a short distance from her. Her hand went up to her mouth to stifle a cry. She crawled over to where he lay to see if he was hurt.

His clothes were torn and there was a scratch on the side of his face. Dee tried to control her panicked breathing and gasped, "Eric?"

He put his hand against her lips and his eyes flew back up the embankment. The sounds of their pursuer could still be heard, but they were fading into the distance as the bear lost their trail.

"Are you hurt?" Eric asked her as he removed his hand from her lips.

Dee shook her head. "Only shaken up. What about you?"

Eric straightened into a sitting position. "I'll be able to answer that question better in a minute or two."

"I'm so embarrassed!" Dee said.

"Embarrassed? Why?" Eric said as he attempted to rise to his feet.

"If I had been watching where I was going . . ." Her voice trailed off.

"Hey, I tripped, too, remember?" Eric tried to take a step and winced in pain. "I must have wrenched my knee."

"Can you make it back to the lodge?" Dee asked worriedly.

"As long as I don't have to run," Eric quipped, trying to make light of his injury.

Dee looked around them and groaned. "Oh, dear! What is Bert going to say? Most of my berries spilled when I fell."

"Bert will say we are both clumsy," Eric told her. "Let's salvage as many berries as we can and head home."

They gathered their pails and scooped what berries they could find in good condition back into them. Having done that they slowly made their way back toward the lodge.

It was close to suppertime when they came in view of the lodge. Dee was relieved to see it. She had begun to wonder if they would make it back before nightfall. Eric's knee was bothering him, but he had insisted on carrying his pails of berries anyway.

Dee felt sore all over; her dress, not one of her best to begin with, was ruined and her hair was a tangled mess. What she wanted was a hot bath and bed.

Leif was the first to see Dee and Eric as they neared the yard. He was still angry that they had gone without him and was splitting logs to work off his feelings. But seeing the disheveled state of Dee and the smile on Eric's face as he said something to her made Leif see red. He dropped the axe and ran over to where they were.

"Hi, Leif," Dee greeted him with a weak smile. "We took a tumble."

Leif turned an angry look on his brother as he said, "Why you . . ."

Dee set her pails down and flexed her fingers as she quickly said, "Leif! It was an accident!"

Eric set his own pails down and tried to hurriedly explain to the angry Leif, "It's not the kind of tumble you're thinking, Leif."

"If it's not, then how do you know what I'm thinking?" Leif growled as he bent down and charged Eric in the middle, causing him to sprawl in the dirt.

"Leif!" Dee exclaimed. "No!"

Eric picked himself up and wrapped his arms around Leif in a bear hug, saying, "Calm down and listen to me. We were—" But his knee refused to hold him up and they both fell to the dirt with Leif on top of him.

"Stop it!" Dee cried.

Hearing Dee's cry, Sven came out the back door. Seeing his brothers wrestling in the dirt, he muttered a curse and marched over to where they were. Bending down, he grabbed them by their collars and jerked them upright. "What the hell is going on here?" he bellowed at them.

Eric tried to maintain his unsteady balance and began to reply, when Leif's flailing about brought his boot in contact with Sven's leg and Sven dropped them both heavily to the ground as he grabbed his shin in pain.

Trying to continue his pummeling of Eric, Leif squirmed about in the dirt as he reached for him. His movements caused Sven to overbalance and come crashing down on top of him. Leif let out a yell of pain that was heard in the house by Kat and Bert.

Kat rushed outside to stand by Dee as she saw what was happening. She put her arm around Dee's shoulders and they watched helplessly.

There was a muddle of flailing arms and legs and

bodies with dust billowing around everything. Grunts and groans came from the pile, but neither girl could tell which brother was making all the noise.

Kat found herself pushed aside as Bert made her way to where the brothers were thrashing about in the dirt. She raised the broom she carried with her and began to bring it down on them, bouncing it off Sven's head, Eric's bottom and Leif's legs with unerring accuracy. Bert punctuated her blows with commands for them to stop fighting.

The sound of Bert's scolding coupled with Sven's swearing, Leif's howling and Eric's moans. Kat looked at Dee and saw that her former fright had changed to amusement. It was a funny sight to see.

Sven's inarticulate swearing slowly turned into grumblings and Leif's howling subsided into gasps for air, while Eric's moans stopped altogether as they lay exhausted in the dirt.

Dee looked over at Eric and said with a laugh in her voice, "I think you would have been safer facing the bear."

"Bear?" Leif gasped.

"What?" Sven growled.

Eric started laughing and could not answer either of them. Slowly rising to his feet, he looked over at Dee and laughed even harder.

Bert stepped back and viewed them all with disgust. "I don't want to know what started all this. I probably wouldn't believe a word any of you said." Having said this, she turned and headed back to the house, pausing at the back door to add, "Supper in twenty minutes."

Kat looked at Dee. "What's this about a bear?"

Dee laughed. "I'll tell you while I clean up."

Sven saw how Eric was limping as he made his way toward the back porch and called, "You had better wrap that leg of yours."

Leif brushed as much dirt off his pants as he could and said, "I don't know what to say. I guess I jumped to the wrong conclusion when Dee said she and Eric had taken a tumble."

Sven stared down at him, shaking his head. "Then you jumped Eric?"

"Yeah," Leif admitted, shamefaced.

The two followed Kat and Dee to the back door and Sven smiled at Leif. "You forgot something a lawyer should never forget."

"What?" Leif asked in surprise.

"Innocent until proven guilty," Sven replied as he entered the house.

Kat had heard Dee's story as she cleaned up and then left her to finish changing. She was heading toward the parlor when she heard a muffled curse from Eric's office. She went to the partially open door to investigate and saw a shirtless Eric trying without much success to pull his pants leg up over his swollen knee.

Without thinking why she was doing it, Kat entered the room and picked up a pair of scissors lying on the table, saying, "You look as though you could use some help."

Eric looked up at her, startled to hear her voice.

Kat tried to ignore the way the light danced off the golden hairs on Eric's chest and bending down, she examined his pants leg. "Your knee is too swollen. I'll have to cut your pants," she said as she slid the scissors into position and snipped the material.

The tightening of his calf muscle as she neared his knee sent a strange tremor through her. She tried to cover her reaction by saying, "Am I hurting you?"

When he did not answer, she looked up at him and was rocked by the look of desire in his eyes. She quickly finished cutting his pants leg open and backed away. She felt uneasy at his continued silence and laid the scissors on the table before her trembling hands dropped them on the floor.

"Thank you." Eric's voice flowed over her, warmly caressing her.

Kat mentally shook herself to fend off the feelings his voice aroused. "Is there anything else I can do?" she asked, half praying he would say no.

"If you will go into the cabinet over there, you will find some bandage. I'll need it to wrap my knee," he replied.

She found the bandage and held it out to him. He shook his head slowly. "I'm not at the right angle to wrap it correctly. I'm afraid you will have to wrap it for me."

Kat took a small step backward. "But I don't know how."

"I'll tell you what to do." Eric destroyed her excuse.

Kat moved nearer to him and bent down where she could reach his knee as he sat in the chair by his desk. "What do I do first?"

Eric directed her in how to place the bandage and wrap it around his leg to give his knee the best possible support. She followed his instructions in silence, her touch as light as a feather.

Eric had a hard time not reaching out and caressing her hair as she bent over him working. Her nearness made his pulse quicken and her fragrance tickled his nose as she moved. Finishing, she stepped back and asked, "Is that all right?"

His voice was ragged to his ears as he answered, "Fine. Thank you, Kat."

They stared at each other wordlessly. He had made up his mind to kiss her when she quickly stammered,

"If that's all, I'll leave you to tend the scratch on your face" and hurriedly fled from the room.

Eric knew why she had fled, but it was no comfort to him. He had wanted to take her in his arms and feel her pressed against him as he kissed her. The time will come when you won't escape me so easily, Kat Thorsen, he thought as he rose from the chair.

Chapter Eighteen

LAUGHTER CAME EASILY THAT NIGHT AS THEY FEASTED ON fresh berries and cream for dessert. Bert grumblingly told them that she was no miracle worker and they would have to wait if they expected berry pie.

Dee explained the encounter that she and Eric had had with the apparent boss of the berry patch. Her colorful description of tumbling down the hillside evoked gales of laughter from her listeners, all but Kat.

Kat tried to join in the merriment, but her heart wasn't in it. She was too aware of Eric as he sat nearby, his every move, expression, even inflection when he spoke. Having run from his office, she was still running, but this time from her own feelings.

She had known that Eric was going to kiss her and it had not frightened her. What had frightened her was the realization that she had wanted him to kiss her. Her mind had shouted no, but her emotions were insisting yes. If she had not fled as she had, she would have lost the control she had always prized. There had never been a situation that she could not cope with before that look in Eric's face had destroyed her reason. Now she did not know what to do, she was a mass of conflicting emotions.

Eric's warm laugh as he accepted Leif's embarrassed apology drew her eyes to his face. His sensuous mouth held her attention and a warm feeling of awareness tingled over her.

Thankful when the meal was finished and she could politely excuse herself, Kat went out onto the front porch, hoping the fresh air would help her think more clearly. She knew it would be foolish to join the others in the parlor. She needed time alone, to think.

She stood near the porch railing and breathed deeply of the pine-scented night air. The once-feared isolation was a balm to her tortured thoughts. Why couldn't she think straight? Why had she wanted Eric to kiss her?

She folded her arms protectively in front of her as the gentle night breeze brushed her cheek. Why did she feel so empty inside?

She was so lost in her thoughts that she didn't hear the creak of a board as Eric limped near her.

Seeing her staring out into the velvet blackness, her arms hugging her, Eric knew he had to hold her. He moved behind her, slipped his arms around her and drew her back against his chest, saying, "Are you cold?"

Kat jumped, startled at the feel of his warm breath on her ear and his strong arms holding her close. She tried to pull away, but he tightened his hold, murmuring, "Relax. You're too tense."

She could not speak; her voice stuck in her throat as his breath caressed her neck. She leaned against him and welcomed the strength of his hard chest. Part of her warned that she was asking for trouble, but she ignored the warning and let the feeling of his arms about her ease the emptiness inside her.

They stood unspeaking and listened to the night sounds around them. Eric held her close to him and slowly she relaxed against him. He could feel the beating of her heart against his arm as it rested under her breast. It was rapid and uneven, as was her breathing. He lowered his head and tenderly kissed the side of her neck. She held her breath in surprise, exhaling slowly as he trailed soft kisses up to her ear. She moved her head slightly and his lips found the sensitive hollow behind her ear.

Kat felt on fire. Eric was attacking her senses, his kisses making it impossible to think. She moved her arms over his as he held her. His hand cupped her breast as he nuzzled her neck, and a soft moan escaped her lips as she felt her breast swell in response to his touch.

Turning her in his arms, Eric's lips sought hers and claimed them. She raised her arms and clasped them around his neck as his kiss deepened and awoke feelings in her she had never felt before. She arched her back, molding herself against his length. Her breasts tingled through the thinness of her dress as they were crushed against his muscular chest.

Eric's hands caressed her back, moving down to draw her even closer to him. He could feel her response as she flowed against him. Her hands moved up the back of his neck and entwined in his hair. He feathered kisses over her eyes and cheeks, his senses alive with the feel of her.

Kat could not get enough of his kisses and moaned again as he reclaimed her lips, pressing them open and exploring the sweetness within. A feeling of fire burned in her loins and spread through her. He broke off the kiss to trail fire down her throat and across the tops of her breasts as they swelled above her low neckline. He lowered his head and took the tip of one between his lips, the silk of her dress adding to the stimulation as he teased. She pulled his shirt free of his pants and ran her hands under it, across the skin of his back. A sound came from his throat and he pulled her tightly against his hips, his desire for her increasing.

Kat knew she should pull away, make him stop, but she couldn't. She no longer had control. This is what she had wanted, what she had craved. Eric had replaced her feeling of emptiness with a new feeling. A feeling that gave birth to another aching emptiness deep inside her. An emptiness she knew only he could take away.

"Eric?" came Leif's voice from inside the entryway. "Did you want coffee?"

Kat swayed against him at the sound of Leif's voice. Eric grabbed her to keep from falling as his injured knee threatened to give way under him. His breathing was ragged and his voice hoarse as he called back to Leif, "Sounds good. We'll be in in a minute."

Kat buried her head against his chest, unable to look at him. She was overcome with embarrassment at her actions. He must think her a wanton.

Eric raised her head slowly with a hand on her chin and stared into her eyes. She lowered hers in shame and he kissed her eyelids softly, saying, "Don't. You've nothing to be ashamed of. I took advantage of you."

She opened her mouth to protest that she was as much to blame for what had happened as he was, but he silenced her with a finger to her lips and a shake of his head.

A trembling spread through her and unbidden tears coursed from her eyes. Eric inhaled sharply at seeing them and gently kissed them away, whispering, "No tears, my love."

"Eric, are you coming?" Leif called again. "Your coffee's getting cold."

"Yes. Be right there," Eric answered him as he gazed down at Kat.

"I can't go in there," Kat whispered tremulously, too disturbed to face anyone else.

"I'll tell them you were tired." Eric smiled at her. He kept her close to his side as they went back into the house. Stopping at the foot of the stairs, he placed one last kiss on her brow and stood watching her as she went up to her room.

Closing the door to her bedroom, Kat was still shaken. Eric had called her his love. Did he love her? Or was it only words of comfort he had spoken?

Climbing into bed, she faced the question she had been avoiding all night. Did she love Eric? She didn't know. She knew she desired his kisses. But was it because she loved him? Sleep was elusive and dawn was breaking as she fought for the answer.

Kat surveyed the bedroom and smoothed the quilt on Leif's bed. She had changed the sheets and straightened everything. She was glad to have work to keep her busy. With Bert laid up with her arthritis, it meant that she and Dee were responsible for seeing things were done.

Bending down, she gathered the dirty clothes and linen she had piled by the door. Carrying them to the head of the stairs, she saw that the others she had left there were gone. Dee must have carted them down to add to the other laundry.

She tried to lose herself in her work, not wanting to think about the night before. But her traitorous body kept reminding her, as she could still feel Eric's lips on hers.

Piling the things Dee had dropped along her way onto what she was already carrying, Kat awkwardly made her way through the door and joined Dee on the back porch. Dropping her bundle and wiping her brow with the back of her hand, she said, "How does Bert manage this by herself?"

"Someone has to do it," Dee replied as she began sorting things into different piles as Bert had instructed them.

Kat bent down and helped her, saying, "Do we have everything we need?"

Dee thought a moment and nodded. "I double and triple checked everything Bert said. I guess we are as ready as we will ever be."

Dee moved out back and began to fill a galvanized washtub with hot water they had heated on the stove. "Have you seen any of the men this morning?" she asked Kat.

"No," Kat replied, adding to herself, Thank goodness. "Bert said they all left early this morning. Why? Did Sven leave before you woke up?"

Dee looked at Kat in surprise. "You know?"

Kat shrugged and smiled. "I would have to be blind not to know. The two of you have been making eyes at each other for days."

"Oh," Dee mumbled as she stirred the soapy water with a stick.

Kat carried an armload of white clothes to the tub and carefully added them to the hot water as Dee continued stirring. "I love him, Kat," Dee said simply as she stared up at her friend.

Kat wished she could be as sure as Dee. "I never thought you didn't," she told her. "Are you happy?"

"Yes," Dee admitted as she scrubbed and Kat did the rinsing. "I really think I am." She paused in her scrubbing and asked, "What about you and Eric?"

"What about us?" Kat hedged.

"Come on, Kat. It's me, remember. You can't hide things from me," Dee told her as she resumed scrubbing.

Kat removed the sheet she had been rinsing from her tub and hung it up on the line after she had wrung as much of the excess water from it as she could.

"I don't know, Dee. I can't honestly say how we are or if we are at all, for that matter," Kat admitted.

"It will come," Dee advised her. "Don't try to worry it through; let it happen or not. It's not something you can plan."

Kat listened to Dee's words and knew they made sense. Maybe she had been trying to approach things in the wrong way. Maybe she should let nature take its course, whatever that might be. But, her common sense warned, you could get hurt that way. If I do, I will face that when it happens.

Dee's cry of alarm, "Oh no!" made Kat look up.

She dropped the sheet she was rinsing back into the water and went to Dee's side. "What's wrong? Did you break the stick?"

Dee pointed to the tub and Kat saw the reason for her cry. The water was turning blue. "I was stirring this last load of sheets and all of a sudden the water started changing color," Dee explained.

"Give me the stick. There has to be a reason for this to have happened," Kat said as she lifted the floating sheets. She poked and stirred as she peered into the darkening water. Lifting the stick from the water, she said, "Here's the culprit."

Draped over the stick was a pair of dark blue denim pants. She hung the pants out of their way as they hurried to remove the sheets from the tub before they were stained. Dee gasped as the hot water burned her hands and glared at the pants as they marked time dripping blue spots onto the ground.

Dipping pails into the tub, they emptied the tainted water and disposed of it between the rows of vegetables. "What do we do if the carrots, corn and lettuce all turn blue?" Dee asked as they emptied the final pail.

"We blame it on the impurities in the soil," Kat told her with a straight face.

"What impurities?"

"If they were not there before, they are now," Kat laughed.

It took the rest of the morning for them to finish the laundry, and Dee was almost paranoid about checking to be sure all the right clothes were in the correct load. By the time they were finished, they were both exhausted.

Kat pinned the last clothespin on the final shirt and stepped back from the clothesline, flexing her tired shoulders. "I couldn't lift another thing," she groaned.

Dee was farther down the line looking at the pants that had almost caused disaster earlier. "Kat, I think we have another problem."

"I don't want to hear it," Kat told her. "I'm too tired to handle any more problems."

Dee took the pants off the line and carried them over to where Kat stood. Holding them up to her waist, she said, "They shrank. They look like they might even fit me. I never knew things could shrink so much."

"They are yours. I make you a gift of them. Now, take them away," Kat ordered. "I said I was too tired for any more problems."

Dee looked down at the pants. "What am I supposed to tell Leif when he asks what happened to his pants?"

"That sounds like another problem," Kat warned her. "Don't expect any answers from me."

Dee shrugged as she folded the pants over her arm. "I guess I'll wait and see if he notices they are missing before I worry about any explanations."

"You're learning." Kat smiled as she rested on the back step. "Don't go looking for trouble. It will find you soon enough by itself."

"You're probably right." Dee laughed as she carried the pants up to her room and stored them in her wardrobe. Closing the wardrobe door, she sighed as she saw her bed. She had not slept in it since the night she had gone to Sven, but now she felt tired enough to crawl into it and forget the rest of the day.

Her thoughts returned to earlier that morning, when she had awakened to find Sven gone. A pleasant glow in her limbs and a dent in the pillow next to her head were the only signs he had been there. She had a fleeting memory of him kissing her and telling her to sleep, but she missed not having seen him all day.

Reluctantly, she forced her tired body to move. She went out onto the landing and decided to see if Kat had come upstairs yet. She went to Kat's room and knocked on the closed door. Hearing no response, she opened the door, thinking that maybe Kat had lain down and fallen asleep.

The room was empty and the afternoon breeze was billowing the curtains away from the open window.

Dee moved to the window to close it and, looking out, saw Kat with Eric and Sven. They were all talking to a man she had never seen before.

She hurried downstairs to join them, curious to find out what they were discussing with such serious faces.

Slowing her headlong rush as she neared the porch, Dee looked to see if anyone had noticed her and saw Sven smiling at her as he looked over Kat's head. Smiling back at him, she moved down the front steps and over to where the others were. Standing close to Sven, she slid her arm about his waist in a natural gesture as he put his arm around her shoulder and they listened to the heated discussion between Kat and Eric.

"If what Mr. Flynn says is true, we must warn my grandfather," Kat was insisting as she glared at Eric.

"I've already told you we can't warn him," Eric was trying to explain. "His train is on the move and there is no way to contact him."

Kat felt frustration at the truth of Eric's words. "Then someone should try to intercept the train," she declared.

Eric shook his head. "We can't spare the manpower. Besides, I think the trouble will be at this end of the line and not on the train itself."

Kat stamped her foot stubbornly, raising a small puff of dirt. "I disagree, Eric. The attempt on my grandfather's life could come anywhere at anytime and he must be warned."

"I agree with Kat," Dee volunteered, unasked.

Sven shushed her with a frown. "Stay out of this, Dee."

Eric put both his hands on Kat's shoulders and faced her, looking into her eyes, trying to make her understand. "All the sabotage has been at this end of the line. We feel that whoever is responsible will try to ruin the line here as well as make an attempt on your grandfather's life. So we think it will be a joint effort at our end, and until he reaches here, your grandfather is not in any real danger."

"I understand your reasoning, Eric. But I still can't agree with you," Kat told him, trying desperately to make him see her side of the argument and her real concern for her grandfather's welfare.

Eric drew her stiff body into his arms and tried to comfort her. "I know you're afraid for him, I understand your fear. But you are going to have to let us handle things the way we think is best."

"And what way is that?" Dee asked as she looked from Eric to Sven.

"Don't worry about it," Sven told her.

"But I *am* worried about it. Why won't either of you

tell us what you are planning on doing? We have a right to know. It is Kat's grandfather who is in danger." Dee protested vehemently.

"Sven, can't you talk some sense into her?" Eric asked.

Sven tried to pull Dee into his arms, but she pulled away from him, not trusting his motives. He shrugged his shoulders and said, "We will be returning with Flynn to the rail camp. You and Kat stay here with Bert where it is safe and you won't be able to get into any trouble."

"What!" Dee exclaimed in shock.

"We are to be pushed to the side and left here to wait and worry?" Kat could not believe what they had asked them to do.

Eric leaned over and kissed Kat on the cheek. "We can't waste time standing here arguing. We have to leave."

With this he and Sven moved to the horses that were tethered nearby and mounted to ride out with Flynn, leaving their angry wives behind.

Chapter Nineteen

ERIC REACHED DOWN AND RUBBED HIS LEG AS THEY RODE away. His knee was protesting the strain as he rode. Sven looked over, saw him rubbing it and said, "Wrenched it pretty good, didn't you?"

Eric straightened in his saddle and replied, "Not as badly as Kat would like to wring my neck about now."

A slow smile spread across Sven's face. "I know what you mean. I'm not in Dee's good graces, either. We may have trouble when we come home."

"Knowing those two, we will be lucky if they wait that long." Eric nudged his horse forward.

Kat watched the men until they disappeared from sight. Turning to Dee, she said, "Are we going to do what they say? Or are we going to do what should be done?"

Dee turned and started back into the house, answering, "You have to ask?"

Bert came into the kitchen and saw Kat filling a saddlebag with food she had wrapped. "I suppose it wouldn't do me any good to try to stop either of you?" she commented.

"No, it wouldn't, Bert," Kat agreed as she moved across to the stove and grabbed a handful of matches.

Bert followed her out of the kitchen to the foot of the stairs and shook her head. "I think you are taking unnecessary risks. You should let Eric and Sven handle things," she told Kat as Kat started up the stairs.

Kat paused and looked down at Bert. "I know you are worried about us, Bert. But someone has to warn my grandfather. Dee and I are the only ones to do it." She moved back down the stairs and hugged the older woman. "Thank you for being so concerned. I promise we will be careful."

"Kat? I've gathered some bedrolls I found in Leif's and Eric's rooms. Can you think of anything else we might need?" Dee peered down from the top of the landing. She had changed into the pants she had hidden in her wardrobe and added a long-sleeved flannel shirt she had purloined from one of the brothers. With her hair braided and pinned to the top of her head, she looked like a young boy.

"You look ready to me," Kat called up to her. "I see the pants did fit you. I think I'll go and see if I can find anything that might fit me."

"Dee?" Bert called up to her.

"Yes, Bert?" she replied as she came down the stairs.

"Do you know how to handle a handgun?" Bert asked her.

Kat paused as she reached the top of the stairs and a cloud passed over her features. "Do you think that will be necessary, Bert?" she asked.

"It doesn't hurt to be prepared in case it is," Bert responded.

Dee reached Bert's side and shifted the weight of the bedrolls she was carrying as she said, "I'm afraid I am barely familiar with handguns. You don't use those when you are hunting."

"Come with me, then. I'll try to show you what you will need to know," Bert told her as she moved into Eric's office.

Opening the door on one of the cabinets, she reached inside and withdrew a revolver. Holding it up for Dee to see, she said, "This is a Colt Army .38 caliber. It holds six shots and is pretty reliable."

Dee listened carefully as Bert explained the workings and handling of the gun and repeated them to Bert as she asked to be certain Dee understood.

Kat moved about in Leif's room, searching through his wardrobe for another pair of pants she could wear. She knew she would have to roll the pants legs and wear a belt of some kind, but it was better than trying to ride cross-country wearing a dress. Finding a pair, she stripped off her dress and tried them on. They were way too long for her to walk. She sat on the floor and rolled up the pants legs until her feet showed. Rising, she had to hold them about her with one hand as she walked to keep them from falling off because they were so big in the waist. "Damn!" she swore as she hunted through the wardrobe looking for a belt.

"You look ridiculous," Dee commented from the doorway as she watched Kat.

"Don't stand there and make rude remarks. Come help me find a belt or something I can use to hold these pants up," Kat complained.

They found an old belt of Leif's and Kat threaded it through the belt loops on her pants and tried to buckle it. "That is no help at all," Dee observed as she watched the pants start to slide off Kat's hips.

"Do you have any bright ideas, Miss Helpful?" Kat groused as she struggled to keep the pants from tripping her as she walked.

Dee shook her head at the sight Kat made in her camisole and bare feet, with Leif's pants rolled to her knees and the waistband crumpled in her hands as she tried to hold them up. "I think we had better see if Bert has any ideas. This will never work," Dee told her as she moved from the room.

Bert laughed as she saw Kat and said, "I've helped you this far, I might as well go all the way."

The two girls followed her as she moved into her room off the kitchen. They watched as she rummaged through a stack of clothes until she smiled and said, "Here we are."

She held up a very faded pair of pants of the same style Kat was struggling to keep up and Dee was wearing with no problem, saying, "Leif outgrew these a while back, but I hate to throw things out. You never know when they might come in handy." She handed them to Kat and told her to try them on for size.

Kat slipped out of the pair she was wearing and pulled on the ones Bert handed her. Fastening the waist, she smiled. "They are still a little big. But much better than the first pair."

Dee stood back and checked Kat out with a nod. "A vast improvement. You will only have to roll those a couple of times and they'll be the right length."

Reaching back into the pile of clothes, Bert extracted a long-sleeved shirt similar to the one Dee was wearing and said, "Try this."

Kat slipped it on over her camisole and tucked its hem into the pants. Looking down at herself, she said, "This will do fine. Thank you, Bert."

"Don't thank me. I'd be in worse trouble if I didn't see that you were properly outfitted," Bert told her.

Moving out to the barn, they saddled two horses and packed their gear on the backs of their saddles with Bert showing them how to strap everything on so it would stay.

Bert followed them as they led their mounts from the barn. Watching them mount up, she said, "You sure you want to go through with this?"

"We have to, Bert." Kat smiled down at her.

Dee looked at the fading daylight and said, "We had better get on our way. I want to be well away from here when Sven comes back."

Kat looked over at her and added, "I'm with you. Eric will come unglued when he finds out we've taken off."

Bert looked at both of them with concern on her face. "Can you at least tell me which way you'll be heading?"

"That's easy. East," Dee answered.

Gathering the reins in her hand, Kat took pity on Bert and said, "We are going to try to intercept my grandfather's train. We'll follow the tracks eastward until we do."

"That sounds rather chancy to me." Bert shook her head.

"Bert," Kat admonished kindly. "You can't talk us out of it. So don't waste your breath."

Bert shrugged. "You can't blame an old woman for trying. You two be careful. And Dee, remember what I told you about that gun."

"I will on both counts, Bert," Dee replied as she followed Kat out of the yard.

Riding alongside of Kat in the growing twilight, Dee asked her, "What now?"

"The rail camp is over that way." Kat pointed off to her left. "We will have to skirt the camp to reach the tracks."

"I wish we didn't have to," Dee moaned.

"It's the fastest way I know of to reach the tracks," Kat explained. "But if there were any other way to go I would. I have no desire to meet up with Eric, or Sven, either."

They rode in silence for what seemed like ages before Kat reined in and waited for Dee to move beside her.

Leaning over, she whispered, "The camp is over the next rise. We had better walk our horses and hope they don't have too many guards posted on this side."

Dee nodded and dismounted, her muscles protesting at the strain of riding added to the laundry she had done that day.

Kat led the way through the trees, praying they would not be spotted. The last thing she wanted now was to have to make any explanations to Eric or Sven as to why she and Dee were out riding dressed as they were.

As she followed Kat, Dee could see the huddled tents of the camp through the trees and wished they could move faster. It was slow and tedious directing their horses over the strange terrain, and Dee breathed a sigh of relief when they left the rail camp behind them.

They mounted up again and rode along the tracks until it was too dark to see where they were going. Dee's arms and wrists were feeling the strain and her backside was reminding her that she was not accustomed to riding this way. She was thankful when Kat pulled up.

"I think there is a small clearing ahead near the tracks," Kat whispered to her. "We can rest there until dawn. We'll be able to see the tracks more clearly in the morning."

Another ten minutes brought them to a small break in the dense trees lining the side of the tracks. It was bathed in the waning moonlight like a beacon of welcome to the exhausted pair.

They settled their mounts and unloaded their bedrolls, with Kat saying, "One of us should keep watch." She plopped exhaustedly under a towering pine and unrolled her bedroll, adding, "You try to get some sleep. I'll take the first watch."

"No. You look as though you need the sleep more than I do," Dee told her. "I'm not that tired." She sat down next to Kat, resting her arms on her upraised knees.

Kat needed no other encouragement and slept, too tired to notice the biting chill of the night air.

Dee was not sure what it was she was supposed to be watching for, but she scanned their shadowy surroundings anyway.

The cry of a raucous jay startled Dee awake and her head jerked up from her knees, where it had sagged in sleep. She looked around and saw that their horses were placidly chomping on the dew-coated grass, their breath coming out in frosty puffs from their nostrils. Turning, she saw Kat curled in a ball on the fallen pine needles next to her. Some kind of watchdog I am, she scolded herself as she watched the first rays of dawn streak the horizon.

Rising to her feet, she could not help but groan aloud at the stiffness of her body and the cramping of her legs from remaining in such an awkward position for hours.

Her groan woke Kat, who blinked up at her. "Don't tell me it's morning already."

"Afraid so," Dee answered as she hobbled to the bushes to answer nature's call.

"I said not to tell me," Kat moaned as she crawled from her bedroll.

Returning, Dee found Kat sitting up and looking miserable. "Is it always this cold first thing in the morning out here?" Kat chattered.

Dee shrugged. "Your guess is as good as mine. I'm as new at this as you are. Maybe it will warm up after the sun's up."

"I hope it hurries." Kat rose and stomped her feet, trying to restore the circulation to her legs and feet.

Dee was fastening the last of their gear to their horses when Kat emerged from the bushes saying, "Are we ready to go?"

Tightening the last knot, Dee replied, "We have to start sometime. It might as well be now."

The sun had been shining brightly for hours and Kat had thawed out to the point of being almost too warm as she and Dee followed the line of tracks eastward.

"How far do you think we have come?" Dee called to her as they rode single file.

Kat turned in her saddle. "I would guess five miles or so. We've been riding since dawn and it feels close to noon. Do you want to stop and rest?"

Having eaten some of the bread they brought with them as she rode, Dee could see no reason for them to stop and replied, "Not now. Maybe a little later. We will need to rest our horses."

"Fine," Kat agreed as she urged her mount forward, anxious to reach her grandfather as soon as she could.

Sven knocked a second time on Dee's door. "Dee? Are you going to sleep all day?"

He and Eric had returned with Leif very late the night before and gone straight to bed. He had not been too surprised not to find Dee waiting for him in their bed. He guessed she was mad at him and returning to her own room was her way of showing him. But he had been knocking on her door now for a few minutes and had not received any answer. He opened the door and entered the room. It took only a few seconds for him to see that the room had been unoccupied for some time. Moving back to the landing, he called downstairs, "Eric! Dee's gone."

"What!" Eric yelled back as he came up the stairs. "Check Kat's room," he ordered disgustedly.

Finding Kat's room vacant, Sven turned to Eric and said, "You don't think they took off on their own, do you?"

Eric scowled. "What do you think?"

"I was afraid you would agree with me," Sven grunted as they went back down to the kitchen to confront Bert.

"All right, Bert. Where are they and when did they leave?" Eric demanded angrily.

Not bothering to pretend she did not know what they were talking about, Bert replied, "They went to warn Kat's grandfather and left shortly after you did yesterday afternoon."

"What now?" Sven asked in a hard voice.

"We can't go looking for them now," Eric answered. "We will have to finish things at camp first."

They left Bert and went to Eric's office. Opening the long cabinet near his bookshelves, Eric withdrew a rifle and handed it to Sven, saying, "There are shells in the bottom desk drawer."

Sven removed a box of shells for each of them and said, "You know they could be heading straight for trouble."

"Yes, I know," Eric answered tersely. "Let's hope they find Gwyn before trouble finds them."

Leif joined them. "What's this Bert has been telling me about Kat and Dee?"

"You heard her correctly. The fools took off yesterday to warn Gwyn," Sven informed him as he pocketed his shells.

Taking a rifle for himself, Leif said, "I'm going with you." He took a box of shells and followed his brothers outside.

Entering the barn, they discovered the missing horses they had overlooked the night before. They saddled their own mounts and headed out of the barn.

Climbing into his saddle, Eric noted, "At least they didn't try using the wagon this time."

"They might not be as conspicuous, but that doesn't make what they did any less dangerous," Sven growled as he mounted and followed Eric.

The three prodded their horses forward and rode in the direction of the rail camp.

"I'm ready. How about you?" Kat asked Dee as she watched her closely. They had stopped to rest their horses and grab a bite of food and Kat was anxious to be on their way.

Dee looked up from her position on a fallen bough. "If someone had told me three months ago that today I would be sitting in the wilderness of Montana eating a sandwich of homemade bread and jam, I would have laughed in their face."

"You have jam on your chin," Kat told her as she moved toward her horse.

Dee wiped her fingers against her chin and licked the jam off them with a dainty tongue. Rising to her feet, she stretched, lifting her arms over her head as she walked over to her mount and climbed into the saddle, saying, "Do you think we will find the train?"

"It's not a matter of if, but of when," Kat returned as she headed her horse down the tracks.

Dee caught up with her as the track curved out of sight, dwarfed on either side by towering trees. Time became meaningless as they traced the twisting and turning route of metal rails. Dee felt tired and sore, but oddly at home. She could grow to love this country with all its wild beauty. She frowned as she looked ahead at Kat and saw how her shoulders drooped with fatigue and how her face was etched with strain as she looked back to see if Dee was still following.

Kat did not see the beauty that Dee was seeing. All

she saw was the rail bed with its path pointing her in the direction of her grandfather. Her mind was a mixture of thoughts as she rode, a combination of fear for her grandfather and a fear of Eric. Eric. He had a hold over her that she could not resist. A hold that frightened her. No man had the effect on her that he did. Not liking the path her thoughts were taking, she kicked her mount to a faster pace and tried to block them from her mind.

The afternoon sun was casting sharp shadows through the trees when Dee called excitedly, "Look! I see smoke up ahead. It's a train."

Kat's head snapped up and she prayed it was the right train as she urged her horse to a gallop with Dee close behind her. They rounded a blind curve in the tracks to be greeted by the sight of a locomotive with two cars behind it, coming toward them on the track.

Reining her horse to a stop in the middle of the road bed, Kat stood in her stirrups and waved her hands wildly in the air, signaling the engineer to stop. Fearful that he might not, Kat almost cried with joy as she saw the billows of white steam from the wheels as the air brakes were applied. The train coasted with a screech of metal to a stop three feet in front of them. The engineer leaned out of the cab and started to swear at them loudly for blocking his way.

Kat laughed at him, making him stop in midsentence with surprise. She was so glad they had found her grandfather that she could have kissed the stunned engineer.

A well-dressed figure descended the steps from the first car and Kat cried, "Grandad!"

Jumping from her horse, she ran as fast as she could toward him with tears streaming down her cheeks.

"Kat?" he exclaimed as she threw herself into his arms and wept.

Dee dismounted and led their horses over to where a dumbfounded Patrick held Kat in his arms. "Are we ever glad to see you," she told him with a grin.

"I got that impression," he said as he patted Kat on the back. "Now, why all these tears? And what are you doing out here in the middle of nowhere dressed like that?"

Kat looked up at him as she tried to regain control of her emotions. "We came to warn you that you are in danger."

"Warn me? Danger?" Patrick looked from Kat to Dee, perplexed. "If you mean Harriman and Morgan are trying to force Jim Hill and me into a corner, I already know that."

A porter came down the stairs behind Patrick and watched with wide eyes. He'd thought maybe a deer on the tracks had caused them to stop, not two females in pants! And Mr. Gwyn was holding one of them in his arms!

Noticing his presence, Patrick ordered, "See what you can do with their horses, George."

Dee handed the reins to the astonished porter and followed Kat and Patrick back aboard the train. She felt an odd twinge as she saw the interior of the private car. It was almost a twin to the one they had traveled in on their journey west. Taking a seat on one of the velvet sofas, Dee listened as Kat tried to explain to her grandfather why they had ridden out to stop him.

"But what is this danger you keep saying I am in?" he asked as Kat finished her explanations. "I still am not clear on what it is I am in danger from. If you are referring to the problems encountered recently at the repair camp, Eric Thorsen wired me about those. He also stated that he felt the next attempt would also be aimed at that site and I concurred with his reasoning."

"You what?" Kat exclaimed, startled.

Patrick shook his head at her. "I am very touched by your rushing to what you thought was my rescue. But I think it was a very reckless thing for the two of you to have done." He poured them each a cup of coffee from a silver urn resting on a side table. "I am also disappointed that the Thorsens permitted such rashness."

"They didn't know," Dee said slowly.

"What!" Patrick sloshed his coffee over the sides of his cup and into the saucer. "You mean to tell me that the two of you took off and did not tell anyone where you were going?"

"We told their aunt," Kat murmured, appalled at her grandfather's anger. He was not supposed to be acting like this at all. He was supposed to be thankful that they had come to warn him in time, not scold them and berate them for coming at all.

"Their aunt? Why not Eric or his brothers?" Patrick stared at them sternly as he demanded an answer.

Dee lowered her head, unable to reply, and Kat spoke up with false bravado, "But they would have tried to stop us!"

Patrick retorted sharply, "And well they should! This is one of the more irresponsible things I have ever seen either of you do."

Kat flinched at his words and Dee chewed her lower lip, knowing he was right.

Looking out the side window at the waning daylight, Patrick said, "We will spend the night here. You will ride back to the Thorsen lodge, where you belong, first thing in the morning."

Neither girl said a word. Kat was numb. Nothing had turned out the way it was supposed to. Now they had the long return ride and the men's anger to look forward to on the next day.

Dinner that night was silent and brief, as Kat was hurt by Patrick's reaction to her coming and Patrick was upset with her. Dee felt sorry for both of them but knew better than to say anything.

Having retired shortly after dinner, Dee lay in her bed thinking of Sven and what he might say to her on the following day. He and Eric were proud men like Patrick. They were also strong and stubborn and did not like to be disobeyed. She drifted into a troubled sleep.

Physically and emotionally exhausted, Kat went right to sleep on retiring. But her sleep was tormented by dreams of Eric telling her he could never love a fool like her.

Chapter Twenty

THE SILHOUETTE OF THE DARKENED TRAIN LOOMED UP from the tracks with only the glow from the porter's lamp keeping vigil like a watchful guardian.

Scanning the length of the train, Grebe saw a muted glow from the hotbox in the engine, and he could hear the voices of the engineer and fireman on the clear night air as they played cards in the engine. Where is the brakeman? he wondered as he stared at the train. He had to be around somewhere, and Grebe wanted his position pegged before he and his men made their move.

The light of a lantern split the night, making him duck back under cover. Voices could be heard at the back of the train. The porter was handing something to the man holding the lantern. It must be the brakeman, Grebe thought as he watched him move to the front of the train and climb up into the cab of the locomotive.

Voices could be heard lifted in welcome, followed shortly by the sound of glasses clinking together. The glow from the hotbox flared brightly as more fuel was tossed onto the bed of coals and the door left open to heat the gathering chill.

Signaling to his left, Grebe crept from his hiding place by the side of the tracks and two men followed him. They sidled up to the side of the private car, keeping low should the porter happen to look out of any of the windows. Reaching the steps, they slowly moved into the car with Grebe in the lead.

Once inside, he motioned for the others to duck as the far door to the car opened and the porter entered from the adjoining car. He came down the short corridor lined with sleeping compartments and stopped at the one nearest him to rap softly on the door.

The door opened and a man's voice could be heard as he answered the porter. The porter's head nodded and he could be heard to say good night as he returned the way he had come.

Grebe waited to be sure it was safe before he motioned for the others to each take a compartment as he crept to the one closest to him.

Kat thought the world must be coming to an end as she was roughly dragged from her bed and a calloused hand closed over her mouth, blocking her scream. She struggled as hard as she could, but her assailant was bigger and stronger than she. He soon had her wrapped helplessly in the blanket from her bed and, lifting her, he tossed her over his shoulder, the impact knocking the breath from her and hurting her ribs. Wrapped as she was, she found it impossible to call for help and tried to fight off the dizziness that engulfed her.

Dee woke hearing a loud thump from Kat's compartment. Without stopping to think why, she rolled out of her bed and hid in the corner. She had reason to be thankful she had reacted on instinct as her door was thrust open and the footsteps of an intruder moved toward her bed. She huddled in her hiding place and watched as the lone figure tore the bedding from her bed and muttered a curse at not finding her there.

She covered her mouth to keep from screaming out loud as she saw the dark figure begin to search around her compartment and head in her direction.

He was close enough for her to reach out and touch him when the sound of shots rang out through the car and a violent struggle could be heard from Patrick's compartment.

Her intruder wheeled and left the compartment, slamming the door behind him. Dee knew she had to get out of there before he came back. She grabbed at the clothes she had discarded earlier and the gun Bert had given her. Opening the window by her bed, she shivered as the cold night air chilled her through to the bone. Levering herself up, she climbed out of the window, glad for the first time in her life that she was small enough to do so.

She dropped to the dirt alongside the car and rolled into the cover of the foliage near the side of the track, holding her bundle of clothes and gun tightly against her and hoping the gun would not go off as she rolled.

Crouching in the underbrush, she brushed as much of the dirt and gravel off as she could before pulling on her clothes and sticking the Colt into her waistband.

She stared at the train and wondered if Kat was able to escape. She knew from the sound of the raised voices and the shots that Patrick was not as lucky. She prayed that he wasn't hurt as she crept alongside the train. Reaching the back of the train, she scurried across the tracks, keeping to the shadows as much as possible as she hid in the cover of the woods on the other side.

The pain in her feet made her regret that she had not grabbed her shoes as well when she had made good her escape. The sharpness of the gravel railbed reminded her that she would need them or something to protect her feet.

Her eyes widened in terror as she watched three men climb down from the steps to the private car. They were all armed and one of them had a blanket over his shoulder wrapped around a body. The slimness of the feet and legs sticking out from the folds told Dee that it was Kat he held. The other two men were half dragging, half carrying the slumped form of her grandfather between them as they hurried away from the train and into the woods.

Dee tried to peer through the trees to see which way they were heading, but as well as shielding her from their gaze, they also shielded them from hers. She could hear the sound of horses being mounted and ridden away.

Wasting no time, she ran to the private car and climbed aboard. Rushing to her compartment to get her shoes, she stopped cold with a scream bubbling from her throat. George, the porter, lay in the hallway by Patrick's compartment with a hole in his chest as his death-glazed eyes stared unseeingly at the ceiling.

The sound of more shots being fired outside broke her frozen stance and she hurried into her compartment and grabbed her shoes. Looking about her, she hurriedly gathered whatever else she thought she might need and left her compartment, closing her eyes as she passed the unfortunate George.

Returning to the main room, she sat down and put on her shoes and stuffed her gun into the saddlebag over her arm. She moved back outside and looked down toward the engine. She could see the brakeman leaning over a wounded man that must have been the engineer, while the fireman was pointing a rifle into the woods.

She hurried down toward them, to tell them about Kat and Patrick. She also told them about the porter, shuddering as she did so.

Not giving them a chance to stop her, she moved away to where she had seen George tether their horses earlier. She was relieved to see their attackers had not found them. Loading her mount, she climbed into the saddle and rode in the direction she had heard the other horses take.

Watching her go, the fireman turned to the other two men and said, "Someone had better tell them at the rail camp what has happened. Will you guys be okay? I'll take the other horse and ride for help."

The brakeman helped the engineer to his feet and said, "We'll manage. You better get going. That damn fool girl could wind up getting herself killed following them like that."

He waited to hear no more and took Kat's horse and started in the direction of the rail camp. He hoped it wasn't a long way.

Kat regained consciousness as the jarring of the horse's gait woke her. She was still trussed like a chicken and had been tossed across the saddle of a horse. She felt nausea rise in her throat as she hung with her head downward and the horse galloped along.

She dimly remembered hearing shots being fired before she blacked out. She prayed that no one was hurt or, worse, killed. It was no comfort to know that she had been right in thinking an attempt would be made on the train.

What about Dee and her grandfather? Had they been taken also? And where were they being taken? These thoughts tumbled through her mind until the misery of her position brought blackness once again.

Dee could not see any tracks in the dark as she rode and could only ride in the direction she thought they had gone. She prayed she was right. She had to do what she could to free Kat and her grandfather. What that might be she didn't know. Right now she was more concerned with finding them. She would deal with how to free them later.

* * *

The morning air was filled with the rumble of men's voices as the brakeman rode into the rail camp. He had reached there as day was breaking and the camp was coming awake.

The men who had been on watch all night were crawling into their bunks, while those who had not were gathered in small groups around the first-aid tent.

The flap on the first-aid tent opened and Sven exited with Eric close behind him.

Leif broke away from the group of men he had been talking to and walked over to them. "There's a rider coming in from the east," he said with a grim expression on his face.

Sven moved toward the oncoming rider as Eric gave orders to the waiting men. Leif watched the rider stop and speak to Sven. He saw Sven's body go stiff as he shouted, "Eric! Leif!"

They both went over to where Sven was speaking with the brakeman from the train. "What is it, Sven?" Leif asked as they joined them.

"This is the brakeman from Gwyn's train," Sven informed them. "They were attacked last night by three men. The porter was killed, the engineer wounded and Gwyn and Kat were taken hostage."

Eric's fists clenched at his sides as he heard the news. Kat had been right after all. But what had it cost her?

"What about Dee?" Leif asked.

"The damn fool took one of the horses and followed them," Sven grated between thin lips.

"We can be ready to leave in a few minutes," Leif replied as he moved away from Sven and returned to the first-aid tent to gather his things.

"Ben!" Eric called to the foreman. "See that this man gets something to eat and a place to rest. We will be leaving to head back up the line. You'll be in charge. Just continue the way we discussed."

"Right, Eric." Ben acknowledged he understood as he watched the brothers move away.

In a short time, the three were riding out of camp and heading back up the line toward the train and the trail they would have to try to follow. None of them spoke as they rode; their faces were set in stone, their minds on one thing.

Grebe looked about the small clearing as they broke through the trees. Holding up his hand, he signaled for the others to stop.

"We'll make camp here," he told them as he directed his mount toward a group of trees, pulling on the lead for the horse that carried Kat.

"But it's daylight now. We can make good time and put some real distance between us and that train," one of his companions complained.

"I said we would wait here," Grebe ordered as he dismounted.

"Wait for what?" the others grumbled to one another as they reined in.

Kat was thankful they had finally stopped. She had been bounced around on the back of that horse for hours and her insides hurt as much as her outsides did.

"Put the old man over by that big tree," Grebe ordered as he untied the ropes holding Kat onto her horse.

She could feel him working and decided she would be better off to pretend she was unconscious than have to face her captors right away. If they thought she was unconscious they might speak more freely and she might be able to learn who they were.

She kept her body limp as she felt herself being

pulled from the back of the horse and carried a short distance. She bit her tongue to hold back the cry of pain that almost escaped as she was dropped heavily to the dirt and the blanket was pulled from her.

She laid there unmoving, her eyes closed, tasting the dirt in her mouth. She could feel eyes staring at her, stripping her nightdress away, and fought the urge to curl up into a ball and cover herself.

Dee pulled up her mount and moved behind a large pine tree. She had been so intent on trying to find tracks that she had come close to riding into the middle of their camp. The sound of their voices warned her and she reined in. Dismounting, she crept forward to where she could peer through the tree limbs at the camp.

In the morning light, she could clearly see the three men. One of them was adding wood to the smokeless fire as another said something to him. Across the camp, she could see the third man unfold a blanket and dump Kat's unconscious form to the dirt. Her grandfather was leaning against a tree, bound hand and foot next to her.

Dee gasped as he moved from where he had dumped Kat. She recognized him as the stranger who had offered to help them on the road the night they had tried to leave the lodge.

Observing the camp, she guessed they were waiting for someone or something. The man by the fire kept looking off to his right expectantly. This was something she had not counted on happening and it worried her. Being outnumbered three to one was bad enough; she did not want to take the chance of the odds increasing against her.

She slipped back to where she had left her horse and

led him back along the trail. She needed to put a safe distance between her and the camp so she could think and make her plans.

She tethered her horse and lowered herself to the ground. Leaning back, she tried to figure out what to do first. She knew she could not count on any help from Kat or her grandfather.

Patrick looked as though he might be wounded and she could not tell how badly hurt Kat might be.

The warmth of the sun on her shoulders made thinking hard. She began to feel very drowsy and fought to stay awake. All she needed now was to fall asleep from exhaustion. She wouldn't help anyone that way. She rubbed her eyes and stretched her aching muscles, trying to throw off her lethargy. You've got to stay awake, she scolded; now try to think of something.

She still had the Colt that Bert had given her, but she would use that only if she absolutely had to. Those men were armed, too, and they knew how to use their guns far better than she did hers.

Maybe if they stayed there all day, come nightfall she could sneak around to the far side of the camp and talk with Patrick or Kat. What good that would do she wasn't sure, but maybe between the three of them they could figure out some way to get out of this mess. Her eyelids grew heavier and heavier and her mind worked slower and slower and in spite of all her efforts Dee slept.

Sven waved at Eric and Leif to caution them as they moved through the woods. He had heard the whinny of a horse up ahead and knew they had found someone.

Motioning for Eric and Leif to wait, Sven dismounted and continued stealthily forward on foot. He moved ahead for about a hundred yards, peering through the gathering darkness. Off to his left, he saw a roan-colored horse tied to a low-hanging tree limb.

It was Dee's. It was one of the missing horses from the lodge. The brakeman from the train had ridden into camp on the other. That left this one for her to take as she trailed her attackers. He made a careful search of the area, looking for a sign that she was nearby.

Not finding a trace of her, Sven crept forward to investigate what lay ahead. He reached the edge of a clearing and paused as he watched the scene before him. His lips drew back from his teeth in a silent snarl and he controlled the urge to move forward.

Across the clearing, he could see Kat sitting with her arms around an older man who must be her grandfather. Sven could see blood on Patrick Gwyn's shoulder and a darkness on Kat's cheek that looked like a bruise.

Standing in front of them was a tall, mean-looking man with his hand raised as if ready to strike Kat a second time.

Sven restrained his desire to rush across the clearing and beat the man to a pulp and turned his attention instead to the campsite itself. He looked around and was not surprised when he saw two other men crouched around a fire. They seemed to be egging him on. Sven could hear one of them say, "That's it. You show the bitch who's boss."

The tall man turned and glared at him, saying, "I told her to shut up and the same goes for you. I don't want the world to know where we are."

The rebuke bounced off the man's back as he turned and grumbled to himself. His partner spat a long stream of tobacco juice into the darkness beyond the fire.

Sven backed away from the clearing and moved to where he had left Eric and Leif. They had dismounted and were waiting impatiently for his return. Eric looked at him and said, "We were about to come after you."

Sven told them what he had found and suggested they move closer to the clearing, but he cautioned that they should wait until the men had gone to sleep before taking any action.

Dee leaned back against the tree she was hiding behind and whispered, "Kat? Are you all right?"

Kat did not raise her head or look around, not wanting to draw any attention as she returned softly, "I'll be fine."

Kat was surprised to hear Dee's voice and hoped she was not alone. This was not something that Dee could handle by herself.

"How badly is your grandfather hurt?" Dee asked her.

Kat placed a finger over Patrick's lips as he was about to speak and replied to Dee in the same low tones, "He's been shot in the shoulder. I can't tell how badly he's hurt."

"I have a plan," Dee told her. "If it works, I'll have you free before morning."

"A plan?" Kat asked as she tore a strip of material from the bottom of her nightdress to make a bandage for Patrick's shoulder.

"Yes, a plan. Now listen to me. I want you to ignore anything you hear me call from the woods," Dee instructed her cryptically as she moved back into the shadows.

Grebe had seen the girl whispering to the old man and moved over to them. Moving in front of Kat, he raised his hand and struck her sharply across the face as he said, "That's so you'll know I mean business when I tell you to forget any ideas you and the old man have about trying to escape."

"Oh!" Kat exclaimed as she put her arms around her grandfather to protect him.

Grebe raised his hand again. "Next time I catch you two scheming you'll both regret it."

He moved back to the fire as he spoke roughly to one of the other men.

Sven moved back through the woods as Dee returned to her horse, determined to make her plan work. She scavenged all the rope and cord she could find on her saddle as her mind frantically tried to remember everything her brothers had taught her.

Unhooking a length of rope coiled near her saddle horn, she froze as she thought she heard the sound of movement in the trees behind her. She listened, afraid to move, and leaned her head against the side of her saddle in relief as the sounds grew fainter as they moved away from her.

Kat tried to whisper to her grandfather what Dee had told her but was cut off by a hard voice from the fire. "Last time I'm going to tell you—shut up!"

She turned startled eyes to the fire, afraid he might return and hit her again. But he remained where he was and poured himself a cup of coffee from a beaten pot sitting on the edge of the fire.

Dee worked for over an hour sneaking around the edge of the clearing. Using her scavenged rope and cord, she had been able to set up only a few snares, but each had been an exercise in patience as she worked in the dark. She smoothed pine needles and dirt over the noose on her last snare and sat back on her heels to view her efforts.

She had used the length of rope to fashion a spring trap. She hoped it would take the weight of a man. She had caught only small animals with her snares when hunting with her brothers, and this time she was after far bigger game.

Dusting her hands off on her pants leg, she moved to the side and said a silent prayer as she put the next step of her plan into use.

Taking a deep breath and a firm grip on the Colt, she called out, "Kat! Help!"

Her calls echoed throughout the clearing. The men around the fire jumped to their feet and stared around them into the night.

"Where's that coming from?" one of them exclaimed.

"Over there," another answered as he started to his left and disappeared into the trees.

Grebe pulled his gun and moved to stand by Kat and her grandfather as he kept a close eye on them, saying, "Don't get any ideas."

The seconds turned into minutes and still there was no sign of the first man. His companion looked anxiously across the fire at Grebe.

Grebe's jaw tightened and the shadows from the firelight as it played across his face made him look vicious. He jerked his head in the direction of the woods and said, "You'd better check on him."

The man by the fire hesitated. He was not keen on going into those trees. One man had already gone in and not come back out. His head came up as he heard his friend's voice calling, "I've found her. Come give me a hand."

Grebe nodded for him to go and he moved off into the trees. Away from the fire, his eyes were slow to adjust to the blackness and he had to move slowly. Brushing by a tree limb, he saw his friend and opened his mouth to yell. A blinding flash of pain cut off his cry as he collapsed to the dirt.

Dee backed away from him, holding her arm. It was

numb from the shock of hitting him on the back of the head with the butt of the Colt. Her eyes moved from the man in the dirt to her snare with its prey hanging upside down from the tree limb it was attached to.

Catching the man entrapped in the snare had been more a matter of luck than of skill. He had come up from behind her and was about to make a grab for her when his boot had stepped on a dry twig. She had turned in time to see him. Fear had choked her as she had backed away from him as he'd come at her. He had called out to his friends by the fire and made a lunge for her. She had closed her eyes in terror, certain it was the end.

But a swish of air had made her open her eyes, and she saw him swing up into the air, hitting his head on the ground as her snare had caught him in its grip.

She had never dreamed the snares might really work and was elated at this success. But her elation had been cut short as she had heard the man at her feet as he'd approached her. She had waited until he had moved by her and then hit him as hard as she could with the butt of the revolver.

Eric put his hand on Sven's arm as they heard Dee's voice cry out. Sven shook free of Eric's hold and motioned for him to move to the far side of the clearing behind Kat and her grandfather. He pointed for Leif to watch the man at the fire while he moved slowly in the direction of Dee's cry.

Dee turned her back on the two men she had eliminated and directed her attention to the third man holding the gun on Kat. This is where she made her second mistake. Her first had been in not making sure the man she had hit was unconscious.

He wasn't and was now crawling towards her from behind as she stared at the camp.

His hand snaked out and grabbed her by the leg, pulling her down next to him. He rolled on top of her, pinning her to the ground and knocking the gun into the bushes. "Hit me on the head, will ya!" he growled as he backhanded her across the mouth, splitting her lip with the force of his blow.

Dee kicked and struggled, trying to get free. But he had her arms pinned above her head and his weight was too heavy to dislodge, no matter how hard she struggled.

"I'll show you what happens to little girls who like to play rough," he grated as he ripped open her shirt and grabbed her camisole, tearing it apart with ease.

She stared up at his ugly face with terrified eyes and choked, "No!"

He laughed as he grabbed her breast with his free hand and cruelly dug his fingers into it.

Her scream of pain and terror cut through the night, triggering an explosion of reaction.

Sven answered her cry with a roar of rage as he yanked her attacker away from her and smashed his face with a massive blow. He started to hit him again, but Leif's warning stopped him. "Don't kill him, Sven."

Sven looked up and saw Leif pointing a gun at the head of the man trapped in the snare, who ceased his attempts to get free as the cold barrel rested against his temple.

Sven dropped the unconscious body of the man he held by the neck and kicked him away. Bending down, he gently pulled Dee's shirt closed and lifted her into his arms as she sobbed his name.

He held her close to him and watched as Leif

released the rope from the tree limb, letting his prisoner crash to the ground.

Shifting Dee in his arms, Sven covered the two men with his gun as Leif used the rope to tie them together. Leaving them, Leif followed Sven as he moved through the trees.

Dee's sobs had eased to whimpers as she clung to Sven for protection. He murmured to her softly as he made his way toward the camp.

A shot rang out from the camp as Sven broke into the clearing. He saw Eric crash through the trees where he had been hiding and hit Grebe at the knees, sending them both tumbling into the dirt as Kat watched in horror.

Kat felt her life draining away before her eyes as she watched the two men fight for control of the gun. A second shot was fired and the gun went flying through the air, crashing to the ground near Patrick.

The two men lay still in the dirt and Kat felt a coldness grip her heart as she prayed, "Let him live. Dear God, let Eric live."

Dee pressed closer to Sven in fear as she saw Grebe put his hands around Eric's neck and try to strangle him. Sven started to move forward toward the two men and a third shot rang out, freezing him in his tracks.

Grebe slumped on top of Eric and the night was deadly silent.

Kat looked at her grandfather in astonishment as he laid the gun down beside him. She stumbled forward, her hand to her mouth, as she cried, "Eric!"

Eric pushed Grebe's body away from him and rose to his feet. He was barely in time to catch Kat as she fell into his arms in a faint.

Chapter Twenty-one

WHILE SVEN AND ERIC TOOK PATRICK AND THE GIRLS back to the lodge, Leif escorted their prisoners and the body of Grebe to the sheriff in town.

Sven carried Dee straight to bed and returned to help Eric settle Patrick as Bert stood by in concern.

Wearing Eric's jacket over her torn nightdress, Kat hovered anxiously around her grandfather. She could not bring herself to look at Eric as he and Sven carried Patrick up to Nick's room.

Knowing how upset Kat was, Eric looked over at Bert as he and Sven moved up the stairs and said, "Bert, Kat should stay with you until I'm through here."

Kat flashed in rebellion at his words; her place was by her grandfather. She started up the stairs, but Bert grabbed her before she passed the first step and pulled her toward the parlor, saying, "Let Eric take care of him, dear. You come with me."

She had no other choice but to go with Bert. She was tired of fighting.

Eric examined Patrick and found the bullet had gone all the way through his shoulder. He cleaned and dressed the wound and told Patrick to rest. It would take time for him to regain his strength and for his wound to heal.

Closing the door to Nick's room, Eric moved to

Sven's room to check on Dee. She lay on the bed in exhausted slumber.

Sven stood by his side as Eric examined her. Finding no other injuries besides her split and swollen lip, he asked, "Are you sure he didn't try to rape her?"

"If he had, he wouldn't be alive now," Sven replied.

Eric drew the covers over Dee and moved to the door as Sven added, "I wanted to kill him, Eric. When I saw him on top of her, all I could think of was killing the bastard. Leif stopped me or I would have."

They moved to the stairs and Eric looked at his brother, saying, "I know how you felt. When I saw that animal holding a gun on Kat, I felt the same way."

Nearing the parlor, Sven asked him, "How is Kat?"

"Scared," Eric replied as they went through the doorway.

Kat jumped up from the sofa, Eric's coat slipping from her shoulders to the floor. She tried to move to the door, but Eric caught and held her.

"I want to see my grandfather," she stammered uneasily.

"Not tonight," Eric told her as he lifted her face to the light. "And not until I've examined you."

Kat kept her eyes tightly closed as she felt Eric's gentle fingers move across her cheek. She winced involuntarily as he found the sensitive area around her bruise. His fingertips traced her cheekbone, sending tremors of awareness racing through her.

"Your cheekbone isn't broken," his warm voice told her. "Do you hurt anywhere else?"

Only my heart, she thought, as she slowly shook her head and tears slipped from her eyes.

"Bert. Let's go make something hot to drink," Sven said as he led his aunt from the room.

Eric pulled Kat into his arms and cradled her near his

heart. "You've a right to cry. You've been through hell," he said softly.

His words opened a floodgate and Kat sobbed in his arms. All her pent-up fear and pain was released as her tears soaked the front of his shirt and her body trembled in his embrace.

Eric held her close and stroked her shaking shoulders as she cried. Her sobs began to grow less and less violent and her breath came in little gasps as she slowly calmed down.

She leaned against him, weak as a kitten, as he gently kissed the top of her head and asked, "Feel better?"

She drew partly away from him and accepted the handkerchief he offered her. "No," she stammered. "I feel miserable."

He lifted her into his arms and carried her upstairs, saying, "What you need is a good night's sleep."

She rested her head on his shoulder, too spent to protest as he carried her to her room, undressed her and put her to bed. She was asleep before her head touched the pillow and did not feel Eric's parting kiss.

Returning to the parlor, Eric found Sven and Bert talking to Leif, who had returned only minutes earlier.

Seeing him, Bert poured a cup of hot cocoa and handed it to him with a smile.

He looked down at it, saying, "No coffee?"

"It was Sven's idea," Bert replied. "He said the three of you had drunk enough coffee the past few days to float a log jam."

"Sven's right," he told her as he sipped at his cocoa and found the mellow taste a welcome change.

"How are the others?" Leif asked him.

"Sleeping," Eric returned as he sank into a chair with a groan.

"Are you okay?" Leif frowned. "You look terrible."

Eric looked down and saw the front of his shirt damp

and wrinkled from Kat's tears, his pants leg ripped and hanging in shreds from his fight with Grebe and he noticed his right eye felt like it might turn black.

"Thank you for the compliment," he groaned as other aches and pains began to make themselves known. "Believe me when I say I feel worse than I look."

"Leif was telling us what the sheriff had to say," Sven informed him.

"And what was that?" Eric asked tiredly.

"I turned our two felons over to him and gave him the description of Spencer that Gwyn gave us. I left the body with the undertaker," Leif said as he rubbed the back of his neck.

"Did the sheriff say anything about trouble at the camp?" Sven asked as he tried to stifle a yawn.

Leif echoed his yawn and complained, "Don't do that! You've got me doing it now!"

"The rail camp?" Eric reminded him as he rubbed his sore leg.

"He said he took a ride out there earlier in the evening and spoke with Ben," Leif answered through another yawn. "Things looked calm and under control."

"That's enough!" Bert scolded all three of them. "You're all dead on your feet. Go to bed! You can continue your talking later."

"Bert's right." Eric grimaced as he rose slowly from his seat. "I think we had better pack it in for tonight."

They kissed Bert good night and dragged themselves up to their rooms.

Eric made a final check on Patrick and Kat before going to his room and collapsing on his bed.

Leif crawled into bed certain that he could easily sleep for a month. Even his teeth felt tired.

Sven climbed carefully into bed, trying not to disturb

Dee. He pulled the covers over him and laid his head on the pillow next to hers.

She stirred in her sleep and murmured, "Sven?"

He put his arm out and drew her next to his side. She cuddled near him and they both slept.

Spencer slammed his fist against the window frame in frustration as he looked out into the street. He had heard the voices of a crowd gathering and gone to see what the commotion was all about.

He saw the youngest Thorsen brother riding in with two men tied to their horses and a third horse bearing the covered form of a body.

He recognized the two tied to their mounts as no-accounts Grebe had used from time to time to help him sabotage the railroad.

His eyes strayed to the third horse and he slammed his hand down again. Damn fool! he thought. He went and got himself killed. He's no use to me now, Spencer complained. His eyes narrowed as he thought, This means Gwyn and his granddaughter are probably still alive.

Damn those Thorsens! Now he would have to do the job himself!

He grabbed a gun from the dresser and checked to be sure it was loaded before stuffing it into his pants and storming from the room.

Taking the back alleys, he moved to the livery stable and saddled his horse. He would ride out to the lodge and wait for his chance to silence Gwyn and his know-it-all granddaughter once and for all.

Dee woke to the feeling of gentle kisses on her cheek. She opened her eyes and saw Sven smiling down at her. He lowered his head and kissed her lips.

"Ow!" she murmured as her swollen mouth throbbed.

Sven lifted his head, concern in his eyes as he said, "Sorry. I tried to be careful."

She trailed her fingers over his strong jawline and replied, "I know you did. It wasn't that painful."

Sven looked down at her and knew how close she had come to being badly hurt. His protective instincts said she would never have to face such a possibility again. He would make sure of that.

"Why are you staring at me like that? Do I look that ugly?" she asked him sleepily.

"No," he whispered as he nibbled on her ear.

Dee tried to turn her head and look at his face, but he buried it in her hair as he kissed the side of her neck. She moved her head the other way, loving the feel of his lips on her skin. "Sven?" she murmured.

He lifted his head and looked down at her again as he let his finger trace her collarbone. "What?" he whispered.

"Was it all a bad dream? Or did it really happen?" she asked him.

Not pretending he didn't know what she meant, he replied, "It wasn't a dream. But it's all over now. Try not to think about it."

She closed her eyes and shuddered against him. "How is Kat?" she asked him. "Is Eric okay? And what about Kat's grandfather?"

"You are full of curiosity this morning, aren't you?" He tried to tease the frightened look from her face.

"Sven," she said. "I want to know. Please tell me."

He told her everything that had happened since she had passed out with exhaustion the night before. Finishing his tale, he kissed the hollow of her throat as he added, "You had me scared, little one."

"I know," she softly replied. "I scared myself as well."

Sven made love to her. Slowly, tenderly, he caressed her and she responded in his arms. He prolonged his awakening of her desire until she moaned with heightened delight. Taking her, they flowed together to a beautiful fulfillment of their love.

"Kat. Take that tragic look off your face," Patrick ordered from his bed. "I have no intention of dying for a long time yet."

Kat looked at him and shook her head. "You are lying there pale as a ghost, swathed in bandages and still you give orders. I do not have a tragic look on my face. It is one of concern," she told him.

"What is there to be concerned about?" Patrick demanded. "I have received medical care, am resting as comfortably as possible under the circumstances and have no intention of doing anything without my doctor's permission."

"What is wrong with my being concerned?" Kat asked him. "I did come pretty close to losing you. And it frightened me."

"I appreciate your concern. But unless you promise me there will be no more long faces, I'll send you away," he informed her gruffly. "You of all people should know how I hate being fussed over."

"You win. I promise," Kat said as she crossed her heart. "Grandad? Do you think there will be any more trouble?"

"I hope not, Kat. We've had enough of that already," he answered her. "I will say that I still think that Elias Spencer was mixed up in this somehow. Don't ask me why, because I can't explain. But until he's caught and brought to justice, I won't be able to rest entirely at ease."

"Do you think he may be around here somewhere?" Kat asked as she plumped the pillows behind his head.

Leaning back, he replied, "That is why I gave his description to the Thorsens. Spencer might be thousands of miles from here, but I doubt it. He was too heavily involved in Paul's death and the power play by Harriman and Morgan not to be lurking in the shadows around here somewhere."

"Grandad! You make him sound like he might jump out at any second," Kat protested. "Surely now that the sheriff has his description, he will think twice before showing his face?"

"I sincerely hope you're right," Patrick replied. "Now, tell me. How are you feeling?"

"Me? I'm fine," Kat answered in surprise.

"You've dark circles under your eyes. Didn't you sleep last night?" Patrick accused her.

"I slept fine," Kat replied. The memory of her falling apart in Eric's arms made her face turn red and her grandfather look at her strangely.

She was saved from having to answer any embarrassing probes from him as the door to the room opened and Eric came in.

"Afternoon, Doctor," Patrick greeted him. "I have been following your orders to the letter, and aside from a damnable soreness in my shoulder am feeling much better than I did."

"Why do I get the impression that you are trying to get rid of me, Patrick?" Eric asked as he took Patrick's pulse.

"Because he is," Kat supplied with a stern look at her grandfather.

Checking the bandages to be sure there was no fresh bleeding from the wound, Eric asked, "And why is that?"

"Because he hates being fussed over," Kat replied softly.

"I also hate being talked about as though I am not even in the room," Patrick complained.

"Sorry." Eric grinned.

"I accept your apology," Patrick replied. "I also would like to thank you for the aid you and your brothers gave my granddaughter and myself. At considerable risk to your own well-being, I might add. We are all in your debt."

"Are you always so pompous?" Eric asked him bluntly.

"Oh!" Kat gasped.

Patrick eyed Eric with a stern look. "Are you always so rude?"

"I am your grandson-in-law," Eric reminded him. "There is no need to be so formal."

Patrick looked over at Kat and saw the red color creep up her neck and into her face as she lowered her eyes in embarrassment. Hmmm! he thought. So that's the way the wind is blowing. Smiling at Eric, he said, "So you are, so you are. Then tell me, Eric, how long before an old goat like me will be fit to travel?"

"I can't say about old goats, Patrick, but you should be able to travel in three or four days," Eric replied with a laugh.

"If you will both excuse me, I'll leave you to talk," Kat said as she rose and left the room.

Patrick watched her go and said to Eric, "Do you love her?"

"Yes," Eric answered.

"Does she love you?"

"I think she does," Eric replied.

Patrick thought a moment, then asked, "What does she think?"

Eric looked at the closed door before answering him. "She thinks if she avoids me she can avoid the truth."

"The truth being that she loves you?" Patrick smiled. "If you would not mind some advice from a grandfather-in-law, I would suggest that you make it impossible for her to avoid you."

The two men looked at each other in perfect understanding.

Kat hurried to her room and closed the door. Her cheeks still felt warm with embarrassment. Why did Eric say that to her grandfather? There was no reason for him to bring up such a subject. After all, she had only married him to save his family's reputation. The marriage would be annulled as soon as she returned to New York with her grandfather. And why had her grandfather looked at her like that? Kat put her hands to her face as she gasped aloud, "Oh, no!"

The only possible explanation for such a look was that Patrick thought she and Eric really were man and wife in the true sense of the words.

A knock sounded on the door behind her. She called, "Who is it?"

"It's Eric. I would like to talk with you, Kat."

She leaned against the door as panic filled her. "We have nothing to say to one another," she answered him.

"I think we do. Now are you going to open this door or do I have to knock it down?" Eric told her.

"You wouldn't dare!" Kat exclaimed.

"Wouldn't I?" Eric said as he pushed against the door.

Kat could feel the pressure and moved to open the door before he did knock it down. Opening it all the way, she turned and walked across the room.

Eric entered and closed the door behind him. The click of the latch made Kat turn around. "Why did you do that?" she gasped.

"Because I did not want any interruptions while we talked in private," Eric answered her as he advanced toward her.

Confusion made it hard for her to think and Kat backed a few steps away from him as he neared her. "What could we possibly have to talk about in private?" she tried to stall him.

Eric stopped and smiled at her as he replied, "Us."

"Us?" Kat choked. "There isn't any us, as you call it. I will be returning to New York with my grandfather as soon as he is able to travel. So how could there be anything between us?"

"It's no use, Kat." Eric shook his head. "You can't run away from it."

She wrung her hands together nervously. "I am not running away from anything."

"Yes, you are," Eric told her as he took a step closer. "I know you love me."

"I what! Of all the conceited, arrogant . . . that is ridiculous! How could you possibly know such a thing!" Kat flared at him.

Eric moved closer to her as he answered softly, "I can tell by the way you respond when I kiss you."

Kat stared at him in shock. "Just because I don't slap your face does not mean I love you. What you're saying doesn't prove a thing."

"It doesn't?" he replied. "Then prove it. Let me kiss you."

Kat backed away from him, her eyes wide with apprehension. "I'll do no such thing!"

"Afraid I might be right?" Eric accused with a slow smile.

"Of course I'm not afraid!" Kat denied heatedly.

"Well?" Eric waited.

Kat held her hands at her side and steeled herself, knowing he had her trapped. If she did not let him kiss her, he would go on insisting that she loved him. And who knows how he might embarrass her by telling others. She would have to prove to him he was wrong and let him kiss her. "If you insist." She glared at him.

"Oh, but I do," he whispered as he took her in his arms and lowered his lips to hers.

Kat tried to keep her mind blank. She tried not to feel his lips as they moved slowly on hers. She resisted the weakness in her that made her want to respond to the pressure of his arms as they held her close. She thought she had won, but he deepened his kiss, sending flares of response throughout her.

She put her arms around his neck and opened her lips to his probing onslaught. Flames licked at her senses as he crushed her tightly against him, molding her hips to his.

His lips moved from her mouth to her ear, where they nibbled and teased. She felt cool air across her back as his hands undid the buttons on her dress. He reclaimed her lips with a fiery kiss as he slipped her dress from her shoulders. She was alive with sensations she had never felt before as her dress fell to the floor around her feet.

His lips followed his fingertips as they moved the straps of her camisole out of their way. Kat made a sound in her throat as she felt him lift her camisole and pull it off over her head.

Bending, Eric lifted her in his arms and carried her over to the bed. Laying her down, he removed his clothes and lay down beside her. His warm mouth teased the rosy peaks of her breasts as she ran her hands through his hair. He was making her feel like she was floating on a cloud of pleasure.

His fingers slipped under the waistband of her silken drawers and she lifted her hips so he could take them off. As they lay there naked in each other's arms, Kat knew that she loved him. She loved him so much it made her mind spin.

Eric worshipped her body with his lips and Kat thought she would die with the waves of feeling that washed over her. She ran her hands over him, reveling in the solidness of his muscles and the feel of his skin. An aching need began to build inside her and she moaned as he kissed her lips.

Eric knew that she loved him; no woman had ever reacted to him so openly and with such trust. A fever of desire ran through him. He would make her his forever.

He tried to be gentle when he took her, going slowly until he felt the curtain of her innocence. Kissing her deeply, he broke through the curtain and made her his.

The world exploded in stars and colors around her as Kat felt herself being lifted higher and higher until a cresting of pleasure sent her cascading over into a realm of infinite sweetness.

Drifting back to reality, she smiled up at Eric as he placed a gentle kiss on the end of her nose. "You win," she whispered.

"We both win," he softly whispered back as he smiled in return.

"I'm going with you," Dee told Sven as she followed him to the barn.

"No, you're not," he told her. "We can't be sure there won't be trouble."

Dee stood there with her hands on her hips and stared at him stubbornly as he saddled his horse. "Leif told me that the sheriff spoke to Ben personally and that everything was normal at the camp."

"I don't care what Leif or anyone else said," Sven told her. "You're still not going."

Dee marched over to one of the other horses and

began to saddle it. "You have two choices, Sven Thorsen. Either you let me ride with you or I follow you. Which is it going to be?" she told him.

Sven looked up from tightening the girth of his horse and stared at her. "Damned if I don't think you would follow me, you stubborn minx," he exclaimed.

"Which is it going to be?" she asked him again.

He shook his head in resignation. "I guess I'd better take you with me. Someone has to protect the country-side from the likes of you."

"Sven Thorsen!" She reached down and grabbed a handful of hay and threw it at him.

He ducked it and climbed into the saddle laughing. "Well, woman, are you coming or not?"

"Coming!" Dee exclaimed as she hurriedly finished saddling her horse and joined him.

That's two of them accounted for, Spencer thought as he stared from his hidden vantage point on the side of the woods. Now, where are the others?

He had been keeping his watchful vigil for most of the day, waiting for the opportunity to slip into the lodge when the brothers were gone.

He knew Gwyn was in there and so was his grand-daughter.

As they rode to the rail camp Sven decided now was as good a time as any to tell Dee of his decision. He looked over at her as she rode alongside him and said, "Dee? I've been thinking."

"From the look on your face, I would say you have been thinking some pretty serious thoughts," she answered him as she saw him frown.

"I've decided that it would be safer for you if you returned to New York when Patrick leaves," he told her.

"Wait a minute!" Dee exclaimed. "You've decided? You think it would be safer? What about what I think?"

Sven reined in his horse and looked at her. "You know New York. Your family is there. It is the kind of life you are used to." He tried to explain his reasoning to her.

"Don't you love me anymore?" she demanded to know.

"Of course I love you!" Sven exclaimed. "It's because I love you that I think you should go back to New York."

Dee shook her head. "It sounds like a funny kind of love that says I can't learn to live here, that I don't have any family here, when the man I love lives here."

"But you could have been killed!" Sven told her.

"Now the real reasons come out," Dee said as she rode her horse close to his and reached over and put her hand on his arm. "Yes, I could have been killed. But I wasn't. Yes, it was something that would not have happened to me in New York. But you listen to me, Sven Thorsen, and you listen good. I met and fell in love with you in Montana, not in New York. I want to make my life here with you and our children, not in New York!"

Sven stared at her in wonder. She was serious! "Are you saying that you are staying?" he asked slowly.

"No, I'm insisting that I'm staying!" she replied. "And I do not want to hear any more nonsense out of you about me leaving."

"I promise!" Sven grinned. "You really have a temper, don't you?"

"You made me mad!" Dee told him. "I would not advise you to do that too often."

"Why not?" he teased as he pulled her up and kissed her soundly. "You're magnificent when you're mad!"

"Oh, you think so?" She dimpled up at him. "Maybe I should stay mad at you?" She tried to pull away.

"That would make me mad," Sven informed her. "I would much rather do this." He pulled her from the saddle and across his own as he kissed her.

Kat smiled shyly as Eric watched her dress. "Don't look at me like that!" she scolded him.

"Why not?" Eric lifted an eyebrow. "I enjoy looking at you."

"You enjoy it too much! You make me think you're going to make love to me." Kat blushed as she fastened the buttons on her dress.

"Sounds like a good idea to me," Eric said as he started to rise from the bed.

"No!" Kat put up her hand.

"No?" You don't think it's a good idea? Or no, don't stop," he teased her as he stood up.

"No to both." Kat smiled at him. "You have to go into town with Leif, remember? You can't spend all day in here; someone will come looking for you."

He grabbed her and pulled her into his arms. "Let them look. I would rather make love to you than ride into town with Leif."

"Eric!" Kat laughed as he growled in her ear.

"Love me?" he asked.

"You know I do," Kat replied as she placed a kiss on his cheek. "But the sheriff and your brother are waiting for you."

"Sheriff?" Eric mumbled as he kissed her.

Kat pushed away from him and held him at arm's length, saying, "Yes, sheriff. You are supposed to ride into town with Leif to give your statement."

Eric shrugged. "I guess you are right. But you had better watch out. When I get back, nothing will stop me then."

Turning to go to the door, Kat said over her shoulder, "I wouldn't want it to."

Spencer smiled in self-satisfaction as he saw the youngest Thorsen brother come out of the barn leading two horses.

He watched as Leif moved to the front of the lodge and stood waiting. A few minutes went by and Spencer saw Katherine Gwyn come out onto the porch with her arm about a man. Good, Spencer thought, good. That makes three.

He bided his time as he saw the three talk and laugh. Then Kat kissed the third brother and stood waiting until he'd mounted his horse.

The two brothers waved and headed out of the yard in the direction of town.

Kat stood watching them with a smile on her face until they were out of sight. Then she turned and went back inside the house.

Now was his chance. He started carefully forward toward the lodge.

Kat moved from the kitchen carrying a tray. "Bert, this smells delicious! My grandfather will enjoy it," she said.

"There's more where that came from, if he wants it," Bert replied as she lifted the basket from the counter. "I'll be in the garden if you need me for anything," she told Kat.

"I don't think I will, but if I do, I'll call." Kat smiled.

Kat carried the tray carefully up the stairs to her grandfather's room. Entering the room, she said, "I've your lunch, Grandad."

"Set it down where I can reach it, dear," Patrick said from the bed.

Kat placed the tray across his lap and sat down next to the bed.

Patrick looked over at her warily, saying, "You're not going to feed me?"

"You can feed yourself." Kat smiled. "I don't want to be accused of fussing."

Patrick lifted the spoon by the side of the bowl and sampled the hearty broth before him. "Pretty good," he commented.

"Bert's an excellent cook," Kat agreed.

"You and that husband of yours settle your differences yet?" he asked, watching her out of the corner of his eye as he ate.

Kat beamed at him. "If it is any of your business, yes, we have."

Patrick looked up at her and studied her face. "I take it you won't be returning with me to New York?" he said with the hint of a grin.

Kat leaned over and kissed him on the cheek. "You sly fox. No, I won't be going back with you. My place is here with Eric." She laughed.

"High time you saw that." Patrick nodded, pleased with the way things were working out.

Spencer slunk across the yard and onto the porch. His eyes darted furtively about as he listened near the parlor window to see if anyone was near the front of the house. Not hearing anyone, he moved to the front door and tested the handle.

A smirk of satisfaction crossed his face as the knob turned easily in his hand. Country clods! he thought. At least New Yorkers knew enough to lock their doors.

He slipped through the door and closed it silently behind him. Keeping his gun ready in his hand, he paused to listen at the foot of the stairs.

The sound of laughter drifted down from above, followed by the rumble of a man's voice. A voice he knew and hated. It was Patrick Gwyn.

He crept up the stairs toward the hated voice. Laugh while you can, he thought, but the last laugh will be mine.

Gwyn and his uppity granddaughter had made a fool of him for the last time. Always treating him like he was dirt. At least Morgan and Harriman recognized his talents and appreciated his business sense. If it hadn't been for Gwyn's granddaughter getting cold feet at the last minute, she would be married to his stooge, Forbes, and Gwyn would be in his power.

Forbes, the spineless fool! Telling him when he met him that day at the Blaine Building that he was going to make a clean breast of it all and talk to Gwyn.

He had to kill him. If Forbes had spilled his guts to Gwyn, all would have been lost: his dealings on the side with agents and shippers, charging them a percentage to do business with the Great Northern and then pocketing the money for himself; going through Gwyn's papers and keeping his ears open to report Gwyn's business moves to Morgan and Harriman. All would have been exposed.

Spencer moved across the landing. The voices were coming from behind the closed door ahead of him.

Kat screamed as the bedroom door crashed open and Elias Spencer stood pointing a gun at her and her grandfather.

A feral gleam lit his eyes as he advanced into the room, saying, "One more sound out of you and it will be the last sound you ever make."

Bert cursed as her arthritic fingers fumbled with the cinch on the saddle. She had to get help.

She had come in from the garden and heard a sound

on the front stairs. Thinking it might be Kat wanting her for something, she had gone through the kitchen and dining room to see. What she saw took ten years off her life: a man with a gun was disappearing up the staircase.

She knew she was no match for him by herself and had rushed out to the barn to saddle a horse and go for help.

She prayed she could find it before anything terrible happened. It hadn't been that long since Eric and Leif had left for town, and she hoped she could catch them before they had gone very far.

Leading the horse around to the back of the barn, she mounted and, taking a long curving path through the woods, avoided the front of the lodge as she rode to intercept the road to town.

"Get up!" Spencer snarled as he pointed the gun at Patrick. "I don't plan on letting you die in bed."

Kat started to help Patrick as he struggled to rise from the bed.

"Stay where you are," Spencer snapped at her.

Fear and concern filled Kat as she watched helplessly as Patrick rose painfully to his feet and leaned against the side of the bed for support.

Spencer laughed cruelly. "The rich and powerful Patrick Gwyn caught in his underwear." He stared at Patrick as he leaned bare-chested, except for the bandage across his shoulder, and clad only in his long knit drawers.

Moving to the side of the door, Spencer motioned with his head. "Come on. Move it. We're all taking a little trip outside."

"He can't manage the stairs by himself!" Kat protested.

"Then you will help him," Spencer informed her.

"But don't try anything or neither of you will live to see the bottom of the stairs," he warned as he watched Kat put her arm about Patrick and let him lean on her as they slowly made their way to the door.

Kat's eyes flashed her hatred as they passed in front of Spencer and she glared at him coldly. Their progress was slow. Patrick had to pause and rest every few steps. Going down the stairs, he almost stumbled and fell, but Kat grabbed him and yelled at Spencer, "He can't make it. He's too weak from loss of blood."

"We'll rest here a minute to make sure he does make it," Spencer replied nastily. "Hear me well, Gwyn. You will make it or you'll see your precious granddaughter die right here." He pointed the gun at Kat's head.

"I'll make it all right, you bastard!" Patrick gritted through his teeth. "But, only because I want to give you the dissatisfaction of seeing me do it."

"Eric! Leif!" Bert yelled as she saw them.

Hearing her yell, they turned in their saddles and pulled up.

She raced up to them and gasped, "There's a man with a gun at the lodge. He's after Patrick and Kat."

As she spoke, Sven and Dee came into view on their return from the rail camp. Seeing her and his brothers, Sven urged his horse forward and Dee followed.

"Sven!" Eric called. "Bert says there's a man with a gun back at the lodge."

"Spencer!" Sven spat.

Dee paled and fear clutched her heart as she listened to the men speak.

"He was going upstairs when I left the back way," Bert explained hurriedly as they turned their horses and headed for the lodge.

"We can't go barging in there like a herd of buffalo,"

Sven said as they rode. "That's the surest way to get someone hurt."

"We'll leave the horses at the back of the barn and circle round the house," Eric said.

"Leif, you stay with the horses and protect Bert and Dee," Sven told his brother as they neared the path Bert had used for her escape.

Reaching the back of the barn, they dismounted and handed their reins to Leif. They could hear what sounded like a man's voice coming from the front yard of the house and a woman's voice edged with fear as it answered.

"They're out front," Leif said.

"Sven, you go around the side and take him from the front. I'll go around and try for him from behind," Eric instructed as he moved away.

Dee stood with her arms around Bert and a lump of fear in her throat as she watched the brothers leave.

Patrick was leaning heavily on Kat and the bandage on his shoulder was stained with fresh blood. He was breathing hard and there was a grayish tinge to the color on his face.

Spencer looked around them, saying, "Enjoy the fresh air. It will be your last time to do so."

"If you are going to kill us, do it and get it over with!" Patrick hissed.

"Oh, no! I've waited a long time for this moment. I am going to savor every second of it," Spencer gloated. "I want to see you sweat with fear before you die in the dirt you tried to keep me down in."

"You're insane!" Kat gasped.

"Shut up!" Spencer snarled as he cocked his gun. "Insane, am I? I'll show you who's insane." He aimed the gun at Kat.

"Kill me, not her," Patrick told him. "Why shoot her? She's never done anything to you."

"And I want to keep it that way," Spencer coldly replied as he started to pull the trigger.

Two bodies flashed through the air and the gun went off in the sky. Eric tackled Spencer from behind and wrestled with him as Sven grabbed Patrick and Kat and rolled with them protectively on the ground.

Spencer fought like a wild animal as Eric grabbed his wrist and repeatedly slammed it against the ground until the gun dropped to the dirt.

Sven moved to retrieve it and aiming it at Spencer said, "That's enough."

Eric's fist caught Spencer on the chin, knocking his head back into the dirt. Eric hauled him to his feet as all the fight drained out of him. Pushing him to Sven, Eric said, "Get this trash out of here before I kill him."

Sven yelled for Leif, who came running with Bert and Dee close behind him.

Kat lifted Patrick's head onto her lap as tears streamed down her face. "Don't die, Grandad, don't die," she softly cried over and over again.

Eric knelt beside her and lifted the bandage on Patrick's shoulder. "Shh, love. He'll be all right as soon as we get him inside and I can stop this bleeding."

"I told you I was a tough old goat." Patrick coughed as he opened his eyes.

It was three weeks later and Elias Spencer was sitting in a jail cell in New York awaiting trial for murder.

Patrick Gwyn was sitting on a bench in front of the lodge enjoying the Montana sunshine as he smiled at his granddaughter and Eric, walking toward him arm in arm from the porch.

Leif pulled the wagon to a stop in front of the house and climbed down to load luggage aboard.

"Are you ready to go, Grandad?" Kat asked Patrick.

"I was just taking a last look around," he answered her. "Beautiful country to live in, Eric."

"We think so, Patrick," Eric agreed as he moved his arm around Kat's shoulders.

"Big and free," Patrick commented as he smiled slyly at Kat. "Plenty of room to raise a family."

"Grandad!" Kat scolded him lovingly.

Rising from the bench, Patrick asked, "Where are Sven and Dee?"

"They're coming," Eric laughed.

Patrick looked at him, puzzled.

"When we left them, they were arguing over what to name their first son," Kat laughed.

Patrick raised his eyebrows. "Is Dee?"

"No." Kat shook her head. "She just wants to be prepared for when it is time."

"I will not have my son stuck with the tag of junior!" Sven roared as he and Dee came out the front door.

"And no son of mine is going to be named after some Indian chief!" Dee shouted back at him.

"Hey, you two!" Eric called. "Don't you think you have plenty of time before you have to worry about that?"

Dee's face blushed bright pink and Sven smiled sheepishly as he replied, "We do sound pretty silly, don't we?"

"Speak for yourself, Sven Thorsen," Dee said as she jabbed him in the ribs with her elbow.

"Oof!" Sven gasped. "Why, you . . . !" He grabbed her and planted a big kiss on her mouth.

When he let her go, she stared at him in surprise. "Why did you do that?"

"I was reminding you who's the boss." Sven grinned at her.

She followed him down the stairs and put her arm

around his waist as they watched Patrick climb aboard the wagon next to Leif.

Bert came out on the porch to say good-bye to Patrick and was in time to hear Dee say sweetly to Sven, "Why, we both know I'm the boss."

Everyone laughed as Sven crushed her to him in a bear hug and she cried, "Okay! Okay! You're the boss!"

"Good-bye, Bert," Patrick called. "Thank you for everything."

Bert eyed the two happy couples in front of her and smiled at Patrick. "I should be thanking you. There hasn't been this much life around here in years. Don't be a stranger. Come back and visit us sometime."

"Leif, you have those addresses I gave you?" Kat asked him.

"Right here," Leif replied as he tapped the breast pocket on his suit.

"Don't you worry about him," Patrick told her. "I'll be keeping an eye on him."

"You study hard and make us proud of you, Leif," Bert told him.

"I will, Bert." Leif grinned as he lifted the reins.

Kat stood on the side of the wagon and kissed Patrick on the cheek. "Good-bye, Grandad. Take care of yourself. I love you."

"Good-bye, dear. You take good care of your husband," Patrick told her as he watched her step down into Eric's arms.

"I'll make sure she does." Eric grinned.

"See that you do that." Patrick laughed. "Good-bye, everyone."

"Bye." They waved as Leif moved the wagon forward.

Bert went back inside and Sven bent and whispered

something in Dee's ear that made her giggle as they followed her.

Kat and Eric watched the wagon until it disappeared.

"Are you sorry you stayed?" Eric asked her.

"No. Are you?" she replied as she leaned against his shoulder.

He hugged her tightly in response as he asked, "What were those addresses you gave Leif?"

Turning and moving toward the stairs, she smiled. "Young ladies Dee and I know in New York."

"What!" Eric said, dumbfounded, as he followed her.

"Since the four of us are so happy, Dee and I decided Leif deserved a chance," Kat informed him.

"Poor Leif!" Eric shook his head. "He won't stand a chance with those city girls."

Kat turned and put her arms around his neck and kissed him, saying, "If he is anything like his brothers, those city girls won't stand a chance with a Thorsen man."

Tapestry

HISTORICAL ROMANCES

Breathtaking New Tales

of love and adventure set against history's most exciting time and places. Featuring two novels by the finest authors in the field of romantic fiction—every month.

Next Month From Tapestry Romances

DELPHINE
by Ena Halliday

FORBIDDEN LOVE
by Maura Seger

POCKET BOOKS

If you've enjoyed the love, passion and adventure of this Tapestry™ historical romance...be sure to enjoy them all, FREE for 15 days with convenient home delivery!

Now that you've read a Tapestry™ historical romance, we're sure you'll want to enjoy more of them. Because in each book you'll find love, intrigue and historical touches that really make the stories come alive!

You'll meet brave Guyon d'Arcy, a Norman knight ... handsome Comte Andre de Crillon, a Huguenot royalist ... rugged Branch Taggart, a feuding American rancher ... and more. And on each journey back in time, you'll experience tender romance and searing passion... and learn about the way people lived and loved in earlier times.

Now that you're acquainted with Tapestry romances, you won't want to miss a single one! We'd like to send you 2 books each month, as soon as they are published, through our Tapestry Home Subscription Service.℠ Look them over for 15 days, free. If not delighted, simply return them and owe nothing. But if you enjoy them as much as we think you will, pay the invoice enclosed.

There's never any additional charge for this convenient service — we pay all postage and handling costs.

To begin your subscription to Tapestry historical romances, fill out the coupon below and mail it to us today. You're on your way to all the love, passion and adventure of times gone by!

HISTORICAL *Tapestry* ROMANCES

Tapestry™is a trademark of Simon & Schuster.